FRANCIS VIVIAN
THE LAUGHING DOG

Francis Vivian was born Arthur Ernest Ashley in 1906 at East Retford, Nottinghamshire. He was the younger brother of noted photographer Hallam Ashley. Vivian laboured for a decade as a painter and decorator before becoming an author of popular fiction in 1932. In 1940 he married schoolteacher Dorothy Wallwork, and the couple had a daughter.

After the Second World War he became assistant editor at the Nottinghamshire Free Press and circuit lecturer on many subjects, ranging from crime to bee-keeping (the latter forming a major theme in the Inspector Knollis mystery *The Singing Masons*). A founding member of the Nottingham Writers' Club, Vivian once awarded first prize in a writing competition to a young Alan Sillitoe, the future bestselling author.

The ten Inspector Knollis mysteries were published between 1941 and 1956. In the novels, ingenious plotting and fair play are paramount. A colleague recalled that 'the reader could always arrive at a correct solution from the given data. Inspector Knollis never picked up an undisclosed clue which, it was later revealed, held the solution to the mystery all along.'

Francis Vivian died on April 2, 1979 at the age of 73.

The Inspector Knollis Mysteries
Available from Dean Street Press

The Death of Mr. Lomas
Sable Messenger
The Threefold Cord
The Ninth Enemy
The Laughing Dog
The Singing Masons
The Elusive Bowman
The Sleeping Island
The Ladies of Locksley
Darkling Death

FRANCIS VIVIAN

THE LAUGHING DOG

With an introduction by Curtis Evans

DEAN STREET PRESS

Published by Dean Street Press 2018

Published by licence, issued under the UK Orphan Works
Licensing Scheme.

First published in 1949 by Hodder & Stoughton

Cover by DSP

ISBN 978 1 912574 35 3

www.deanstreetpress.co.uk

INTRODUCTION

Shortly before his death in 1951, American agriculturalist and scholar Everett Franklin Phillips, then Professor Emeritus of Apiculture (beekeeping) at Cornell University, wrote British newspaperman Arthur Ernest Ashley (1906-1979), author of detective novels under the pseudonym Francis Vivian, requesting a copy of his beekeeping mystery *The Singing Masons*, the sixth Inspector Gordon Knollis investigation, which had been published the previous year in the United Kingdom. The eminent professor wanted the book for Cornell's Everett F. Phillips Beekeeping Collection, "one of the largest and most complete apiculture libraries in the world" (currently in the process of digitization at Cornell's The Hive and the Honeybee website). Sixteen years later Ernest Ashely, or Francis Vivian as I shall henceforward name him, to an American fan requesting an autograph ("Why anyone in the United States, where I am not known," he self-deprecatingly observed, "should want my autograph I cannot imagine, but I am flattered by your request and return your card, duly signed.") declared that fulfilling Professor Phillip's donation request was his "greatest satisfaction as a writer." With ghoulish relish he added, "I believe there was some objection by the Librarian, but the good doctor insisted, and so in it went! It was probably destroyed after Dr. Phillips died. Stung to death."

After investigation I have found no indication that the August 1951 death of Professor Phillips, who was 73 years old at the time, was due to anything other than natural causes. One assumes that what would have been the painfully ironic demise of the American nation's most distinguished apiculturist from bee stings would have merited some mention in his death notices. Yet Francis Vivian's fabulistic claim otherwise provides us with a glimpse of that mordant sense of humor and storytelling relish which glint throughout the eighteen mystery novels Vivian published between 1937 and 1959.

Ten of these mysteries were tales of the ingenious sleuthing exploits of series detective Inspector Gordon Knollis, head of the Burnham C.I.D. in the first novel in the series and a Scotland Yard detective in the rest. (Knollis returns to Burnham in later novels.) The debut Inspector Knollis mystery, *The Death of Mr. Lomas*, which was published in 1941, is actually the seventh Francis Vivian detective novel. However, after the Second World War, when the author belatedly returned to his vocation of mystery writing, all of the remaining detective novels he published, with two exceptions, chronicle the criminal cases of the keen and clever Knollis. These other Inspector Knollis tales are: *Sable Messenger* (1947), *The Threefold Cord* (1947), *The Ninth Enemy* (1948), *The Laughing Dog* (1949), *The Singing Masons* (1950), *The Elusive Bowman* (1951), *The Sleeping Island* (1951), *The Ladies of Locksley* (1953) and *Darkling Death* (1956). (Inspector Knollis also is passingly mentioned in Francis Vivian's final mystery, published in 1959, *Dead Opposite the Church*.) By the late Forties and early Fifties, when Hodder & Stoughton, one of England's most important purveyors of crime and mystery fiction, was publishing the Francis Vivian novels, the Inspector Knollis mysteries had achieved wide popularity in the UK, where "according to the booksellers and librarians," the author's newspaper colleague John Hall later recalled in the *Guardian* (possibly with some exaggeration), "Francis Vivian was neck and neck with Ngaio Marsh in second place after Agatha Christie." (Hardcover sales and penny library rentals must be meant here, as with one exception--a paperback original--Francis Vivian, in great contrast with Crime Queens Marsh and Christie, both mainstays of Penguin Books in the UK, was never published in softcover.)

John Hall asserted that in Francis Vivian's native coal and iron county of Nottinghamshire, where Vivian from the 1940s through the 1960s was an assistant editor and "colour man" (writer of local color stories) on the Nottingham, or Notts, *Free Press*, the detective novelist "through a large stretch of the coalfield is reckoned the best local author after Byron and D. H. Lawrence." Hall added that "People who wouldn't know Alan

Sillitoe from George Eliot will stop Ernest in the street and tell him they solved his last detective story." Somewhat ironically, given this assertion, Vivian in his capacity as a founding member of the Nottingham Writers Club awarded first prize in a 1950 Nottingham writing competition to no other than 22-year-old local aspirant Alan Sillitoe, future "angry young man" author of *Saturday Night and Sunday Morning* (1958) and *The Loneliness of the Long Distance Runner* (1959). In his 1995 autobiography Sillitoe recollected that Vivian, "a crime novelist who earned his living by writing . . . gave [my story] first prize, telling me it was so well written and original that nothing further need be done, and that I should try to get it published." This was "The General's Dilemma," which Sillitoe later expanded into his second novel, *The General* (1960).

While never himself an angry young man (he was, rather, a "ragged-trousered" philosopher), Francis Vivian came from fairly humble origins in life and well knew how to wield both the hammer and the pen. Born on March 23, 1906, Vivian was one of two children of Arthur Ernest Ashley, Sr., a photographer and picture framer in East Retford, Nottinghamshire, and Elizabeth Hallam. His elder brother, Hallam Ashley (1900-1987), moved to Norwich and became a freelance photographer. Today he is known for his photographs, taken from the 1940s through the 1960s, chronicling rural labor in East Anglia (many of which were collected in the 2010 book *Traditional Crafts and Industries in East Anglia: The Photographs of Hallam Ashley*). For his part, Francis Vivian started working at age 15 as a gas meter emptier, then labored for 11 years as a housepainter and decorator before successfully establishing himself in 1932 as a writer of short fiction for newspapers and general magazines. In 1937, he published his first detective novel, *Death at the Salutation*. Three years later, he wed schoolteacher Dorothy Wallwork, with whom he had one daughter.

After the Second World War Francis Vivian's work with the Notts *Free Press* consumed much of his time, yet he was still able for the next half-dozen years to publish annually a detective novel (or two), as well as to give popular lectures on a plethora of intriguing subjects, including, naturally enough, crime, but also fiction writing (he published two guidebooks on that subject), psychic forces (he believed himself to be psychic), black magic, Greek civilization, drama, psychology and beekeeping. The latter occupation he himself took up as a hobby, following in the path of Sherlock Holmes. Vivian's fascination with such esoterica invariably found its way into his detective novels, much to the delight of his loyal readership.

As a detective novelist, John Hall recalled, Francis Vivian "took great pride in the fact that the reader could always arrive at a correct solution from the given data. His Inspector never picked up an undisclosed clue which, it was later revealed, held the solution to the mystery all along." Vivian died on April 2, 1979, at the respectable if not quite venerable age of 73, just like Professor Everett Franklin Phillips. To my knowledge the late mystery writer had not been stung to death by bees.

Curtis Evans

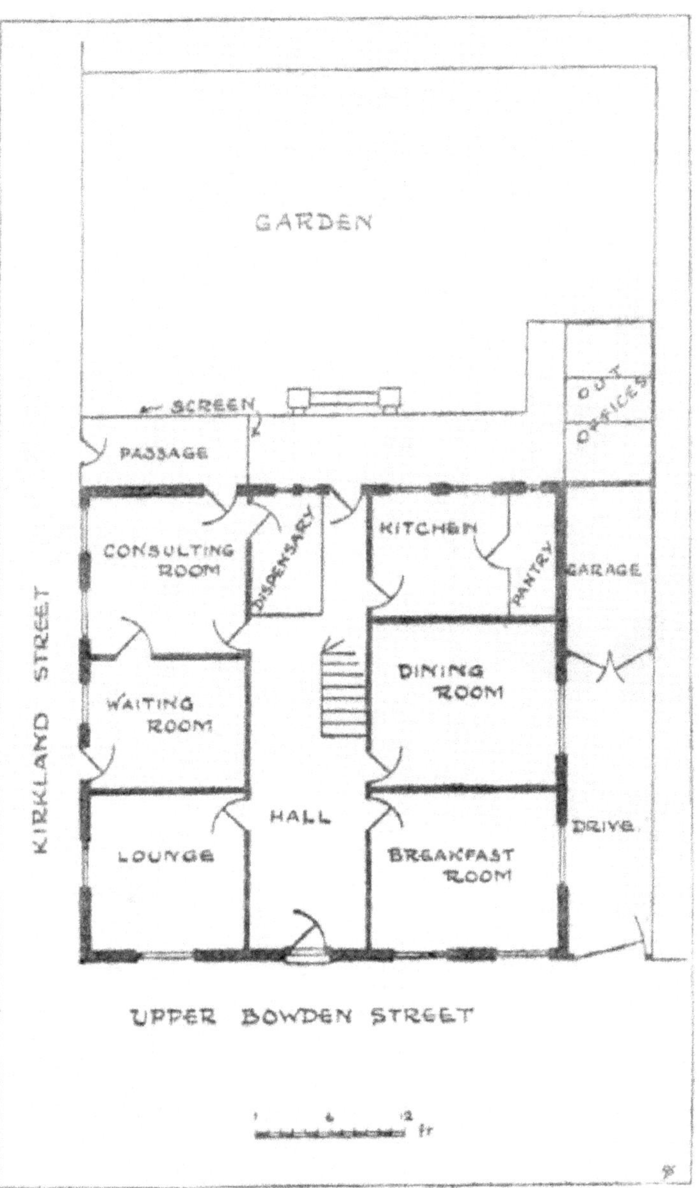

DR. CHALLONER'S HOUSE

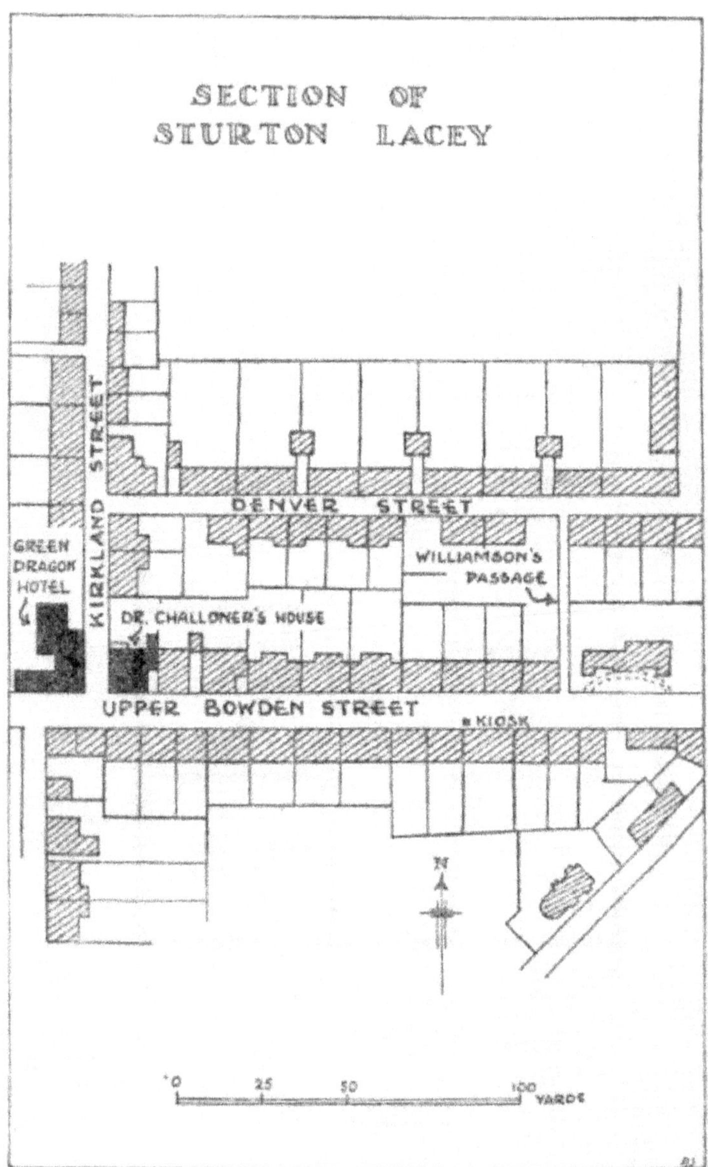

SECTION OF
STURTON LACEY
KIRKLAND STREET
DENVER STREET
GREEN DRAGON HOTEL
WILLIAMSON'S PASSAGE
DR. CHALLONER'S HOUSE
UPPER BOWDEN STREET
KIOSK
N
0   25   50   100   YARDS

STREET PLAN

PROLOGUE

AT TWENTY-FIVE MINUTES past ten on an August morning, Dr. Hugh Challoner strode from his hotel in the Rue d'Isly, pulling the brim of his panama over his eyes against the brilliance of the sun. He hurried down to the corner, bought a copy of the *Continental Courier* from the kiosk opposite the Hotel de Postes, and turned right into the Rue Michelet, along which he proceeded at a brisk pace, a short, dark little man of fifty-six whose eyes wandered whenever a pretty girl passed—which was every few seconds in Algiers.

The city was fully awake, as it had been for four hours or more. The citizens rose early, and got their business and house-work done before the heat of the day, when all but the most ambitious observed siesta as religiously as the Mahomedan observed Ramadan, or the Hebrew observed Yom Kippur; but for now it was all activity in the city, and under the striped awnings of the cafés and bars the tables were fully occupied; business-men transacted deals, ladies-about-town gossiped, confessed loungers discussed the latest political situation; one ardent couple made love, oblivious to the bustle around them.

Challoner strode on happily. An appreciative glance at the unsullied blue sky, a saucy smile at a young matron in a black-striped dress, a muttered' apology as he bumped a fat and perspiring barrel of a man; it was all part of the scene.

At the corner of the Michelet and the Rue Jean Mace was a shop with a large entrance porch. A throng of small boys were gathered inside, and it was just possible to tell that a man was sitting somewhere beyond them, a man with copper-coloured hair. Whether the shop was occupied in the normal sense could not be ascertained, for the window was hung with lines of crayon drawings, portraits, and caricatures which all but touched the glass, so that they looked like a great poster.

An inquisitive coppery eyebrow lifted above the boys as Challoner stepped into the porch. Then a pair of arms waved excitedly, and a still more excited voice bade the boys take themselves away, jump into Algiers Bay or under a tram, or dispose of themselves in any other way providing they did not further impede the progress of the English gentleman. The boys grinned, and backed a few feet, so that it was now possible for Challoner to see a small folding table on which stood four boxes of crayons, and against a leg of which rested a large red and green portfolio. Beside it was a camp stool, on which sat the copper-head. He was about the same height as Challoner—five feet five—and wore a sporty moustache, the ends of which were tightly twisted and waxed. He was good-looking, nonchalant in manner, and apparently used his eyebrows, which twisted outward like horns, as auxiliary means of expression. He wore bright green trousers tied at the waist with a red necktie, and a yellow open-necked shirt whose sleeves had been severed three inches above the elbow.

"M'sieur Aubrey Highton?" said Challoner. "Bonjour!"

"I speak English fairly well," Highton replied easily. "So the messenger from the Hotel Bretagne delivered the message. You never know," he said with a rueful smile. "If the tip is not big enough, or a friend is met on the way—who knows?"

"You speak excellent English," Challoner exclaimed with un-disguised astonishment.

Highton laughed. "I was educated at St. Bertrand's School, in Kent. I am quarter-French only. Now this matter of the portrait I'm to do of you; you'd like a straight portrait, or one of my almost famous caricatures? I warn you; my caricatures are cruel! I see people as birds, or animals, or even flowers. I don't care which way you want it. The price is the same—five hundred francs."

He nodded towards the window display.

"You see the ostrich? The woman is the wife of a successful business man. I saw her like that, so I drew her. She was angry, and refused to pay, so I exhibited the drawing. Everyone knows her, and they all laughed—and still do. Her husband has offered me three thousand francs for the drawing, but I've taken a fancy to it, and shall keep it. Now which manner do you prefer?"

Hugh Challoner looked into the artist's eyes, and a curious smile crossed his face. "Oh wad some power the giftie gie us . . ." he quoted.

"Burns hadn't met me," grinned Highton. "The inner eye of the artist is all-revealing. You toy with danger if you let me draw you. Mind you, I won't understand what I draw, but it will be there. It is the client, not myself, who perceives the revelation."

"That is a dare," said Challoner, "and I never refuse one. A caricature it shall be, whether I turn out to be animal, vegetable, or mineral. I'll double your fee if I like it."

"And I will give it to you for nothing if you don't," said Highton. "One moment, please!"

He dived into the shop and returned with another camp-stool, which he placed on the edge of the step leading down to the pavement. "You're my first client to-day. I'm an idle fellow and can't rise early like these city people—but then I don't go to my bed in the afternoon."

"Then where do you find your clients?"

Highton shrugged. "They come! It entails little effort to sit here and be sketched, and if the truth be told they rather enjoy being subject to the whims of a temperamental artist. I play up to them. Actually, I'm not temperamental—I'm a business-man. Now please sit there. A little more this way. Right! You have a paper, so I suggest you read it as I work. That way you will relax, and your character is allowed to creep into your features."

Highton took a large sheet of buff-coloured cartridge paper from the portfolio, fastened it to a square of stiff cardboard with an alligator clip, and rested it on his knees with its back against the edge of the table. He considered Challoner for a time, began work, and after a time began to make conversation. "On holiday in Algiers?"

"A fortnight," said Challoner. "I fly home in three days."

"Been here before?"

Challoner glanced up from his paper. "Er—no, although I've travelled extensively in Europe—the Scandinavian countries, the Netherlands, Germany, France, Italy, Greece, and the Levant proper."

"Quite a traveller!"

"I'm a doctor," Challoner explained. "I take my vacations this way. It was horrible during the war, being confined to our tight little island. There's nothing wrong with it, mind you!"

"But no sun," observed Highton.

"No sun," Challoner agreed. "That is all we miss."

"I hope to go to London in November," said Highton. "You like Algiers?"

"No mean city," said Challoner. "I'll be back next year, or the year after, God willing."

"Been far out of it?"

"Only as far as Retour de la Chasse and Fort d'l'Eau. Of course, I flew in to Maison Blanche. Now next time I want to get out to the oasis of Bou Sada!"

Highton glanced up and chuckled. "The Street of the Ouled Nails, eh?"

"You know Bou Sada?" Challoner asked quickly. Highton kissed his bunched fingers and tossed a kiss into the blue sky. "The girls! My God!"

"Then you've been there!" persisted Challoner.

Highton nodded. "I was in the *Regiment étranger*, the Legion, during the war."

Challoner looked down at his shoes and then flashed a glance at Highton over the top of his *Courier*. "They—the girls—were worth seeing?"

"From an artist's point of view, definitely," Highton said gravely. He added: "If one isn't an artist—give me a fast camel and a bottle of nerve tonic!"

"I see," murmured Challoner. He jerked his head towards the window display. "Why are you doing this type of work? Your drawings are surely—"

He sought for a word and did not find it.

"I'm earning money to take me to Paris and London," Highton explained easily. "I have introductions to Pierre Ferry of Paris, and George Darby of Gray's Inn Road, both of whom, I'm told, can dispose of my work. I hope to cross to Marseilles in the third week of October, and on to London as soon as my business is finished."

He laid his crayon on the table, opened a case and threw a cigarette into Challoner's lap. He then threw one in the air, caught it neatly between his lips, and fished for his lighter.

"Truth to tell, I'd like to get myself a steady job as a commercial artist in England—advertising, or textiles, or something. The more Bohemian aspects of art, as practised by myself at present, are certainly interesting, but they don't pay any more than they did in Murger's day." He cocked a copper eyebrow. "Don't suppose you can advise me?"

Challoner blew a cloud of smoke into the stuffy air. "I may be able to help you," he said slowly. "There's scope in my district. We've quite a few industries which could absorb a man of your talent."

"I don't want absorbing," said Highton. "I want a chance to do some individual work and at the same time possess some degree of security."

"Well, you know what I mean," Challoner said shortly. "I mean they could use your talents. Look, I'll give you my card. If you care to let me know when you're in England I'll see what I can do."

"That's decent," said Highton.

He waited quietly as Challoner took a card from his wallet and handed it to him. *"Dr. Hugh Challoner, Bowden Street, Sturton Lacey."* He let it drop inside the bosom of his shirt and reached for the crayon.

"Er—doctor!"

"Well?"

"I hope this is not one of those impulsive gestures that you'll regret later, like a sea-courtship, because I feel that I shall attempt to take advantage of your offer."

Challoner leaned forward in an earnest manner. "I am not a man of impulse, Mr. Highton. No doctor can afford to be that; he must be reflective. Now I cannot accommodate you at my own house, but if you'll wire me when you arrive in England I'll book a room for you at an hotel straight opposite my house, and then see if we can find you a job."

Highton continued his work silently for a time, and then looked up with a quizzical air. "I wonder why you're doing this for me?"

Challoner himself appeared to be puzzled. "I don't know," he admitted. "I think I've taken a liking to you. Do you believe in affinities?"

Highton's lips twisted into a crooked smile. "Part of me does—the French part."

"I either like people, or hate them," said Challoner.

Highton nodded. "That explains something that came into my head when I began drawing you."

"What?"

"You will see! You will see!"

An hour passed, and then Highton laid down his drawing-board and rose to stretch himself. "If you have time for a drink, Doctor? I know a little place round the corner . . ."

"That is the Englishman in you," chuckled Challoner. "An Englishman always knows a little place round a corner. Yes, a vermouth, or a muscatel, would go down the hatch very nicely."

"And a talk," added Highton gravely.

Challoner took his arm as if they were old friends, and allowed himself to be led round the corner. "So you were in the Foreign Legion . . ."

At twelve o'clock Highton renewed his work on the caricature, and at half-past he rose with a rueful smile on his lips. "I shouldn't have done this, but it is what came! You're not going to like it, my friend!"

He stared at Challoner, and then tossed the drawing, still clipped to its backing, across to him. He came and stood looking over Challoner's shoulder, tapping a foot anxiously on the terrazzoed floor of the porch.

"A dog," Challoner said softly.

"The friend of man," said Highton. "It either loves or hates, and there can be no compromise. It is the English fox-terrier, quick, intelligent, alert, and a faithful friend. See the cock of its head as it looks up and awaits approbation or otherwise—a bone to eat, a stick to fetch, or a stone to send it yelping back to its kennel. It came from the realm of the subconscious. I know nothing of you. I have never met you before. There is a generation between us. I am thirty-two years of age—"

"Fifty-eight," said Challoner.

"The appointment was made by an intermediary, a mere servant obeying an order and being paid for his errand."

"A dog," said Challoner.

"Laughing," said Highton.

"A laughing dog?" asked Challoner, and winced.

"You're upset," said Highton.

"How the devil did you know!" Challoner demanded in an angry voice. He shook himself. "You couldn't know. It's idiotic of me to suggest it. . . ."

"I've revealed something to you," said Highton.

Challoner shook his head. "No matter, my friend. It is the long arm of coincidence. No more and no less. Now I must pay you for your work."

Highton stayed him with a gesture. "There can be no talk of payment between us. You spoke of affinities, and I feel it myself now. We're men of a kind; we each have a string that vibrates to the same note. Perhaps when I come to England we'll discover what we have in common—if you still mean what you said!" Challoner forced his eyes from the crayon drawing, and gave a sad half-smile. "I never go back on my word, Highton, no matter how much it costs me—and whatever I do for you will cost nothing."

Highton extended a hand. "Then, until November!"

"Until November," said Challoner, returning a firm grip.

He returned to his hotel in the Ruc d'Isly, and for the remaining days of his holiday stayed away from the shop at the corner of the Rue Michelet and the Rue Jean Mace. He was due to fly home via Marseilles and Le Bourget on the Thursday morning. On the Wednesday evening he paced his room, ill at ease, casting occasional glances at the caricature now propped against the mirror of the dressing-table. At last he grabbed his hat and ran down to the vestibule, demanding a taxi. Utilizing the services of the hotel interpreter he asked if the driver knew the studio of Highton on the Michelet. The driver knew both M'sieur Highton and his studio, but the artist would not be there now. He might be at his favourite bar in the Rue de Constantine, or in his room over the Café Tabard in the Rue Sidi Carnot. Challoner pressed a wad of franc notes into the man's willing claws. "Find him!"

Highton was not to be found at his studio—and all the drawings had been removed from the window so that it was possible to see that the shop was completely empty. At the American Bar on the Rue de Constantine they only knew that M'sieur Highton had not been seen for three days. At the Café Tabard they could only say that he had paid his bill and gone. Where? Who knows? To India or to the devil, and who cares?

Early in the morning Challoner went the round of the shipping offices. None could tell him of any Highton on their lists. Neither could the traffic manager at Maison Blanche when Challoner went to join his aircraft, so he climbed aboard the Douglas Dakota *en route* for London, where he would charter a Blue Vine aircraft back to Swinnerton, a few miles from Sturton Lacey.

At the bottom of his suit-case there lay, face down, a sheet of buff cartridge paper on which was drawn a caricature of himself. It portrayed him as an English fox-terrier, quick, intelligent, and alert. Its head was cocked as if waiting for approbation, or a stone that would send it yelping to the shelter of its kennel.

I

THE LAST PATIENT

MRS. MADELEINE BURKE was prepared to swear that she was Dr. Hugh Challoner's last patient on that Tuesday evening, the fourth of November, and that he was alive and in good spirits when she bade him good night at approximately twenty minutes past seven.

"He seemed preoccupied," she admitted, "although only in the way you would expect a doctor to be—you know, as if one half of his mind was on his work and the other half concerned with the social courtesies, as you might say. He made several little jokes, and courteously opened the door for me when I left. It was twenty minutes past the hour by the watch on his table."

She smoothed her brown hair with a slim hand, and awaited comment. None came. She flicked long dark lashes over vivid blue eyes, fidgeted with the lace at her neck, and hurriedly continued:

"Mr. Highton, the artist, can corroborate my statement. He was the last patient to see Dr. Challoner before I went in. He locked the door of the waiting-room at seven o'clock, at Dr. Challoner's request."

She cast an appreciative glance at her inquisitors. They regarded her stonily across her dining-room table. She licked her lips, and lowered her eyes, her fifty-four years suddenly apparent behind the mask of makeup.

Inspector Manson she knew well enough as the head of Sturton Lacey's crime bureau, or detective department; a fat, jolly man who turned up at most of the social events in the town in an unofficial role, or so she assumed; a happy man who knew how to enjoy himself, and who could be relied on to lead the floor in the old-tyme dances. Mr. Manson was all right.

It was the other who disturbed her, the lean-faced, long-nosed, grey-eyed man whom Manson had introduced as Inspector Gordon Knollis of New Scotland Yard. He regarded her through near-closed eyelids, and spoke in curt, incisive tones. She was sure that she was an object of the utmost suspicion to him.

It was he who tapped on the table with his pencil in a peremptory manner, for all the world as if he were examining her knowledge of history or geography. He tapped on the table with the butt of his pencil, and said: "Tell me, Mrs. Burke; what was the doctor doing when you left the surgery?"

She toyed with the grocer's bill which had arrived five minutes before Manson and Knollis, rolling it into a tight cylinder, screwing it tighter and tighter.

"He was scribbling something or other in a large diary, one of those page-a-day diaries. Then he got up and opened the door for me."

"I see," said Knollis. "You say that this Mr. Highton locked the outer door?"

"The outer door of the waiting-room; yes."

Knollis slid a square of paper across the table. "You will see that this is a rough plan of the surgery, which comprises the waiting-room, consulting-room, and dispensary. Mr. Highton locked the door leading on to Kirkland Street?"

She nodded assent.

"Tell me about it," Knollis said abruptly.

She made a feeble gesture with her hands. The grocer's bill unrolled itself with slow deliberation.

"There is really nothing to tell. He simply locked the door."

"How did it come about that he locked it? Did the doctor call through to the waiting-room?"

She wrinkled her brows, apparently not understanding why Knollis should be interested in such a silly question.

"He—he—well, Mr. Highton walked through to the consulting-room when the bell rang."

Knollis looked up. "The bell? Explain that, please."

"Dr. Challoner has a bell-push on his table. It rings a bell in the waiting-room as a signal that he is ready to see the next patient."

"Thank you. Please continue."

"Well, Mr. Highton went through. A moment or so later he came back, smiled at me, and said he may as well do it himself now that he was here. I judged by his tone that Dr. Challoner had asked him to pass the message to me—the last patient. Mr. Highton went to the door and dropped the latch. The clock of St. Aidan's was striking seven as he returned to the consulting-room and closed the door behind him."

"St. Aidan's is in Lower Bowden Street," Manson interpolated in a deep rumble that came from his diaphragm.

"I see," said Knollis. "Tell me, Mrs. Burke; at what time did you enter the consulting-room?"

"It would be about twelve or thirteen minutes past."

Knollis glanced at his notes. "And you left at twenty minutes past."

Mrs. Burke inclined her dark head. "That is correct."

Knollis leaned across the table and dropped the point of his pencil on the plan. "The exit from the consulting-room leads to a fenced-off portion of the yard and garden, forming a narrow passage which leads on to Kirkland Street a few yards before the waiting-room entrance. Tell me, Mrs. Burke; would it, in your opinion, be possible for anyone to conceal himself or herself in that passage?"

She gave him a pitying smile. "Good gracious, no! It cannot be more than four feet wide!"

"The lock on the waiting-room door is a latch-lock, similar to a Yale or Chubb?"

Mrs. Burke agreed that it was.

"You heard Mr. Highton leave?"

"I heard him call good night to Dr. Challoner," she said cautiously. "The doctor answered, and then the outer door slammed. The bell rang a few seconds later, and I went in the consulting-room."

Knollis suddenly smiled. The unexpected change from ice-cold inquisitor to friendly sympathizer threw her into momentary confusion.

"It was nothing serious that took you to the surgery?" Knollis inquired in a soft voice.

She smiled back at him; he seemed such a charming man! "Oh no, not really, Inspector. The boy has two hammer toes, and Dr. Challoner was arranging for his admission to hospital for a corrective operation."

Knollis nodded his understanding. "Ah yes! Nothing really serious, but of great benefit to the boy if performed."

"Er—Inspector?" she ventured, encouraged by the change in his manner. "How did you know I was the last patient?"

Manson beamed on her, and rushed in to supply the information before Knollis could gather his thoughts. "It was in the desk-diary," he boomed. "*Mrs. Burke. Leslie's toes. Ring Dayson ten-thirty Wed.* Simple, isn't it?"

Knollis's elbow took him in the ribs. He cast an offended glance at his colleague and subsided.

"So you knew why I went to see Dr. Challoner," said Mrs. Burke, somewhat tight-lipped.

Knollis shook his head, and still smiling replied: "We didn't know, Mrs. Burke; we only assumed. Your verification was necessary before we could say that we knew. A subtle difference, but a vital one."

"I see," she said primly. She was back in her place again, a witness to be suspected.

"You made a further appointment with the doctor?" Knollis asked with an air of bland innocence.

"He was going to ring me when he had consulted Dr. Dayson," she replied sulkily. "I was then to call for a letter of recommendation to present at the Out-Patients' Department at the hospital. He hoped to arrange it for next Tuesday—a week yesterday, in which case I was to collect the letter on Monday evening."

Knollis reached for the plan, and folded it inside his wallet. He swung his grey trilby from the table by its brim, and prepared to leave the house.

"I think that is all, Mrs. Burke. Thanks for your willing co-operation."

She ventured a further question as she stepped ahead of them to open the outer door, and again it was Manson who answered her.

"Heart failure consequent on an attempt to strangle him, Mrs. Burke. Yes, it counts as murder. Looks as if someone had thrown a noose over his neck, drawn him back over the chair, and tied the free end of the rope to one of the back legs. He must have struggled until he overturned the chair, and that loosened the running noose round his neck. He might easily have freed himself if his heart hadn't given out."

Mrs. Burke pressed her clenched fists into her cheeks, and stared with bulging eyes. "How awful! To think that only a few minutes before—"

"Horrible," Manson agreed. "He looked pretty grim when we first saw him. His face was as black as the kitchen grate and—"

"Manson!" Knollis snapped irritably.

"Eh?" Manson murmured. "Am I saying too much? She did ask me, y'know!"

"She doesn't want the autopsy report," said Knollis. He touched Manson's elbow and led him from the premises.

"Who is she?" he demanded as they settled back in the police car and were driven away.

"Mrs. Burke. Widow of local government official. He was our rating officer, and also secretary of the local branch of N.A.L.G.O.—y'know, the local government officers' trade union. Nice bloke, he was. Died of pneumonia two years ago."

"What is she living on?" Knollis asked.

Manson turned to regard him with surprised eyes. "Living on?"

"Living on!"

"How the deuce should I know?" asked Manson. "I expect she'll have a widow's pension, won't she? And they may have managed to put a bit away. Doesn't that sum up the position?"

"I'm asking you," said Knollis.

He stared at the driver's back for a few seconds, until his head came round with a jerk as he shot another question at his colleague. "How old is the boy?"

"Oh, about thirteen. Why all these questions, any-way? They don't strike me as being relevant."

Knollis shrugged. "I'm merely trying to establish the back-ground and reliability of the witness. Normal routine, surely?"

Manson wriggled uncomfortably. "Suppose so," he admitted, "but it seems a bit queer when you know folk as respectable townspeople."

"You may know her as such," said Knollis. "I don't know her at all, and I happen to be in charge of the investigation."

"This is my first murder case," Manson grunted.

"Every murder case is a first one," Knollis sighed softly. "I have yet to meet two with similar features."

The driver drew in to the kerb and applied his brakes. "You said Hodson and Spender, sir?"

Manson nodded. "That's right. Wait for us."

"Who do we see here?" asked Knollis.

"Young Eric Lincoln. He's courting the doc's daughter, Joan. Clerk to this firm of solicitors. He was thoroughly approved by Challoner as a prospective son-in-law."

He dropped from the car and proceeded towards the double doors of the building. Knollis delayed him with a tap of his finger on the shoulder. "I can't remember any reference to a Mrs. Challoner."

"You won't," replied Manson. "She died five or six years ago of a malignant tumour. Joan ran the house for the old man, with the assistance of a day-girl and a rough char or Part Time Domestic Aid as they are known in these days of new-found social dignity."

"A doctor who is a widower, and a witness who is a widow," Knollis murmured more to himself than his companion.

Manson stared at him with dismay written on his face. "Oh lord! Don't start on those lines. There's nothing in the notion, nothing at all."

"Lincoln and the girl engaged?"

"No-o, not officially, but it's generally accepted that they are booked for the altar."

"It's accepted by themselves?"

"Ye-es, I think I can say so, Knollis."

"With what effect on the Challoner ménage, assuming that the doctor had lived?"

"Well," Manson hesitated. "I don't know all the affairs of all the people in Sturton, but I think it was generally understood that Lincoln and Joan would live with her father and look after them all. She's a nice girl, Knollis! One of those really nice girls. Twentyish, with fair hair and a natural wave, and frank blue eyes and an open countenance. Lincoln'll have something worthwhile as a wife when he marries her."

"She'll be the sole beneficiary!"

Manson regarded him with shocked awe. "Why yes, I reckon so, but surely to God you aren't suspecting *her—*"

"I'm not suspecting anybody," Knollis countered. "How can I at this stage of the game? I'm trying, as I've already explained, to visualize the background and general set-up of this affair. I'm not jumping to conclusions, and I'm not suggesting that Lincoln, Joan Challoner, or Mrs. Burke, or all three together bumped off the doctor for benefits to be received. Nevertheless, even you must admit that his statement reads a wee bit thin! It doesn't convince."

"He was nervy, and suffering from shock," Manson muttered between his teeth.

"We must encourage him to open up!"

Manson said something beneath his breath, and led the way into the building.

Eric Lincoln, a dark-haired young fellow of twenty-two, rose to meet them as they entered his office at the rear of the building and on the third floor. He smiled uncertainly at Manson, and avoided Knollis's penetrating gaze. "Didn't expect to see you this morning, sir," he said in an anxious voice.

"This is Inspector Knollis, of the Yard," Manson rumbled. "He'd like to ask you a few questions. Nothing to worry about. Just a few straightforward questions."

"But—but I made a statement," Lincoln protested.

"Which is quite satisfactory," Knollis assured him easily. "I merely wish you to amplify it if at all possible. Being engaged in the law you'll be aware that witnesses seldom tell the full story at the first recital. They omit minor details which seem unimportant—to them!"

Lincoln nodded. "Yes, that's right enough, Inspector, but I thought I'd reported everything—not like some of the witnesses we get in divorce proceedings. We generally have to go over and over their stories."

"Then you'll appreciate my point," said Knollis. "The tables are turned on you. Now according to your statement, you were sitting in the house when Dr. Challoner was murdered?"

"I think that must be right," said Lincoln with a shudder. "I let myself into the house by the front door about twenty to twenty-five past seven. Joan was upstairs. She called down to ask if it was me, and said she would be down in a few minutes. I went into the lounge and ran through the cartoons in some new magazines that were on the table."

"The lounge door? You closed it, or left it open?"

"Closed it, Inspector. There's a deuce of a draught runs through the house."

"You heard no suspicious sounds?"

Lincoln paused a moment before answering. "I don't know about suspicious sounds. I heard a door slam, but I can't say which door it was. It was just a dull thud, and I can't even guess at the direction from which it came. It may have been Joan closing one upstairs."

"It could have come from the consulting-room?" asked Knollis.

"It isn't likely, Inspector. The waiting-room is between the lounge and the consulting-room, and the door from the consulting-room to the rear hall is baize-lined."

"I see," said Knollis. "Tell me, Mr. Lincoln; why did you go to the consulting-room?"

"It was past surgery hours and I thought I'd have a chat with the doctor while Joan was getting ready for dinner."

"It was then you found him?"

Lincoln gulped, and nodded his dark head.

"Tell me about it," invited Knollis, his lean features tense as he watched Lincoln's wandering eyes.

"He—he was lying behind the table, across the carpet. He was lying on his face, which was nearly black—he looked horrible! His left arm was straight down by his side, and the fist was clenched. The right hand was underneath his body, and across his chest. It looked as if he had felt a sudden pain in his heart and clutched at it as he fell or rolled over."

"The chair?" Knollis asked keenly.

"It was lying on its side, Inspector. The rope was tied to the back leg that was uppermost, and the other end round the doc's neck, although very loosely. There was a mark round his neck, more distinct at the throat and under his ears than at the nape. I noticed all that, and then I'm afraid I bolted."

Knollis ignored the young man's embarrassment.

"You are familiar with the layout of the consulting-room, Mr. Lincoln?" he asked in a casual voice.

"Well, yes! I know the whole house pretty well by now."

"Are you of the opinion that anything had been removed from the room? Had the room or its furnishings been interfered with in any way, as far as you could see?"

Lincoln stared his bewilderment. "I don't think so, Inspector! What could have been taken away?"

"I'm sure I don't know," smiled Knollis. "I merely wondered."

"It was Miss Challoner who 'phoned us, wasn't it?" inquired Manson, anxious lest his presence should be overlooked.

Lincoln gave an uncomfortable shrug. "She used her wits better than I used mine. I shouted upstairs that something had happened to her father, and bolted into the street to look for a policeman. I found one against the kiosk in Bowden Street, just a few yards from the house. Joan came downstairs while I was out, discovered her father, and 'phoned to the police station."

"You know a Mr. Highton?" asked Knollis.

"The artist? Fairly well. He has a room at the Green Dragon, and I've had a few drinks with him in the saloon bar at one time or another."

He added: "The Dragon is straight opposite the house—Inspector Manson knows that, of course. I've slipped across a few times when Joan—Miss Challoner—hasn't been home when I've called."

Manson leaned forward. "Directly opposite the surgery, Knollis. Stands on the opposite corner of Bowden Street and Kirkland Street."

"Interesting," Knollis murmured in a tone that suggested something very different. He turned to Lincoln again. "You know a Mrs. Madeleine Burke?"

"Mrs. B-burke?" faltered Lincoln.

Knollis raised one eyebrow, and instantly lowered it again. With innocence written across his face he repeated the name. "Mrs. Madeleine Burke."

Lincoln twisted his fingers together and looked awkwardly from Manson to Knollis. "Well, I do, and I don't."

"Tell me what you know, and skip the rest," Knollis suggested with a rare spark of humour.

"She's well known in the town, Inspector!"

"She may be, Mr. Lincoln, but my home is in London, and Inspector Manson is the only Sturtonian I know, and I've only known him for a few hours. What is Mrs. Burke like? A quiet domesticated woman, or a fly-by-night? Is she quiet and reserved, or is she regarded as a town socialite?"

"Well . . ."

Lincoln cast an appealing glance at Manson. Knollis intercepted it, and waved an impatient hand. "I'm asking for your opinion, and not Inspector Manson's."

"Well, she's all right," Lincoln muttered. "She goes to church, and attends the whist drives, and helps with the buffet at the dances."

"Hectic sort of a life," murmured Knollis. He sucked a tooth for a minute or so, and then returned to the attack. "I suppose you knew Dr. Challoner really well?"

"I've been visiting the house for nearly two years," Lincoln replied.

"Did Dr. Challoner indulge in that harmless occupation known as doodling?"

Lincoln laughed nervously. "Doc. Challoner? He was a very busy man, Inspector. I shouldn't imagine he ever had the time to spare for doodling."

"Do you doodle? That sounds like a new tongue-twister, but nevertheless, do you doodle?"

"Sometimes, when I'm waiting for the exchange to put through a 'phone call."

"I'd like to see a few samples, please."

Lincoln glanced inquiringly at Manson, who merely shook his head and raised his shoulders in a gesture indicating his helplessness.

Knollis walked round the room to the telephone, and studied the note-pad intently. "Impatience and nervous apprehension," he remarked. "Your dotted lines indicate the former, and the spirals the latter. Challoner was a doctor, a man capable of reaching decisions. . . ."

He glanced up at Lincoln. "You never draw dogs?"

Lincoln's brow furrowed. "Dogs?"

"Of course you don't," said Knollis. "Now Dr. Challoner did! Under the last entry but one in his professional diary he drew a dog, a dog recognizable as a dog and yet bearing some of the characteristics of a man, a dog that had its mouth open and its tongue lolling out, and was laughing in human fashion."

He watched Lincoln keenly through near-closed eyes. Lincoln's jaw dropped. "Laughing? A laughing dog?"

"It suggests nothing to you?"

"Only sheer lunacy, Inspector! It's fantastic!"

"It was very well executed," said Knollis.

"The doc did a bit of sketching in his younger days. Joan has shown me some of his work."

"Any sketches of dogs?"

"No-o! I can't remember any. It was mainly old streets, and mountains, and scenery generally."

Lincoln scratched his head and looked from one to the other. "A laughing dog! I've heard some queer things in this office, but this is the silliest yet. A laughing dog."

He began to laugh, somewhat hysterically. Then he suddenly sobered and said: "What does it mean, Inspector?"

Knollis reached for his hat. "Anything—or nothing."

II

The House Without a Dog

Gordon Knollis was at all times fully conscious of the state of mind of any bereaved person in a murder case, and acted accordingly. They were shocked by the tragic event into a mental bewilderment which made them slow of comprehension and tardy in realizing the correspondences between vital points of evidence, so that while his professional curiosity urged him to force the pace and question and cross-question, a better sense born of long experience bade him treat them gently, with a show of almost casual interest. In the earlier stages of an investigation he was prone to humour them, winding up the pace only when he had gained their confidence and put them at their ease. His own mind was keen and alert throughout, his grey eyes watchful for the slightest change of expression in a face, his sixth sense switched on to detect a fractional degree of evasion or untruthfulness.

Joan Challoner's impression of detectives had been derived from the films and sensational thrillers, so that she pictured them as bullying District Attorneys, uncouth and crude in their methods. The morning had been spent in a state of nervous apprehension, and on opening the door to find Manson and Knollis facing her they suddenly appeared through a wavering mist. Then Manson raised his hat and asked if they could step inside for a minute or two. He urged her indoors, gently closed the door, and introduced Knollis.

"Just a few routine questions," he explained apologetically. "My colleague will not keep you long."

She took a grip on herself, nodded acquiescence to Manson's request, and showed them into the lounge.

Knollis noted a great deal as he entered the room. He noted that the window on the long side of the room opposite looked out on to Kirkland Street. He noted that the Green Dragon was directly opposite, and that a long green signboard announced the name of the hotel, in gold leaf. He noted that the shorter wall on his right would also be the wall of the waiting-room, and that this lounge was the room in which Lincoln had waited for his fiancée, in which he had heard the slamming door, and from which he had gone to find Challoner dead in the consulting-room.

He turned to Joan Challoner with a friendly smile. Manson had given a good description of her. She had pretty fair hair, framing a frank, open face showing signs of her present sorrow. Her wide blue eyes had nothing to conceal; her skin was without blemish and carried little make-up. She wore a brown skirt which revealed legs of which she had no need to be ashamed, and a golden-yellow jumper which perhaps over-emphasized the fullness of her breasts.

She waited with parted lips. "I—I don't know what I can do for you," she said hesitantly.

Knollis encouraged her with a broader smile. "There is very little you can do, unfortunately, Miss Challoner. Your statement is crystal clear, but I would like to hear the story from your own lips if the recital will not distress you. I regret, of course, the necessity of disturbing you at such a time. . . ."

His gesturing hand made it abundantly clear that he was the victim of circumstances with no alternative to his present distasteful errand. She rushed to help him, as he had anticipated.

"I know," she said, "and I must do all I can to help you."

"Perhaps you will tell us what you can," Knollis murmured in a caressing voice.

She pushed her hair back from her face with a trembling hand, and stared through the wall that separated the lounge from the waiting-room. "There's so little to tell. . . . What exactly do you want to know, Inspector?"

"When did you last see your father alive, Miss Challoner?"

"About ten to six, when he was going to open surgery. His evening hours were from six to seven, but he used to sign club-notes and so on before the surgery began. He knew all his regulars, and when they would be coming, and why, and he hated wasting time."

"Yes?" prompted Knollis.

"I was getting dinner ready for half-past seven. It was practically ready for serving just after seven, so I went upstairs to change. Eric came in about twenty past, and I called down to him and told him there were some new magazines in here. I heard him come in, and close the door. It was some time after that when I heard him go and tap on the consulting-room door."

"Which is baize-lined," Knollis observed mildly.

"Yes, but it's possible to tap on it so that you can be heard inside."

"I see," said Knollis. "Please go on."

"It didn't seem to be many minutes after when Eric ran to the foot of the stairs. . . ."

"Yes, Miss Challoner?"

"He—he shouted that something had happened to Father, and I ran downstairs. Eric was running along the front path. I went to the consulting-room and—and saw what had happened. I knelt beside him and tried to make him speak to me, and then somehow or other made my way to the 'phone. Eric came back with a policeman shortly after, and they gave me some brandy and brought me in here."

Knollis found a seat, and leaned forward, his eyes gleaming keenly. "Tell me, Miss Challoner; can you suggest who killed your father, and for what reason?"

She raised moist eyes, and shook her head. "There doesn't seem to be a reason, Inspector. He had no enemies. He was well-liked in the town, and was a good doctor and a conscientious man."

"No one ever threatened him?" boomed Manson.

"I never heard of anything like that."

"Look," said Manson, "I don't want you to get me wrong, but can you recall any case of his within recent years in which the patient died—despite your father's efforts—and the surviving relatives attributed the death to negligence on his part—say, an error in diagnosis or treatment? Such things do happen, you know, in Harley Street and Bowden Street."

There was something akin to pitying contempt in her expression as she replied: "My father was a good and conscientious doctor!"

"I'm aware of that," replied Manson with a trace of irritation. "I'm not accusing him of being anything else. I'm merely suggesting that somebody else might have conceived the notion. That would create an enemy!"

"My father had no enemies," she said firmly, and tossed her head.

Knollis tut-tutted. No murdered man ever had an enemy if you believed the surviving relatives.

"Someone must have had a reason for killing your father," he suggested, and added hurriedly: "Or shall we repeat that they thought they had a reason. Inspector Manson's idea is a sound one, you know."

Joan Challoner dabbed at her eyes with her now bedraggled handkerchief. "He was a kind man, and everybody liked him."

"So somebody killed him because they liked him, eh?" Manson commented caustically.

Knollis grimaced at him.

"Of course he was a good man, Miss Challoner. He was a good doctor, too. By the way, wasn't he something of an artist in his younger days?"

"He could have been a very good artist," she retorted between sniffs.

"A valuable gift," said Knollis, and waited.

She gave her eyes a final dab, and parked the hand-kerchief in the sleeve of her golden-yellow jumper: then took a deep breath, and exhaled it in one great quivering sigh.

"He—he was very good!"

"I'm sure of it, Miss Challoner," said Knollis. He could exhibit great patience on occasion.

"Everybody said he could have been a great artist."

It was Knollis's turn to sigh. *Everybody* and *They* were his pet aversions, mainly because neither legendary party could be pinned down as exhibits in the way demanded by the orderly

Knollis mind. Even in his hobbies he had no use for abstractions, and collected butterflies.

He pulled himself together, and forced a smile to his thin lips. "I've always been interested in sketching," he said in an innocent manner.

Now she had been steered away from the events of the previous evening, and the appalling possibility of her father being disliked by someone, Joan Challoner was showing signs of interest in her visitors.

"You must see some of his work!" she said. "Delighted!" murmured Knollis. He glanced sharply at Manson. "We've time, haven't we, Inspector?"

Manson blinked, grunted, and hurriedly agreed that they had all the time in the world. "Charmed, I'm sure!"

Joan Challoner was probably more surprised than was Manson. "Now?" she asked with a nod.

"There's no time like the present, Miss Challoner!"

"Oh, well I won't be long. His sketch-books are in the attic. If you don't mind waiting. . . ."

"You're a cunning so-and-so," said Manson as she sped from the room and up the stairs.

"We're detectives," Knollis replied with a grim smile. "The laughing dog intrigues me. I like murderers to leave tokens and trademarks; they are right in the tradition, and make the case more interesting—but we have to make sure that it wasn't Challoner's own work. Damn' silly when you come to consider the matter; our man did what I would call a pretty sound job, looking at it from his angle, and then spoils everything by doodling in the diary."

"Challoner did that, surely!" Manson protested. "A clue for us to follow. You said so yourself!"

"I've changed my mind," said Knollis. "I wasn't using my imagination. Put yourself in Challoner's place. Would you be in any condition to draw a dog when you had just escaped strangulation by throwing yourself bodily from the chair to which you were tied? Again, surely Challoner would conclude that he was free and to live when once the noose slackened? He expected to live, and had no need to leave a clue for us."

"He turned ill again," Manson retorted.

"Apoplexy. He hadn't time to draw a breath, let alone a dog. More to the point, to reach the diary he would have had to free himself from the rope, or alternatively would have had to drag the chair to the desk—and you'll remember that the chair had fallen away from the desk, and not towards it!"

"He—" began Manson, and then said: "Oh, nuts!" and closed his mouth.

"I'm willing to be proved wrong," said Knollis, "but I'll wager a month's salary that the dog was drawn by the killer."

"I don't bet," said Manson. "Y'know, Knollis, Highton is an artist. He attended the Organ-Fund bazaar at St. Aidan's, and did lightning sketches of people at two bob a time. He generously gave the proceeds to the fund."

"Interesting, but not necessarily significant," said Knollis. "The population of Sturton Lacey is over ten thousand, isn't it?"

"Thirty-five at the last census."

"We can surely assume that more than two people out of thirty-five thousand are capable of drawing a laughing dog."

Manson rubbed the nape of his bull neck. "I can't make you out, Knollis. Why the devil do you want to see Challoner's sketches? Waste of time. A sheer waste of time."

"I'm looking for a laughing dog, or some appropriate clue that will lead us to the meaning of it. Know anything about drawing?"

"Apart from corks and my screw, not a ruddy thing," Manson admitted. "I suppose you do! You seem to know something about everything!"

"I don't know the first thing about the subject," Knollis admitted in his turn. "On the other hand, I'm quite good at encouraging other people to believe that I do understand their interests, and at encouraging them to enlighten me without realizing that they're doing it."

"I can believe that," said Manson. "I said you were cunning."

He subsided as Joan Challoner returned with an armful of sketch-books, which she laid on the table.

"Most of these are ages old, of course! Father travelled a great deal in his younger days. This one is the German tour in Nineteen-twenty-four. He did the traditional trip down the Rhine—Bonn, Coblenz, Cologne, and so on. He always took his holidays abroad except during the war years, of course! Now this is the Italian book. Here's the Arch of Victory at Milan, and La Scala, and the Cathedral, and the Fountain of St. Anthony. Further on—here we are—are Como and Maggiore. And see, he went to Venice in the same year. There are lots more sketch-books in the attic!"

She poised a finger on her lip. "He did all the Netherlands, and Scandinavia, and France, Germany, Italy, Greece, and Turkey. Quite a lot of the world to see, isn't it?"

Knollis put a question. "Always in Europe we might say, apart from Turkey."

Joan Challoner nodded. "Until this year, when he went to Algiers for a fortnight."

"I'd always seek the sun if I went abroad," said Knollis. "He doesn't appear to have done anything in the way of sketching people, does he? Always buildings and scenery!"

"Why yes! I hadn't noticed that before," said Joan Challoner in a surprised tone. "Unless you can regard the odd human beings in the sketches as breaking the rule."

"He never drew animals, Miss Challoner?"

Her blue eyes opened wide. "Why no! I can't remember him ever doing so."

After which she asked the eternally feminine question.

"Why?"

Knollis appeared to hesitate for a moment. "Er—you didn't happen to glance at his desk-diary when you were in the consulting-room last evening?"

"No, I certainly didn't, Inspector. Why?"

"Someone drew a laughing dog in the book," said Knollis. "Just the head of a dog, laughing."

"A—a laughing dog!"

Joan Challoner was incredulous.

"It strikes no chord in your mind?"

She stared blankly. "It doesn't seem to make any kind of sense, Inspector."

"Silly, isn't it?" he murmured. "Almost as senseless as the idea of your father having an enemy."

She glanced suspiciously at him, but nothing was to be gleaned from his bland features.

"Tell me," said Knollis; "do you happen to know a Mr. Highton?"

She nodded towards the window. "At the Dragon? Why yes, Eric and I have met him at dances."

"How long has he been in the district?"

"Oh, no more than a week or two." She glanced sharply at Knollis. "He—he's an artist, isn't he?"

"Don't put ideas into my mind, Miss Challoner, please," said Knollis. "It just happens that he was the last patient but one to see your father last night, and I shall have to question him in case he saw anyone hanging round the surgery when he left. I like to know something of my witnesses before I approach them."

"He seems very nice," she offered gratuitously.

"He and your father were acquainted?"

"Well yes. They met in Algiers, and Father offered to help him find a job when he came to England."

Knollis blinked, and instantly wreathed his manner in innocence. In a non-committal manner he said: "I see!"

"He came to see Father professionally last night?"

"It would seem so, Miss Challoner."

"I wonder why he didn't come to the house?" she asked with a perplexed frown.

"Did he know your father well enough for that?"

"Well, ye-es, I think so, Inspector."

Knollis nodded. "However, he was not the last patient to be seen by your father."

She raised her eyebrows. "No . . . ?"

"A Mrs. Madeleine Burke was the last patient."

Something indefinable flashed across her face. She closed her mouth a shade too tightly, and then tried to look disinterested. "Really, Inspector?"

"You know her, of course?" asked Knollis.

"Well yes, in a way."

"What way, Miss Challoner?"

"Well, she's a prominent member of St. Aidan's Church, and a good charity worker. She's also regarded as a pillar of strength to the local Women's Unionist League."

"Of which you are a member?"

"Yes."

"Then you should know her quite well, surely!" protested Knollis.

"Well, I suppose I do in a way."

A grim smile crossed Knollis's lean features. "Miss Challoner," he said, "please give me a direct answer. Do you, or do you not, know Mrs. Burke?"

"As an acquaintance. Perhaps that's the best way to put it."

"She and your father were acquainted?"

"As doctor and patient, yes."

"And as members of St. Aidan's church?"

"Well, yes," she admitted grudgingly.

"We must be tactful with the wording of the next question," said Knollis, "for we do not wish to be misconstrued. Were your father and Mrs. Burke acquainted outside his surgery and outside the church? Could they be regarded as friends?"

"No-o, not really."

"Mrs. Burke could have no motive for harming your father?"

Joan Challoner screwed up her eyes and looked at Knollis in a bewildered manner. "I—I don't understand, Inspector! I hope you are not suggesting an affair!"

"We are coming back to Inspector Manson's notion," said Knollis. "Mrs. Burke lost her husband two years ago, and your father attended him professionally during his illness. That is correct?"

"Yes."

"Mrs. Burke still engages your father's professional services?"

"She does," Joan Challoner said simply.

"Then we can safely assume that she was completely satisfied with his doctoring," smiled Knollis. "We can assume that she harbours no false notions about any imaginary lack of efficiency?"

"He was a good doctor," said Joan Challoner.

Knollis prepared to leave. "Tell me, Miss Challoner; have you a dog?"

"A dog? Why no! We've two cats. Why?"

"Can you remember the time when a dog was kept in the house as a pet?"

She shook her head vigorously, and her honey-coloured hair danced. "We've never had a dog in the house, Inspector. Father hated them—and said he could never understand why."

And then, as if the statement was a slur on his character she hurriedly added: "He adored cats!"

"Mrs. Burke; does she keep a dog?"

"I—I don't know her well enough to say," she said in a defiant tone.

"Thank you," said Knollis. "Good morning, Miss Challoner."

They returned to the car in silence, and then Manson smiled. "Very nifty, that one about the doc keeping a dog. I still think you're a cunning so-and-so. But look, who are you after?"

"The Burke woman," said Knollis, without offering to qualify the statement.

Manson jumped. "Don't be a darned fool, old man. She's as innocent as a new-born babe!"

"I didn't say I was after her for murdering Challoner, my friend," Knollis said with a grin. "Look, I'll tell you how I'm regarding this case up to now, and you can sort it out for yourself. Something hit that girl between the eyes when I mentioned Mrs. Burke. Lincoln also shied away from the subject. There's some reason why neither of them want to talk about her. Both of them use the word *well* too often when answering questions. A too-frequent use of the word indicates a state of mental uncertainty, or a playing for time. There's something connected with Burke that needs uncovering."

"How?" asked Manson.

"It's ten to one," said Knollis. "What about dining at the Dragon? Highton may take his lunch there and it will give us a chance to look him over before we interview him. You know him by sight?"

"Can't miss him," chuckled Manson. "Bohemian type, with ginger hair and moustache. Medium height, and almost as lean as a chop. Brown eyes with a sardonic sort of smile in 'em. Long slender fingers like a pickpocket's."

"Sounds interesting," said Knollis. "You know, I'm pretty hungry now I come to think about it!"

III

THE LUNCHEON GUEST

THEY FOUND a table in a corner of the room from which the doorway could be watched, and five minutes later Aubrey Highton walked in. He stood for a few seconds in a brief appraisal of the assembled lunchers, and then strode forward, weaving between the tables until he stood before them, his hands plunged deep into his jacket pockets.

He bowed. "Scotland Yard, I presume?"

"No, Dr. Livingstone!" retorted Manson. "You're Mr. Aubrey Highton?"

Highton grinned. "No, my name is Stanley. Now I wonder if I might join you at this table and tell you about my adventures in darkest Africa?"

Knollis took a turn in the game. "I'm afraid we are a course ahead of you, Mr. Highton, but we should still be honoured by your presence."

Highton drew out a chair, and seated himself at the table with his back to the door. He was thus facing Knollis, and had Manson on his left.

"We have a point in common," he said to Knollis. Knollis raised an eyebrow. "I wasn't aware of it."

"You have chosen my seat, my usual seat, and for the same reason, Inspector."

"Which is?"

"To watch your fellow-men as they enter the room, eat, and think."

"I didn't know I had a reason," said Knollis.

A mocking smile came to Highton's face. "We've a reason for every action we take, surely? My reason for choosing your present seat is a professional one. I regard any person who enters this room as potential material for the execution of my art—sorry if that sounds highfalutin. You also regard them as potential material for an execution."

Knollis turned to Manson. "Our Mr. Highton is a wit," he said dryly.

"Well, don't you?" challenged Highton. "Weren't you waiting for my appearance?"

Something akin to a mischievous quirk came to Knollis's lips. "I chose this seat because I'm afraid of being attacked from the rear."

"It could be!" Highton admitted. "According to the morning papers we have a murderer stalking the town."

The waitress approached for his order. Highton flirted extravagantly with her in the process of choosing his lunch, and turned to Knollis and Manson with a smile as she left the table.

"A shocking attitude, isn't it? And yet I find that a little subtle flattery serves better than the bribery known as tipping. If people like you they'll do anything for you without thought of other reward."

"A bit Scotch, isn't it?" Manson grumbled with his mouth full of roast beef and potato.

Highton looked at him in pained surprise. "Good heavens, no! I tip better than most people, but my tips follow the service, and cannot be regarded as bribes."

Knollis laid his knife and fork on his plate. "Mr. Highton," he said quietly, "I cannot believe you joined us merely to discuss the ethics of tipping, and I'm afraid my curiosity can't be restrained until after coffee."

"Too true!" Highton admitted amiably. "That was the curtain-raiser, the ice-breaker, the aperitif, the few words by the chairman to put the speaker at his ease. Quite frankly, I'm interested in the murder that happened under my nose, or at any rate straight opposite my bedroom window."

Knollis waited until the girl had served Highton's soup, and his own and Manson's sweet before replying: "In short, you are impelled by vulgar curiosity?"

Highton scowled over his plate, and twitched his coppery moustache. "Not vulgar, Inspector! Come, come! Give me credit for my sensibilities!"

"You've a natural interest in the doctor's death?"

Highton grinned in a provoking manner. "Have I?"

"You knew him in Algiers!"

Highton straightened his features. "True enough. He was one of my clients."

"Would you care to tell us about how you met him?" suggested Knollis.

"And eat soup at the same time? Well, I'll try. You must know, in case you don't know, that I am an artist. For several months I had a pitch—for want of a better word—on the Rue Michelet in Algiers. My line was portraiture, with a spot of caricature thrown in. For five hundred francs I would spend an hour to an hour and a half in portraying the noble lineaments of such citizens as cared to submit themselves to me. Sometimes they were casual passers-by, and sometimes they were people of dignity who made appointments. Dr. Challoner was one of the latter. An emissary from the Hotel Bretagne, where he was staying, made an appointment on his behalf. The doctor rolled up at ten-thirty the next morning, and one way or another we spent the rest of the morning together—I freely admit that some of the time was spent in a bar where we necked the local vin rouge, vin blanc, and muscatel. We got on famously. We told each other our troubles and ambitions, and on telling him that I hoped to find a steady job in England he offered to help me."

"He invited you over to Sturton Lacey?"

Highton nodded. "To Sturton Lacey, yes, but not to England. I was coming in any case. That Algiers stunt was fun, but not good pay, and the good artist despiseth not hard cash. I'm pretty good at pictures for calendars and Christmas cards. Any picture drawn for a postcard can be made seasonable by a few deft touches. I mean, I can do a vivid white and Reckitts'-blue picture of a street in the Kasbah, and it will go for a picture postcard of the kind loved by tourists. Stick a star on it, and make no comment, and it is taken as a street in Palestine and regarded as a religious subject. So I went to see an agent in Paris, and old Darby of Gray's Inn Road, and they've managed to fix me up with a few quite decent commissions. All I want now is a steady job as a designer or commercial artist, and I'm made. Doc. Challoner was going to provide that job. And now he's gone, and I've got to fish around for myself."

He glanced lugubriously at his soup. "Cold! Where's Milly with the rossbif?"

He waved his soup-spoon hectically and the girl vanished from the room, to return a minute later with his meat course.

"You and Challoner got on well together?" asked Knollis.

Highton shrugged. "We did until the last few minutes. He didn't like my interpretation of the Challoner soul."

"Meaning what, in plain English?" Knollis asked with a furrowed brow.

"Well," said Highton, "I gave him a choice, and I told him the truth. My caricatures have not always been popular, but they are revealing. Some inner eye sees my clients as they really are, and not as they think they are, or pretend to be, or would like to be. I caricatured him, and while he was awf'lly polite over it I could see that he was damned annoyed."

He paused to stoke a fork of meat and potato into his mouth, and while chewing continued: "You see, for some darn queer reason I saw him as a dog."

Knollis came bolt upright. "A what?"

"No, a dog," said Highton. "I drew him as a terrier, with his tongue lolling out, and a funny sort of laugh on his face. That laugh puzzled me at the time, because I'm hanged if I could decide what sort of a laugh it was!"

"A laughing dog!" Knollis breathed heavily.

Highton filled his mouth again, and nodded silently. After a few moments he gulped, and went on: "I think it was a smug laugh, such as a dog gives when it knows it has got its master and mistress for fools—you know, running about after it and making too much fuss."

"Look," said Knollis in a puzzled tone, "why draw him as an animal, anyway? Why didn't you do what I might call a straight caricature—y'know, exaggerated features or a large head on a small body? Why an animal?"

Highton made him wait for an answer until he had disposed of his meat course. "Just a hobby of mine. I see things that way— people, I mean. Sometimes I've had a pretty girl as a sitter and I see her as a flower. A Madonna-like creature I had earlier in the year, for instance, I drew as a white lily, a Madonna lily. Then I had the devil of a row with a pensioned courtesan who was living with a bloke in Hussein Dey. I drew her as a ruminating quadruped, and there was unholy Harry played about that. She wanted to have me arrested."

"A cow," murmured Manson.

"How did you guess?" mocked Highton.

"And you drew Challoner as a dog!"

"Right, Inspector. I explained to him that it was a compliment. The English terrier is quick, alert, intelligent, and a faithful friend."

"A fair piece of rationalization," commented Knollis.

"He did look like one now I come to think back," said Manson. He nodded his appreciation. "Y'know, Mr. Highton, that's true, but I wouldn't have thought about it without help!"

Highton ignored the waitress as she removed his plate and substituted the apple tart. He was looking thoughtfully at Knollis.

"Inspector," he said slowly.

"Mm?" murmured Knollis, stirring himself from a daydream.

"Am I wrong, or are you inordinately interested in the idea of Challoner as a laughing dog?"

"I'm intrigued," Knollis said frankly. "You were the last patient but one to see him."

"True," said Highton. "I'm wondering if the lady who followed me had anything to do with his death. Had she?"

"She had not, Mr. Highton."

"It could have been deuced awkward for her."

"It could," Knollis said non-committally.

There was a further silence until Highton pushed back his plate, and the coffee was served for all three. "There, but for the grace of God, went I!"

Knollis raised his head. "Hm? Why?"

"I was nearly the last patient. You see, Inspector, I was the last bloke to enter the waiting-room. The lady should have gone in before me, but waived her claim. She said her interview might be a lengthy one. I went in first. That was lucky for me. The lady is apparently well-known in the district, and no suspicion can attach itself to her. Now I'm a stranger, and strangers are suspect in all the best murder cases."

"Is that so?" said Knollis.

Highton waved his cigarette case as he offered it round the table. "You should read the *Views of the World*, Inspector. Marvellous dope on the scarlet sins of the species that populate this planet. Makes Maria Monk read like the diary of a nun."

"It is the diary of a nun," interposed Manson.

Highton clasped his head. "Now you're getting pedantic!"

"Suppose you had been the last patient," said Knollis; "what motive could have been ascribed to you?"

Highton's smile mocked him. "He was trying to use me."

"Oh? In what way?"

"He'd got an idea for writing a book—revelations of a doctor stuff, and wanted me to trim up his own drawings for use in it. Now passing off other people's work as one's own is not honest! He wasn't bad as an amateur artist, but as a professional—ugh!"

"You refused, and quarrelled with him?"

Highton touched his own breast with a reproachful finger. "Me quarrel with him? Not me, Inspector! I never quarrel with anyone. I watch the world, think about it, and paint it, but I never quarrel with it. Why should I when it is the goose that lays my golden eggs?"

"The non-moralizing observer, eh?" said Knollis. Highton screwed up his eyes and appeared to be struggling with a word. "No-o, I wouldn't say that. I moralize, judge, and condemn—being human—but I never let the subject hear the condemnation. In the main I work off my annoyances with pencil, pen, or crayon. Once it is worked out of my system I can regard myself as a free man."

"Sensible outlet," rumbled Manson pontifically.

"Quite a good job you hadn't quarrelled with Challoner, and at the same time been the last patient, isn't it?" said Knollis. He added: "Speaking hypothetically."

"I don't follow you," Highton said with a perplexed frown. "You're perhaps suggesting that I might not have found a mode of sublimation in the usual fashion?"

"Just that."

"Well," sighed Highton, "the sublimation or otherwise would have depended on the intensity of the emotional disturbance. My art deals with the petty annoyances of everyday life, and I'm not sure how I'd react if faced with a really serious situation. The potentiality for murder lies within most of us, I suppose."

"I'm of that opinion," said Knollis. "I'm also of the opinion that the potentiality for sainthood also lies within us. Everything depends, surely, on the way we choose to live, on our reaction to circumstances."

"The roads of destiny," said Highton. He puffed at his cigarette and blew a column of smoke to the ceiling. "This job has disturbed me more than I care to admit, and the grey English skies do little to encourage a cheerful manner. Already I'm wondering if I'll manage to settle in England after all. I can't live without sunshine!"

"I thought you were an Englishman, Mr. Highton."

"Yes and no," Highton replied. "I was born of an English father and an English mother who had an English father and a French mother. Sort out that little tangle and you have the answer. My love of the sun comes partly from my forebears and partly from the years I spent in North Africa."

"During the war?"

"Before and during," replied Highton. "I joined the *Régiment étranger*—the Legion, in thirty-eight, when I was at a loose end. I got out again in forty-five. I can't say that it's a good life. Anyway, I roamed about pretty well between Algiers and Sousse and got to know Algeria and Tunisia, so when they turned me loose I went to Algiers and started this lightning-sketch business while I wondered what to do with my life. Now I want to get back to the sun!"

He looked across at Knollis, and smiled. "I'll stay put until this job is cleared up. I realize that you may need me, especially if I add that I didn't like Challoner at all when I got to know a little more of him. We were attracted to each other in Algiers, but I realize now that it was the attraction of opposites. Being an artistic type, I'm an introvert. Challoner was an extrovert, and almost an exhibitionist—a point which I didn't t realize until he told me about his intention to write up his life. They say everything happens for the best, don't they? If Challoner had lived I should have been beholden to him for finding me a job; I should have had to put up with his company, and been bored to tears—or murder. His death has sorted out quite a few problems that were perplexing me, and as soon as you say I'm free I'll get back to the Med."

"You feel you'll never settle?" asked Manson, anxious not to be left completely out of the conversation.

Highton rubbed his cheek. "We-ell, settle is hardly the word. The business of settling-down anywhere is mainly a matter of adaptation, isn't it? I can adapt myself fairly well to new conditions, but there's something missing in England. Mind you, I was educated in England, and I should be English in outlook, but I'm not. I'm looking for something, and I'm blessed if I know what it is. The Mediterranean countries don't exactly satisfy me, but they've something I can't find in England. Life's crude and somewhat primitive out there, even in the towns and cities, but there is a beauty to be found, and something of a pattern in life. Maybe it's that pattern I'm seeking."

He broke off and laughed. "That brings us back to Challoner, doesn't it?"

"I don't see the connection," Knollis remarked with a puzzled tone.

"Life in the Med is crude, but it's a primitive crudeness, and therefore natural. Challoner was crude in a civilized way, and so unnatural that it clashed with the pattern of life. You don't understand me, do you? It's the very devil trying to express one's deeper thoughts in words when one isn't a natural word-spinner. Challoner was a little bloke, about my own height. The little fellow generally carries round with him a full sack of inferiority feelings, *but* he is more successful than the big man at finding compensatory devices. To balance inferiority feelings you need to develop a sense of power in another direction. I find it in my art. I kid myself that I'm a first-class artist—which I am. Now Challoner was a good doctor, but nothing outstanding. He wasn't, say, a famous surgeon or diagnostician. No, he was just a doctor. So he developed what I call the Babbitt-complex. He charged round with a hail-fellow-well-met manner, and was, in the words of a local paper—see his obituary at the week-end!—a much-loved, much-respected, and valued member of the community."

Knollis nodded silently, while Manson muttered that he thought he could follow the argument.

"Ostentation is vulgar," went on Highton. "It wouldn't be regarded as such by many people in the town, but I'm an artist, with an artist's sensibilities and temperament. I tell you that if you were to give me the choice of sitting with Challoner—when he was alive—or with a pig, I'd choose the pig. You expect vulgarity from a porker, but not from Homo Sapiens."

Knollis nodded thoughtfully. Manson found his cigarettes and passed them round.

"Y'know, you were correct when you challenged me on first entering the room," said Knollis. "We both study the human race, but from different angles. Tell me, Mr. Highton; does that scalpel of a brain of yours reveal any motive for the death of Dr. Hugh Challoner?"

Highton shook his head. "I've only known him a few weeks. I know nothing of his history. Still, I shan't be surprised to hear that you've unearthed one."

"Haven't we all?" demanded Manson.

Highton turned on him with a quizzical expression. "Didn't someone or other say that the happy nation was the one with no history? Surely we can transfer that implication from the general to the particular, from the nation to the individual?"

"That is what Inspector Manson is saying," Knollis interrupted. "Some incident in Challoner's life must have served as the cause, as the stimulus. A direct sequence of cause and effect—or perhaps I should use the plurals."

"There you exhibit a mind more analytical than my own," smiled Highton; "the mind of a trained observer *and* a trained reasoner. I'm only the trained observer, and the functioning of the cerebral matter doesn't necessarily follow in my case—well, it does, but only after the material has been digested and sorted by the subconscious and thrown up again in the form of somewhat vague intuitions. Y'know, Inspector, I'm rather sorry for the poor devil who killed Hugh Challoner, because I'd like to see him get away, and he'll have to be darned clever if he's going to do it."

Knollis pushed back his chair. "This is developing into a mutual admiration society, Mr. Highton. I'm as vain as the next man, but I can't allow my vanity to obscure my vision. I must be hard, cold, and unsentimental."

Highton favoured him with a mocking smile. "You must have the devil of a time trying to keep up the pose, Inspector. My intuitions tell me you're a family man. Yes?"

"I've a wife and two boys."

"There you are! The happy family man at home, and the cold-blooded head-hunter during your professional hours. It won't do, you know! You'll develop into a schizophrenic. You can't be true to yourself and your alias at the same time. One day your sentimental streak is going to interfere with business, and then you'll go bust either as father and husband, or as detective."

"Thanks for the advice," laughed Knollis. "By the way, you understand that we shall be paying you an official visit during the next few hours?"

"I'll do all I can to help you," said Highton. "I've told you more than you realize during this most interesting *conversazione*."

"Have you?" Knollis asked keenly.

"You'll think it out later," said Highton. "In return, will you do me a very great favour?"

"What is it?"

Highton screwed tight the ends of his moustache, and a horribly mocking smile came to his lips. "Whenever you find out—if you do, please tell me why I portrayed Dr. Hugh Challoner as a laughing dog. You'll do that?"

He laughed straight into Knollis's face, gave a light bow, and walked out of the room.

IV

THE RELUCTANT ADMISSION

SERGEANT GEORGE ELLIS was busy with a file of papers in the sergeants' room of police headquarters when Knollis returned from his initial investigations with Manson. His bullet-shaped head was bent over the table, and his bristly and rebellious black hair standing on end as if the facts contained in the file were of a startling nature. They were not; Ellis's hair was always like that. He glanced round as Knollis entered the office, brushed his walrus moustache away from his mouth and greeted him with a nonchalant: "Hello, Cock!" The two were firm friends, and the more formal modes of address were saved for more official occasions.

"How's it going?" Knollis asked as he joined him at the table.

Ellis shrugged. "Nothing exciting as yet. I've checked the statements against each other and can't find any discrepancies. The bloke who was waiting for his oppo outside the pub says he saw Highton emerge from the passage beside Challoner's house, cross the street, and enter the pub by the private door on Kirkland Street. And that is funny!"

"What is?"

"Why, this bloke's statement. Why do witnesses go all la-di-da when giving statements. Highton, mark ye, didn't come out; he emerged. He didn't go in; he entered. I'll bet the witness never used those two words in normal speech in his life until this morning or whenever he made the statement. Probably got it from reading court cases where the uniformed jobs do the same trick."

"Most interesting, I'm sure," Knollis murmured in a deceptively innocent tone. "You should write a monograph on the subject when you've time. Now if it will not inconvenience you in any way, do you think we might concentrate on Challoner's murder, and leave the academic study of statements for another time?"

"If that's the way you want it," said Ellis. "Now the bobby who was fetched in by this Eric Lincoln was waiting by the 'phone kiosk for the check-call from headquarters. He distinctly remembers seeing Mrs. Burke pass him just after twenty-five past seven. She lives in a side-street off Upper Bowden Street. Sergeant Johnson, whose office this is, has been hunting witnesses all morning; he's looking for people who might have seen suspicious characters going in or coming out of the pub about the time that Challoner is supposed to have died. He's an optimist!"

"Why so?" asked the earnest Knollis.

"A character would have to be very suspicious to be coming out of a pub just after it had opened. Anyway, how have you wasted your morning?"

Knollis gave him a brief resume of the morning's activities, adding: "I'm satisfied that Highton knows more than he cares to say. His connection with Challoner is all too coincidental to satisfy my mind."

"Coincidences do occur," said Ellis.

"I know," nodded Knollis, "and we've been into all this so many times before. A coincidence only appears to be a matter of chance when the reason or cause cannot be seen. Take the Challoner girl and Lincoln as an example. If either one of them had sheered away from admitting acquaintance with Mrs. Burke, then I might have allowed their ignorance, but when both sheer away, and they are almost engaged to be married which means they are pretty close to each other, then I become suspicious and see more than a coincidence in their manner."

He half-closed his eyes, and stared through the window into the courtyard below, meanwhile gently beating his right fist into the palm of his left hand.

Ellis watched with mild interest for some minutes, and then asked: "Might I be permitted to know what great thought is wandering round the Knollis brain?"

Knollis gave a twisted smile. "One day I'll commit mayhem on your person. You're right, of course. I've a bee in my bonnet. Listen, Ellis! Suppose you had known Dr. Challoner really well; how would you refer to him in conversation with strangers like Manson and myself?"

"Why, either *the doctor*, or as—" said Ellis in a deep tone intended to mock Inspector Manson's.

"No, no!" Knollis exclaimed impatiently. "You're a woman, you ass!"

"Dear me! And no one ever told me!"

"You're also a darned fool!"

"I know that," said Ellis. He rocked himself from side to side in the revolving chair for some seconds. At last he suggested: "Either *the doctor*, *he*, or by his first name."

Knollis beat a gentle tattoo on the edge of the table with his knuckles. "Throughout the interview she referred to him in a very formal manner. Dr. Challoner said this; Dr. Challoner did that; Dr. Challoner was arranging for her boy's admission to hospital."

"She overdid it," said Ellis. "Too respectful and too formal. It struck a cracked note?"

"I'm glad you see my point," said Knollis. "I'm suspicious of her relation to the doctor. He was a widower of five years' standing, and she a widow of two years—"

"Impatient sitting," Ellis interrupted.

Knollis chuckled. "Neatly put, and it may be the truth. Now I'm wondering. . . ."

"Which bodes ill for someone!"

"Highton told Manson and myself that he was the last patient to enter the waiting-room. Mrs. Burke was there first. She asked him to take her place in the queue because she expected to be some considerable time with the doctor. I've mentioned that the boy had nothing more wrong with him than two hammer toes. Why, then, should the interview be a long one? Her business was no more than an inquiry as to the date of the lad's admission to hospital!"

"I get you," Ellis commented thoughtfully.

"Got Challoner's desk-diary handy?" Knollis asked.

Ellis swung round to the table and produced the twelve-by-eight diary from under the confusion of papers. "Here we are—fourth of November. Sun rises—"

"Oh, let me have it," Knollis said, impatiently taking the diary from the grinning sergeant. "The Highton entry. *Highton, Green Dragon, Chest*. That is all, and its brevity intrigues me. Look at the previous entries, Ellis! Each gives details of the complaint, and the medicine and regimen prescribed. Then why not in Highton's case?"

Ellis brushed his moustache before answering. "If we're to follow this theory, which is only tentative, I can suggest an answer. He was so anxious to get Mrs. Burke into his lair that he postponed the Highton entry until she had gone and didn't get a chance to do it."

Knollis eased himself on the table, and nodded into Ellis s rotund features. "That must be it, comrade. It's worth following up, anyway. We should now go and give the surgery a good once-over. What have the local people done?"

Ellis clasped his hands over his corpulence and revolved his thumbs. "My dear Inspector Knollis, you are from the Yard—from New—Scotland—Yard. Who are we to presume?"

He leaned forward earnestly. "Honest, Cock, they've done nothing more than photograph the body and the consulting-room, take the usual measurements, and hand over the cadaver to the surgeon. They have a holy respect for us, and have touched little or nothing."

"In which case we mustn't grumble," replied Knollis. "We do know that there will be little or no overlapping, and that is something to be thankful for. Hop off and organize a car and driver—and keep out of Manson's way. I don't want him trotting round with us if it can be avoided. He's a nice fellow, but not too bright at the moment."

"As if I hadn't noticed," snorted Ellis as he swung from the chair and collected his hat from behind the door. "Meet me at the main entrance in five minutes, and I'll have some conveyance waiting for you."

"Here! Where are the photographs?"

Ellis turned in the doorway. "In the table drawer—detective!"

Knollis spent the intervening five minutes with them, and with Ellis's notes on the statements provided by the witnesses. He turned the latter over in his mind as he went through the building to the car, and was silent until the surgery was reached.

They found a constable on duty in the waiting-room. The room was blue with smoke. The constable saluted gravely and tried to look as if he was a non-smoker. Knollis returned the salute perfunctorily, and a humorous smile came to his lips. "You may smoke if you wish," he said dryly. "Time must hang heavily on your hands."

The constable thanked him soberly, and then said: "A gentleman by the name of Highton called, about half an hour ago, sir. He said you had given him permission to go in there. I didn't let him."

"You mustn't," said Knollis, "unless he is with myself or Sergeant Ellis."

They shut themselves in the consulting-room and went to work.

"Brought the diary?" inquired Knollis.

"You were the last out of the office," Ellis reminded him pointedly.

Knollis scratched his head. "Oh yes! I put the stuff in the despatch case. Here we are. It seems to be the only item Manson's fellows took away, other than the body. I'm wondering . . ."

"What, again! What is it this time?"

"Mrs. Burke. She seriously engages my attention."

"Not having met the lady I can't say whether she'd appeal to me or not," Ellis grinned.

"I must either dismiss her from my mind or concentrate on her until I'm satisfied that she was or was not responsible for his death," Knollis went on, not heeding Ellis's remark.

His gaze wandered over the littered table, taking in the pad of National Health certificates, the prescription pad, the pocket note-book, the tattered medical directory, the assortment of pencils, and Challoner's fountain pen. He chose the note-book, opened it at the back page, thumbed his way forward to the latest entry, and then slowly worked backwards to the first page.

Ellis meanwhile turned his attention to the drawers in the pedestal desk in the corner of the room. "There's a private diary here," he announced. "Various references to some M.B. That cover La Burke?"

"Madeleine Burke," Knollis said casually. "The nature of the references?"

"The initials and a time against them in each case."

"Make a list of them, Ellis. I'll do the same with his visiting-book and desk-diary."

Twenty minutes silence followed, broken only by an occasional grunt from Ellis and an oath when the pencil point collapsed and he had to hunt for his pen.

"What have you got now?" Knollis asked as he straightened up from the table.

Ellis brushed his moustache away from his mouth clearing the deck for action. "If M.B. is the Burke, then the main fact emerging is that he was acquainted with her during the whole of last year. A shorthand note suggests that he received the gift of a wallet on New Year's Day."

"Ye-es, that will follow," Knollis agreed. "He would get to know her when attending her husband two years ago even if he didn't know her before. Incidentally, the visiting-book is devoid of reference to her. The desk-diary shows that she visited the surgery three times during the course of the year: February the eighteenth, April the fourth, and June twenty-sixth."

Ellis grunted. "That's interesting!"

It was Knollis's turn to grunt. "Oh? Why?"

"I've got the almanack open at the page giving the bank holidays. The first two dates you gave are Shrove Tuesday and Good Friday respectively, and the latter is two days after Midsummer's Day."

Knollis reduced his eyelids to slits and stared into the realm of thought. "On all three occasions," he said slowly and deliberately, "the boy would be on holiday from school. Almost looks as if the mountain went to Mahomet when the lad was at home—and that surely means that she did not want him to know that the doc was visiting her. Or am I jumping to a conclusion?"

"It seems to be corroborated by my list," said Ellis. "The dates on which the initials occur are in between school holidays, and there are none which fit in with holiday periods."

"The times, Ellis?"

"Eleven in the mornings, and two-thirty in the afternoons. No particular sequence of dates."

Knollis scratched his head. "I could really do with the assistance of Manson's department, but the telephone is in the hall, which means that Miss Challoner would overhear the conversation. I'll give the constable a message to 'phone from the kiosk—"

He broke off as voices sounded in the waiting-room. The inner door was pushed open, and a tall, thin man entered.

"Sergeant Johnson," said Ellis by way of introduction.

"Oh! Just the man I want," said Knollis. "You know Mrs. Burke, of course?"

Johnson intimated that he did.

"I want you to find out whether she has a 'phone in her house, and when it was installed. I want to know what holidays her boy had from school during the year—the School Attendance Officer can help there. Then I want discreet inquiries making with regard to any visits the deceased may have made to her house."

Johnson whistled softly. "Like that, sir?"

"I won't commit myself," said Knollis, "but I think so."

Johnson moved towards the door. "I'll get working on those points straight away. Should have something for you by this evening, sir."

"Good man," said Knollis.

Ellis turned with a handful of cheque-book stubs. "These likely to interest you?"

"Sling 'em across," said Knollis.

A minute or so later he pushed back his chair. "I'm having a chat with Miss Challoner. Hold the fort."

He found her in the kitchen, preparing tea. She expressed no surprise on seeing him, merely smiling and asking if he would like a cup. "I was bringing it through to you," she said.

Knollis cocked an eyebrow. "The door is supposed to be sound-proofed. How did you know we were present?"

"The door *is* sound-proofed," she replied, and showed no trace of confusion at Knollis's implied accusation of eaves-dropping.

"Then how—?"

"The dispensary is a mere lath-and-plaster addition to the consulting-room, Inspector. It was annexed from the rear hall, as you will see if you turn and look through the doorway. If the door leading from it to the consulting-room is left open it is possible to hear every word spoken."

"Your father was aware of that?" Knollis asked quickly.

Joan Challoner tossed the question away with a careless gesture. "I don't know, and I don't see that it matters whether he did or not. None of us were sufficiently interested in other people's ailments as to listen to recitals of them."

"I'm silenced," Knollis chuckled. "You may now get your own back when I ask you to realize that an investigation of this nature entails a great deal of what you might regard as prying into your private affairs."

"I'm beyond adolescence, Inspector," she said, and poured out a cup of tea.

"I've to ask a few delicate questions," Knollis warned her earnestly.

She poured a second cup and placed both on a tray.

"I've had eight newspaper men round this morning, and in half an hour they wrecked whatever ideas I may have held on the inviolability of private life."

"You make it horribly difficult for me," said Knollis.

She looked up with a weary smile. "Sorry! I didn't mean it that way. What is it you want to know?"

"The financial arrangements in the household."

"My father gave me a personal allowance of four pounds a week, and two pounds for petty household expenses. All other bills were paid by cheque."

"On a quarterly basis?"

"Monthly, Inspector. The butcher, the baker, the candlestick maker . . ."

"I see," murmured Knollis. He gave a quick glance to make sure she was watching him, and then ran his tongue over his upper lip and lowered his gaze.

"Go on!" Joan Challoner snapped.

Knollis affected surprise.

"There's something else?" she challenged.

Knollis hesitated. "I—er—was wondering if your father was contemplating a second marriage."

"Seek for the woman, eh? *Cherchez la femme?*"

"You have a penetrating mind, Miss Challoner."

"Isn't that maxim supposed to be one of the basic principles of crime detection? It is according to the books."

"Suppose you tell me what I want to know, Miss Challoner, and cease this fencing?"

"Wait a moment!"

She slid two plates of biscuits on the tray and hurried to the consulting-room. On her return she pushed a cup of tea towards Knollis. "Don't let it get cold, Inspector. I make a pretty good cup."

Knollis sipped the tea slowly. "You certainly do make a good cup, Miss Challoner. I imagine you're one of those people who do everything well."

"You were asking about my father," she said in a sharp voice.

"You were going to tell me about him," countered Knollis.

"It's the same thing, surely?"

"Your logic has gone astray. However, I wait on your convenience."

"He was not going to remarry, if that is what you want to know!"

Knollis said: "Oh!"

She regarded him with a sardonic smile. "That surprises you, I see!"

"Yes, it does," Knollis admitted. "You've pulled my leg, Miss Challoner. Tell me; was there anything in the nature of an understanding between your father and Mrs. Burke!"

She winced, and then forced a too-casual laugh through her lips. "How ridiculous!"

Knollis took his time. He drank the remainder of the tea, pushed the cup and saucer on the table, and folded his arms across the back of the chair.

"Ridiculous, eh? What is ridiculous about a man and a woman wanting to marry? The man had been a widower for five years, and the woman a widow for two years. The middle-aged feel loneliness even more than the young."

"He wasn't lonely! He had myself—and Eric!"

"There are various kinds of loneliness," said Knollis. "It is possible to be lonely in a crowd. A man of fifty-eight or so can be very lonely when surrounded by young people. We must also remember that the man was about to lose his daughter to another man, and although they were to live in the same house he would lose her more completely than if they were to move to a house of their own."

He broke off and shook his head. "The volatile spirit of youth and the heavy wine of middle-age cannot mix, Miss Challoner.

No, there is nothing ridiculous in the suggestion. The implication is unthinking, and somewhat unkind. Might I also add, selfish."

Joan Challoner stared quietly at the floor, one hand pressed into her cheek. "I—I hadn't looked at it in that light," she faltered.

"Yourself and Eric Lincoln opposed his desired marriage with Mrs. Burke?" Knollis said sharply.

She stamped an angry foot, somewhat dramatically.

"There was to be no marriage!"

Knollis regarded her mildly. "You reminded me that you were no longer adolescent, Miss Challoner. May I remind you in turn that I'm supposed to have reached years of discretion myself, and that I'm not simple! You are trying to evade the issue by the use of an ambiguity. You say there was to be no marriage. True, there wasn't—if yourself and young Lincoln could scotch it. The fact remains that your father and Mrs. Burke had discussed the possibility, and fully intended to marry. I'm a trained investigator, and not a bungling theoretician!"

Joan Challoner stood as taut as a bowstring for a full minute, and then relaxed with a deep sigh. "Father was interested in her," she admitted reluctantly.

"And you regarded him as a silly old fool on the verge of an Indian summer?"

"You have no right to speak to me like this!"

"I'm aware of it," Knollis said blandly. "I have an advantage, and I intend to utilize it in the interests of justice. I want your father's murderer."

She clapped her hands over her face, and spoke between her fingers. "My father is dead! What good can it do him, or any of us, for another man or woman to be hanged?"

"It's unusual for the bereaved to believe with the murderer that death is the end of the story," said Knollis.

He returned to the consulting-room.

V

THE NOTIONS OF KNOLLIS

ELLIS WAS MISSING when Knollis reached the breakfast-room on the following morning. This was unusual, for he loved his stomach and seldom absented himself from meals. Knollis made inquiries, and learned that his lieutenant had left the hotel in a hurry some twenty minutes previously, muttering to himself as he went.

Knollis shrugged and sat down to his meal. Ellis obviously had some bee or other in his bonnet, and the story would emerge in due course. An hour later, at police headquarters, he asked Manson if he had seen anything of him. The stout inspector shook his head. "Haven't set eyes on him this morning. Anyway, he's big enough to look after himself, and the Super is down from County headquarters for a conference—which means he wants to know what the devil we're doing, and why. Better not keep him waiting."

Superintendent Lambert, known to the rank and file as Fairyfoot on account of his size twelve boots, received Knollis sadly, almost as if the deceased man had been his own brother. "Murder in my county! A bad job, Inspector! It does us no good! It does us no good."

"Why worry?" Knollis suggested humorously. "You weren't responsible for it—I hope!"

"True enough," sighed the Superintendent, "but the blessed public expect us to do something about it, and waste no time in doing so. However, let's get down to business. What do you make of the case up to now? Mind you, I've read your report, but it doesn't tell me much."

"I think we can pull it out of the bag, sir," Knollis said in a quiet and confident tone.

"You think so? I'm glad you do. I don't feel at all happy about it. How about you, Manson?"

A rumble began in Manson's belly, and slowly resolved itself into recognizable words. ". . . coming all right, I think, sir. Knollis knows what he's doing, and I'm giving all the assistance I can."

"Must do, Manson! Must do. No time for inter-departmental jealousies. The play's the thing. The cause! The cause! *It is the cause, my soul!* That's it y'know!" He wagged his long thin head. "The cause."

Knollis coughed. Lover of Shakespeare though he was, at the moment he was more inclined to agree with the author of Ecclesiastes that there was a time for all things, and was satisfied that this was the time for talk of murder.

The Superintendent took the cough as a hint. "Yes, to business. Where do we stand, Inspector?"

"You know the facts," said Knollis. "I'll present my present opinions for what they are worth. They are subject to alteration at a moment's notice."

"Still welcome," said Superintendent Lambert.

"Mrs. Burke could have done the job. Miss Challoner is afraid that her boyfriend did it."

The Superintendent blinked. "Oh? Why?"

"His motive was somehow mixed with the opposition raised by himself and Miss Challoner to the doctor's proposed marriage to Mrs. Burke. Miss Challoner was very reluctant to admit that the possibility of the marriage had ever existed, and she only admitted it under pressure."

"Psychological clue, eh?"

"The physical clues are almost negligible, sir."

"I've noticed that. Anyway, carry on with Lincoln for the time being, and ignore Mrs. Burke."

Knollis laid his note-book on the table, consulting it from time to time as he outlined his theories.

"Lincoln was in the house before Challoner died. Joan Challoner was upstairs, and there is no reason to believe that she came down until Lincoln called to tell her that something had happened to her father. Until that moment he was supposed to be in the lounge, reading the current magazines. We can take it for granted he'd been in the house so often, and was so conversant with the routine of the household, that he knew, within a minute or two, exactly how long Miss Challoner was likely to remain upstairs.

"He could have killed Challoner after Mrs. Burke left. If he did, I suggest he returned to the lounge for a few minutes, and then went back to discover the body—or to make sure that Challoner had not escaped from the noose. The door between the consulting-room and the back hall is sound-proofed, and the consulting-room as a whole is sound-proof—reasonably so—providing the door leading into the dispensary is closed. Now . . ."

The Superintendent leaned forward. "Yes?"

"We have to make a practical test, but if it was possible for Lincoln, sitting in the lounge, to hear Challoner overturn the chair, then—"

"He would hurry from the lounge with the intention of finishing him off?"

"Exactly, sir!"

"It hadn't occurred to me," said Manson.

"The motive?" the Superintendent demanded urgently.

"I'm not too sure at the moment," Knollis admitted. "There was an understanding between Challoner and Burke, and I'm fully satisfied on that point. They wanted to marry, and the young couple objected. Only thirty-seven hours have elapsed since the murder, and there's the deuce of a lot of spadework to be done. The details regarding the disposition of his estate will tell us a lot, for we've to consider that if Challoner re-married, then his money, or the bulk of it, would logically go to his wife, and the young couple would be out in the cold, financially."

"Good solid motive," grunted the Superintendent. "Can't beat the monetary motive, y'know. Surprising what people will do for money!"

"Even murder!" Manson boomed in a significant tone.

"I've noticed it," Knollis replied dryly. He turned to Manson. "I'd like you to interview the domestics at the Challoner house. You're the local man, and they'll not be so suspicious of you."

The Superintendent nodded. "Your appearance is all against you in this game, Knollis. Dunno how you get away with it. You look too much like a detective as portrayed on films or stage. Can't understand for the life of me how you get folk to talk!"

Knollis smiled. "I'd be a fool if I wasn't aware of my looks after the way the Press treated me over my last four big cases. The secret is that I exploit them, as one should exploit any limitations."

"Quite! Quite!" murmured Lambert. "Surprising, but there you are. Nevertheless, I agree that Manson should do the job. What exactly are you looking for—or expecting Manson to look for?"

"Undercurrents!"

It was Manson's turn to nod. "You've probably got something there." He then added: "What under-currents?"

"Between Challoner and his daughter, and Challoner and Lincoln. You know what to look for!"

Manson flashed a quizzical glance at Knollis. "Not expecting anything in the way of co-operation, are you?"

Knollis frowned. "I don't understand you."

"Well, I mean if Lincoln killed her old man. She might have helped him, or covered him. Depends on what was in it for herself."

"You're inconsistent, aren't you?" asked Knollis. "Yesterday you were rowing me because you thought I was accusing Joan Challoner. Today you bring her in as an accessory before and after the fact. Frankly, the idea has never entered my head. Judging by what little I've seen of her I should say she's not likely to have assisted in killing her father."

"A lot depends on whether Lincoln heard the chair falling, or whether it was a door he heard," interrupted the Superintendent. "You must see about that test."

"We'll do that," Knollis assured him. "I agree that the result may tell us a great deal, and may have a vital bearing on the course of the investigation."

The Superintendent interlaced his fingers and stared keenly across the desk. "How does this Mrs. Burke stand in your estimation?"

"I see no shadow of a motive up to now," Knollis admitted. "She'd a first-class opportunity, and there's no gainsaying that point. Strictly speaking, it was too good, inasmuch as she had no alibi. If she did kill Challoner she'll have to rely on bluff if she's going to get away with it—and few of 'em manage to keep up the bluff to the end of the story. She was the last patient to leave the surgery; the implication is very obvious."

The Superintendent hesitated for a moment. "Er—look, Knollis; on what clues or evidence are you working? I'm aware of the available facts, and I'm aware of the implications that arise from them, but I can't see into your mind. Care to explain your own notions?"

"Well, I thought that was what I'd been doing," he replied, "but I'm prepared to go farther. Frankly, sir, there is all too little evidence at the moment on which to base any theory or theories. Either Mrs. Burke strangled the doctor, or someone dodged into the consulting-room after she left. They may have come from the house, or from the street. Unless further evidence is forthcoming, we are faced with the following possibilities: Burke strangled him before she left, or Lincoln strangled him after she left. As both Lincoln and Joan Challoner were in the house at the time we can safely assume that no one else could get to the consulting-room via the house. If some third person entered the consulting-room after Burke left, then it was either some person who had been in the waiting-room with her, and knew that she was the last patient, or some person who waited on the street and counted the patients both in and out. The latter possibility is not a probability, for a loiterer was bound to be noticed. We must go through the list of Challoner's patients for that evening; we must go thoroughly into Burke's history; we must do the same with Lincoln; and we must know the state of affairs existing between the three parties, and consider Lincoln as a member of the household for that purpose."

"Concise," the Superintendent remarked gravely. "That details the strategy. What about the tactics?" Knollis again turned to Manson. "You are seeing to the domestics, so I'd like you to follow the house, if you will. I'll take Mrs. Burke."

He paused, drumming his finger-tips on the desk. "I'll give you one tip. Right or wrongly, Joan Challoner suspects her boy-friend, and I think she may break down if you keep playing on her nerves and rapping her knuckles. The domestics should be able to give you sufficient information to enable you to hint shrewdly that you suspect this, and that, and the other—nothing definite, you know, but cultivate a mysterious manner to keep her nerves at strain."

"What about this Highton fellow?" asked the Superintendent as he ran a finger down the list of persons concerned in the investigation. "Where does he come in, if anywhere?"

"Highton puzzles me," said Knollis. "There are people, and we've all met them, who have a pathological urge to make people believe they know more than they do. I'm inclined at the moment to believe that he is one of them. He came to Sturton Lacey on Challoner's invitation, and that fact raises one question in my mind; why did he go to the surgery, and during surgery hours, to see Challoner? As an acquaintance, if not a friend, of Challoner's, I would have expected him to go to the house. There may be a simple explanation, and I think it will be worth-while finding it. I don't like loose ends lying round. They make a case untidy. . . ."

Knollis paused and grinned uncertainly. "There is, of course, one other point. Coincidence is anathema to me, and yet I feel I'm up against a genuine one in the matter of the laughing dog. Either that or the connecting link isn't evident. Frankly, I'm puzzled, and I prefer to think about it for a time before dismissing it or seeking a reason."

"You'll interview him, of course?" said the Superintendent.

"Manson and myself have had an unofficial chat with him, but we will have to interview him with regard to his statement, sir. I'll concentrate on Burke and Highton."

"That brings us to the drawing in the diary, Knollis. You regard it as a vital clue?"

"I don't know," Knollis said somewhat unhappily. "It means nothing to me at the moment, and seems to mean as much to everybody else. I'll swear it has no significance for either Joan Challoner or Lincoln."

"It gives you no clue to the mentality of the killer?"

"Only pointing to the type of person who loves to sign his work."

"Such as an artist?" Superintendent Lambert asked in an eager voice.

Knollis refused to admit the point. "It could. I'll go no further than that."

"That surely indicates Highton—the artist!"

"Or the doctor himself," said Manson. "He used to sketch."

"Or it could be a red herring," added Knollis.

His companions grunted their disappointment.

"Frankly," said Knollis, "I incline to the red herring view at the moment. The simple-minded invariably contrive an ingenious murder with the idea of confusing us. The intelligent murderer does a simple job that leaves the fewest possible traces of his work. Highton may be regarded as an intelligent man. Mrs. Burke may be regarded as an intelligent woman—and there you are!"

"Where?" grunted Manson.

Knollis laughed. "In a state of suspension."

"Lincoln!" exclaimed Manson.

"He's young, and the young have tortuous minds."

"He's had a certain amount of legal training," the Superintendent reminded him. "That usually tends to straighten out the mind."

"You'll pardon me if I contradict, sir," said Knollis. "The legal mind is a tortuous one."

"Ah-ha!" exclaimed Manson. "Then you really do suspect him!"

Knollis protested with upraised hands. "For heaven's sake do remember that we can't suspect any one of them at present. I can allow myself to think that Lincoln had the best opportunity, but I dare go no farther. If he could get to the consulting-room without being heard by the girl, then he is the best bet. If he couldn't, then Mrs. Burke is the best bet. Highton only figures in the list because he was in the best position to know that Mrs. Burke was the last patient that evening—and the good Lord knows where you'll find his motive!"

He paused, and added: "The job was premeditated."

"I didn't think so," said Manson.

"Do you walk round with six feet of clothes' line in your pocket?"

"Heck, no!"

"That's a point," said the Superintendent.

"Where would he park it?" demanded Manson. "Even six feet of line makes a bulky hank."

"A man's pocket, or a woman's handbag," said Knollis. "It's winter, remember, and men wear great-coats with deep pockets. Cotton rope is soft and takes up little room. All our killer needed was an excuse to get behind the doc—and do remember that when seated at his desk his back was towards the wall."

Superintendent Lambert chewed on his bottom lip, and then looked across at Knollis with a gleam in his eyes.

"Knollis!"

"Sir?"

"Can you suggest why the doctor should allow his killer to stand between him and the wall?"

"I cannot," said Knollis.

"He was looking over the doctor's shoulder as the doctor was drawing the laughing dog!"

Knollis blinked. "That's distinctly an idea, sir!"

VI

THE DIRECT APPROACH

MADELEINE BURKE waved Knollis to a fireside chair, and took the opposite one herself. She made a great performance of settling herself for the interview. She crossed her ankles, pulled at her scarlet woollen frock, tugged at a black cuff, patted the black collar, regarded her varnished nails critically, and then looked up with an encouraging glance. "What can I do for you, Inspector?"

Knollis stared at her in a thoughtful manner. "Well," he said with deliberate hesitancy, "we are puzzled by certain aspects of the doctor's life, and think you may be able to help."

She stiffened perceptibly. "Oh? In what way?"

"You knew Dr. Challoner fairly well."

"Indeed!"

"You may be able to tell us whether there was a feminine interest in his life."

Madeleine Burke bridled. "Why should I be able to tell you that, and why should there have been? If it comes to that, why shouldn't there have been?"

"These cases so often revolve round a woman," Knollis said in a non-committal manner. His face was an expressionless mask.

Madeleine Burke twisted her hands into each other and assumed an air of indifference. "I cannot help you, Inspector. I knew little about him until he attended my husband in his last illness, and little more now."

"How long had he been your doctor?"

"Well, actually, he was our doctor before my husband's illness. He attended Leslie—our boy—during all the usual childish complaints. Even so, I knew little about him except as a doctor, and he was a very good doctor!"

"So I believe," said Knollis. "Your son has kept well during the past year or so?"

"Oh yes, apart from his toes. He's a healthy boy, I'm pleased to say."

She arched an eyebrow theatrically. "Why do you ask me these questions, Inspector. Are they intended to lead to something, or are we being conversational?"

Knollis lit a cigarette after asking permission, and flicked the first ash into a tray. "You prefer the direct approach, Mrs. Burke?"

"Oh, always! Definitely!"

"In that case," said Knollis, "we know how we stand." He stubbed the cigarette, and bent forward, his fingers interlaced.

"Do we?" she countered vaguely.

"Dr. Challoner kept two diaries, Mrs. Burke; one a desk-diary relating to his practice, and the other a private diary."

She pressed her lips together, and waited.

"From his desk-diary we learn that you saw him at the surgery with regard to Leslie on Shrove Tuesday, Good Friday, and two days after Midsummer's Day."

"During Leslie's holidays, of course," she said gently. "I've tried to avoid disturbing his education."

"The personal diary implies that Dr. Challoner paid visits to your house at various times between those dates."

Her eyebrows rose. "And why not, Inspector?"

"The dates do not interest me at the moment, Mrs. Burke. I find the times intriguing. Eleven in the morning, and two-thirty in the afternoon are times when your boy would normally be at school."

Madeleine Burke nodded slowly as she made his point. She gave a somewhat insolent smile, and asked: "May I ask a question, Inspector?"

"Of course, Mrs. Burke."

"Was my name in Dr. Challoner's private diary?"

Knollis lowered his head to suppress a smile. He had not expected her to call his bluff so readily. He tapped his fingers against his leg for a minute, and then said frankly: "Your initials, Mrs. Burke."

She threw up her chin. "I can't express admiration for your reasoning, Inspector. You have jumped to the conclusion that I am the only person in town with the initials M.B.!"

"They are contributory factors which have led to the conclusions I have suggested if not stated," Knollis said stiffly.

"Suppose we ignore all contributory factors, and the illogical conclusions," she challenged him. "Why not accuse me outright of being Dr. Challoner's paramour!"

"Mrs. Burke!" exclaimed Knollis.

She took her cigarette case from the table-bookcase at her side, and lit a cigarette. Not until she was blowing the smoke down her nostrils did she deign to comment on Knollis's shocked exclamation.

"We did agree on the direct approach, Inspector!"

"There are degrees of bluntness, Mrs. Burke. We may have agreed on the direct approach, and yet to suggest a friendship between yourself and Dr. Challoner is not necessarily to imply it was anything but a platonic friendship."

"You are either a very tolerant man, or a hypocrite, Inspector."

"I hope I am neither, Mrs. Burke, but rather a man who can add two and two together without getting the total higher than four."

She laughed, and wriggled a cushion into position behind her back. Then she shot a straight and serious glance at Knollis. "You believe in platonic friendships?"

"I believe they do exist," said Knollis, "although I'll readily admit I believe that quite a few well-advertised ones are nothing but illicit associations."

"You're not a cynic?"

"I sincerely hope not."

Madeleine Burke leaned towards him, her forearms resting on her knees, the cigarette parked in the corner of her mouth. "We'll imagine the worst, Inspector. We'll assume that Dr. Challoner and myself were intimate; if that were the case, don't you think that the initial of my Christian name would have been found in his diary rather than both my initials?"

"We seem to be swallowing camels, Mrs. Burke," said Knollis.

"You suggested the direct approach," she reminded him tersely.

Knollis narrowed his eyes. "Mrs. Burke, would you care to explain why Dr. Challoner called on you only when your son was at school? You're surely not suggesting that it was with the object of discussing the boy's toes!"

"Did he call on me?" she countered. "You are trying to force me into an admission of some kind of guilt on the strength, or weakness, of initials found in his diary, initials which happen to correspond with my own. I repeat, Inspector; did Dr. Challoner call on me?"

A whimsical smile came to Knollis's lips. "We must ask the neighbours, Mrs. Burke, and the ladies who live across the street, opposite your house. They'll know; they always do. I came to you with the object of getting a straight story at first hand, and avoiding the imaginative efforts of malicious people with wagging tongues. You don't intend to meet me even half-way. And yet I can learn the truth. Every time the doctor called the curtains of the neighbouring houses swayed gently, and the ladies opposite were standing well back in their front rooms to watch, and not be seen. Oh yes, the evidence will soon be forth-coming if I go about the search in the right way."

He sat back, and watched her as an anxious tongue explored her cheek.

"If this was an official call I should have brought a sergeant with me as witness," he went on. "Every word spoken would have been taken down, and in the terms of the usual caution would have been liable to use in evidence. I have come alone, Mrs. Burke. . . ."

The dark lashes fell over her vivid blue eyes. "Hugh Challoner and I were very friendly," she whispered. "There was nothing more to it than that."

Knollis sighed. The first barrier was down. "Marriage had been discussed, Mrs. Burke?"

"Well . . . !"

"You had discussed marriage?" Knollis persisted. The dark lashes rose for a fleeting second, and fell again. "Yes, it had been discussed."

Knollis spread his hands. "There you are! That was all I wanted to know. If the initials had not referred to you, but to some other person, then I had to discover the identity of that person. I do assure you, Mrs. Burke, that I'm not trying to bully you into any damaging admission. Please do not mistake my intentions."

"People talk so," she said lamely. "We've had to be so very careful. A reputation can be ruined overnight in a town like Sturton Lacey."

"I'm fully aware of that," said Knollis. "I chose to come to you rather than make inquiries of your neighbours. Most people have vivid imaginations and are incapable of making two and two come to less than six. I relied on you to give me a straight tale, plain and unvarnished."

She heaved a deep sigh. "There was nothing to it, really, Inspector. He was an angel to us when Edmund was ill. Afterwards he helped me to straighten out my affairs. The friendship grew quite naturally. When he realized that Joan was likely to be marrying in the near future he asked me if I would marry him. There was nothing romantic or passionate in the friendship. The marriage would have been a sensible arrangement on both sides. It would have provided a father for Leslie, and Hugh would have had someone to look after him and his home."

"Yourself?" Knollis asked quietly.

She stirred uneasily. "Life has been a little difficult since Edmund died, and Leslie needed a father's influence. . . ."

"It was with the object of discussing the marriage with Dr. Challoner that you asked Mr. Highton to take your turn in Tuesday night's surgery?"

She looked up, surprised. "You know that?"

"That incident turned my attention to you."

"The little things, Inspector! The little things that change our lives!"

"Tell me, Mrs. Burke; how long ago was your telephone installed?"

"The telephone? Why, perhaps a little over a year."

"It was installed at Dr. Challoner's suggestion?"

"Why, yes!"

"So that he could ring you before he called. To make sure that you would be at home?"

She nodded, twice.

"That's all I wanted to know," said Knollis. "Having cleared the mysterious M.B. from my list I'm free to concentrate on other angles."

A wry smile crossed her rouged lips. "I—well, I got the wind up for nothing, didn't I?"

"Unless you killed him, yes," Knollis retorted with deliberate cruelty.

She regarded him with wide eyes. "Me—kill Hugh! Great God, no! Why should I ever want to kill him? My boy's future depended on Hugh Challoner. The ground is swept from under my feet now. All the plans I made are worthless. I—I don't know what I'm going to do! I really don't. . . ."

"The direct approach," Knollis said softly. "You did engineer this projected marriage, Mrs. Burke? Or perhaps you merely helped it along?"

Something like a sob escaped her. "Of course I helped it along! What would any woman in my position do but that? I've no skill in my fingers with which I can earn a penny. My boy needs an education. If it wasn't for him I'd finish it all. Hugh was paying for his schooling—you may as well know that! I've three pounds a week from all sources, so what else could I do but put myself under an obligation to Hugh? He paid the rent, the fuel bills, and for Leslie's schooling. There was only one possible answer when he asked me to marry him."

She stared at Knollis with abhorence in her eyes. "And you asked if I killed him! Great God!"

"Tell me, Mrs. Burke," said Knollis; "for what especial reason did you want to see him on Tuesday evening?"

She let her hands fall limply into her lap as she answered: "I wanted to ask him how soon we could be married. He said he must see Joan married first, and then find her a house. He said that two women in one house never would agree, and particularly when one of them had been brought up in it, and it was her home. He had something else on his mind. I don't know what it was. I wish I did, because I think it would be the key to everything. . . ."

"This contradicts your original statement," said Knollis.

"I suppose so, Inspector," she faltered miserably.

"What gave you the impression that he'd something on his mind."

"He was a long time answering some of my questions. He looked at me once or twice as if he had not heard me, and I had to repeat myself. He was in ill spirits, Inspector. He had something on his mind. . . ."

"You said he was scribbling something just before you left him. What was it, Mrs. Burke? Can you say?"

She looked directly into his eyes, a square look.

"He was drawing a dog's head, Inspector; drawing it idly, almost subconsciously. I doubt if he knew he was doing it. It was a queer little dog, laughing."

Knollis licked his lips, and gulped. "Er—Mrs. Burke," he said; "are you prepared to swear—in a court of law if necessary—that he drew that laughing dog in your presence?"

"So help me God, I watched him draw it."

"Did you say anything to him about it?"

"Ye-es!"

"And he said . . . ?"

"He answered in French. I've done no French since I was at school, and the only word I caught was *chien*."

"Dog!" said Knollis.

She nodded.

"And then?" asked Knollis.

"He said: 'We must get Joan and Eric married as soon as possible, and then nothing matters.'"

"Yes, Mrs. Burke?" coaxed Knollis.

"I asked him outright if anything was wrong. He gave a twisted sort of smile and asked how long it was since I'd read the Bible. He gave me no time to answer, but came round the table, took my hands in his own, and led me to the door. He said he would see me tomorrow—Wednesday, and then added: 'The man who has no worries doesn't exist, Madeleine!'"

Knollis had his note-book on his knee by now, taking down her statement in shorthand. He looked up as she came to a verbal halt. "Yes, and then?"

She hesitated. "Well, just before he closed the door on me he smiled, and said: 'We're apt to think that living in time is like rowing down a river, and we can leave the past well behind and forget it. We can't, Madeleine, and it's damnably frightening and humiliating when it catches up with you.'"

"That was all?"

"He said good night, and closed the door on me. I heard him walking slowly back to his table, and then I came home. I knew I'd get no more out of him if I stayed."

"You came straight home!"

"I swear I came straight home, Inspector!"

"And that was the last time you saw him?"

She lowered her head.

"The constable waiting by the kiosk says you passed him at twenty-five minutes past seven, Mrs. Burke," said Knollis in a reassuring tone.

"Oh dear!" she sighed. "The relief . . . !"

"Tell me, Mrs. Burke," said Knollis, "what do you know of his past life? I take it you are as anxious as myself to see his murderer brought to justice?"

"That scarcely needs answering, Inspector! As far as his past life is concerned, I know little or nothing about him. He was trained at Edinburgh. I know that, and I know he was assistant to some London doctor for a time after qualifying. His father was a fruit importer, and worth a great deal of money. He paid for Hugh's education, and bought his practice. Apart from those meagre facts I know nothing—except that he travelled a great deal in his younger days and was also something of an artist."

"I see," said Knollis. "Now please tell me: were you aware of any opposition to the marriage?"

"Well . . . !"

"His daughter, Mrs. Burke?"

"Neither of them wanted him to go through with it, Inspector. They were furious with him."

"The reason?"

"Obvious," she retorted bitterly. "He intended providing for Joan in his will, but even so most of his estate would have come to me in the event of his death, because I would have been his legal wife. Joan and Eric would lose by our marriage."

"He admitted the opposition, and discussed the matter with you, Mrs. Burke?"

"Yes."

"You think it might have been this disagreement in his home that was disturbing him on the night of his death?"

She shook her head vigorously. "It was not that, Inspector! He'd made up his mind about the course he intended to take, and had no intention of being side-tracked or persuaded to change his mind."

"You had seen him earlier in the day?" asked Knollis.

"No. He called on Monday, about half-past two. He brought a large box of fireworks for Leslie, and asked me to hide them until Wednesday night."

"Oh!" said Knollis. "He was coming to the house for Guy Fawkes' celebrations, and openly?"

Madeleine Burke nodded. "He was going to ask Leslie how he would like him as a new father."

"And then announce the engagement."

"Openly, yes."

"And how would your boy have reacted to the idea?"

"He would have welcomed it, I think. He was very fond of Hugh."

"Thank you," said Knollis. "One other question, Mrs. Burke. Did you notice anybody loitering near the surgery when you left on Tuesday evening?"

"The street was clear, Inspector."

Knollis thanked her, and excused himself. He found Ellis waiting in the rear seat of the car, smoking his famous meerschaum pipe and infamous brand of tobacco. Knollis held the door wide open to let the fumes escape, and asked if Ellis had been on holiday.

"Been proving you wrong for once in your life," said Ellis happily.

Knollis climbed in beside him, gave the driver the Green Dragon as the next call, and demanded an explanation of Ellis.

"Been doing two queer jobs," he replied. "I ran into Highton, and at his suggestion showed him the consulting-room. Thought he might have some notion or other in mind, but if he had he didn't give it away. Second job, and the original one, was having the ink in Challoner's pen analysed, and compared with the drawing of the dog. A cursory exam seems to prove that it was drawn with his pen."

"That's true," Knollis informed him. "Neither Manson nor myself were completely right about it. Challoner drew the dog before Mrs. Burke left, and under her eyes."

He went on to detail the results of his interview, after which Ellis took a turn.

"Johnson reports that the Burke boy had no absences from school owing to illness or other cause. Inspector Manson has ascertained that Challoner left Mrs. Burke a small matter of two thousand pounds if he died before he married her."

"She can do with it," said Knollis.

"Lincoln's firm, Hodson and Spender, drew up the will," added Ellis.

"So that Lincoln was aware of its provisions?"

"A bit late to knock off the doctor, surely!" Ellis protested.

"I suppose so," said Knollis, "unless they have some idea of contesting the will, and I can't see on what grounds they could approach the matter. Challoner seems to have been in his senses. They've got the balance, anyway, so why should they worry? They might have got nothing more than a bite from the mousetrap."

The car drew up outside the Green Dragon, and Knollis prepared to alight.

"Haven't you forgotten something?" said Ellis.

Knollis turned back into the car. "Such as?"

"The clock. It's lunch-time."

Knollis heaved a sigh, and surrendered. "Your tummy! All right, but we don't eat at the Dragon today. Mr. Aubrey Highton is too much at his ease on social occasions, and our next meeting is to be an official one, with all the advantages on our side."

With a rueful smile, he added: "I hope!"

VII

The Departing Woman

Aubrey Highton's brown eyes rested easily on Knollis as he and Ellis introduced themselves into his room on the second floor of the Green Dragon. He flicked the stub of a cigarette into the grate, nodded his head, and said: "Well, well! The cops!"

"Hope we're not intruding?" Knollis asked. His manner indicated that he didn't care whether he was doing so or not.

"Not intruding exactly," replied Highton, "but I'm darned busy, so if you can get down to business I'll be obliged. I suppose you want to know if I saw any suspicious characters hanging around on Tuesday evening?"

"That's the general idea," Knollis agreed. "There are a few other questions as well."

Highton flopped on the edge of the divan-bed, and waited, completely at his ease.

"First, then," began Knollis, "can you tell me at what time you went across to the surgery?"

"Seven or eight minutes to seven. I always leave such appointments until the last minute, hating to hang around doing nothing. Further to the point, I wanted Challoner to give my chest a good pounding, and I've found on other occasions that even if you are early they send you back to wait until after surgery so that you aren't holding up the queue."

"Had trouble with your chest?" asked Knollis.

"Bronny," said Highton. "This climate sets it going. I've been all right while I've been in the Med, but I've a living to earn. Seems as if I'll have to do with less money and beat it back to Africa for my health s sake."

"You said you were a commercial artist?"

"I did, and I am." He played with his coppery moustaches and cocked an eye at Knollis. "Perhaps I should say I shall be. I told you what I'd been doing, and why I came to England. Old Darby tells me he can find me plenty of work with calendars and Christmas cards, and plenty of book illustrating and jacket designing if I stay in England. Bit of a devil, and I don't quite know what to do. As you know, I had ideas of settling down, but I don't think I can do it. Once I've got Darby organized I'll probably do a steady trek along the North Africa coast from Fez to Alex and Cairo, cross to Crete and Greece, make my way up Italy, and then go back to Algiers from the Italian Riviera. Depends on how I manage to pull in the cash."

"You said you were in the war, Mr. Highton."

"Yes, the old Legion. When I was twenty-three, which was in thirty-eight, I wanted adventure. I got out in forty-five and wouldn't join again for a quid a day."

"A hard life, I've heard," Knollis murmured sympathetically.

Highton whistled. "Hard! They nearly ruined my hands, Inspector. I spent most of my time building roads."

"You took up your artistic work again immediately on leaving the Legion?"

"Mm," Highton said in a reminiscent strain. "Set to work to get my hands back to normal, and rented the shop on the Michelet. You know most of the story that comes after that—as if it mattered!"

"What did Dr. Challoner say about the condition of your chest, Mr. Highton?"

Highton grimaced. "Seemed to think it was a bit dicky, and suspected some congestion in the left lung. He was wondering about me being X-rayed, and said he would think about it."

"Tell me," said Knollis; "why did you go to the surgery? I thought you and he were pretty friendly."

"We were. We were. I could have gone to the house, but I prefer to keep business and pleasure apart."

He paused, and gave a sardonic smile. "Plus the fact that young Lincoln, the fool, thinks I'm trying to push him out of the running with Joan Challoner!"

"And are you?" Knollis asked quietly.

Highton laughed. "Not me. She's a goodly wench withall—and don't ask withall what, because I know that one! A goodly wench withall, as I said, but I'm not interested in the idea of settling down. On the few occasions I've been to the house Lincoln has glared at me, and been as unsociable as a puppy with his first biscuit, so I decided to keep clear. Consequently, I presented myself at the surgery like any other client."

"Challoner comment on your appearance?"

"Didn't seem to strike him that there was anything unusual. He never said anything, anyway."

"You were the last patient to enter the waiting-room?"

"That's right," said Highton. "I seem to remember telling you yesterday. Still, this is your official visit, so I'll play your game! Yes, the lady was present when I arrived. There was also a young fellow waiting. He went in when the bell rang, and Mrs. Burke—I know her by sight—asked me to take her turn as her interview with the doctor was likely to be a lengthy one. Having a rough idea why she wanted to be the last to see him I played ball with her."

"Why did she want to be the last to see him?" asked Knollis innocently.

"You ain't very convincing, Inspector," Highton mocked. "After investigating Challoner's affairs for these past few days you should know the answer. Challoner was courting her."

"He discussed the matter with you?"

"No-o, I wouldn't put it that way," said Highton. "He dropped out odd remarks. Incidentally, I concluded that the idea was not backed by the approval of Joan and young Lincoln, and I think they both suspected me of aiding and abetting the romance."

Knollis smiled. "Were you?"

"Yes. I thought the old cock deserved some comfort in his life—especially as Joan was getting married. I egged him on as hard as I could."

"It was about seven o'clock when you went into the consulting-room. That correct?"

"Just seven when I came back to lock the waiting-room door," Highton corrected him.

"And about ten past when you left?"

"Roughly, yes."

"Quick examination, wasn't it?" challenged Knollis.

Highton blinked. "Dunno? All he had to do was poke his what's-it, his stethoscope, on my chest, and listen. He poked round for a few minutes, and then said I'd better have its photograph taken. I said that was all right with me, buttoned up my shirt, pulled on my jacket and greatcoat, said I'd see him in the smoke-room here at half-past eight, and let myself out."

"You came straight back to your room?"

"Yes, I was feeling a bit untidy. He'd dragged my shirt out of my belt to some extent, and it was bunched round my waist and feeling most uncomfortable. I tidied myself and went down to the bar. I like perpendicular drinking myself, and was going to stay there until Challoner joined me, when we would have gone to the smoke-room."

Highton offered his cigarettes, lit them from his lighter, and then gave Knollis a curious glance. "I don't know whether you'll regard this as significant or not, but I think I should tell you. I didn't remember it until after our chat yesterday. I changed my jacket when I got back from the surgery, and some time after going down to the bar found I'd left my hanky in the other jacket, so I slipped upstairs for it. If you look through my window you'll see that the surgery is directly opposite. The lights of the waiting-room and consulting-room light up this room in the evenings when surgery is on. Well, I didn't bother to switch on my light when I came in. I'd slung my jacket over that chair under the window, and as I was fumbling for the hanky I noticed someone leave the surgery by the waiting-room door."

He paused, obviously for dramatic effect, and added: "I think it was a woman."

Knollis said "Oh!" and allowed himself a few seconds for the new item of information to sink in.

"You didn't see her in the waiting-room before she came out?" he asked. "What I mean is: are you sure that she came from the waiting-room, and did not appear to be coming out? I mean: she wasn't walking past, and was level with the door when you looked up?"

Highton checked off the questions on his fingers.

"I didn't see her in the waiting-room, Inspector, because, as you'll see, if you look, the windows are hammered glass. I did see her leave the waiting-room because she opened the door to come out—quite a normal habit—and the waiting-room light was on, so that I *did* see her leave the waiting-room, which is what I said at first."

Knollis strolled to the window. "So they are. I see that there are two sash windows in the consulting-room, the upper sashes of which are composed of plain glass. Could you see into the room?"

"The blinds were down, Inspector—or perhaps the curtains were drawn across. All I could see were chinks of light at the edges of the curtains—or blinds."

"Which way did this woman go, Mr. Highton?"

"She turned left."

"Your left, or her left?"

"Her left."

"Towards the corner of Bowden Street?" Knollis asked in a surprised tone.

Highton nodded. "She could hardly go in any other direction if she turned left, could she?" he asked sarcastically.

Knollis waved his sarcasm away. "I'm merely checking facts. At what time was this?"

Highton closed one eye, and scratched his ear. "About twenty-five past."

"You're sure of that?"

"Well, as sure as one can be of such things. It was half-past seven by the clock in the bar when I got down again, and that is four minutes fast."

"H'm!" grunted Knollis. "You took no further notice of her movements?"

"Why should I?"

"That's true," said Knollis. "You weren't supposed to know that Challoner had been murdered."

Highton straightened his back, and stuck his chin out. "I don't like that crack. How could I have known that he'd been murdered?"

"You couldn't—unless you killed him, or unless you went back after he had been killed!"

"I did neither, Inspector Knollis," he said gravely.

"Then that's that," said Knollis. "You took no further interest in her, and you had no reason to do so."

Highton rose from the bed and stalked about the room, the cigarette end in his mouth and his hands thrust deep into the pockets of his trousers. "After all," he threw over his shoulder, "Mrs. Burke said her interview might be protracted, and it was only twenty minutes or so after I left. You seem to see something suspicious in the information, whereas I thought it would merely corroborate any statement she might have made."

Knollis glanced at Ellis, taking notes from a chair close to the fire, and winked.

"Mr. Highton; it didn't strike you as queer that she left by the waiting-room door instead of the usual exit from the consulting-room?"

Highton wheeled round, and looked down at Knollis in amazement. "Lord! I never even thought about it from that angle. I probably wouldn't have remembered the incident at all if the morning papers hadn't said that Challoner was murdered five minutes after his last patient had left the surgery."

Knollis wandered over to the window again, and looked down into Kirkland Street. "You're an artist!"

Highton laughed. "I thought we were agreed on that. I kid myself that I am, Inspector. What's the implication?"

Knollis shrugged carelessly. "I'm just wondering about your power of observation. To what degree can you describe the woman's appearance? Her height, dress, or manner?"

Highton joined him at the window, and laid a hand on his left shoulder. "Shall we reconstruct the circumstances, Inspector? It was a dark night, and the sky was overcast. The hammered glass, by virtue of its refractive index, gives a dazzling effect— as it's intended to do. The woman was silhouetted against the light of the room for just so long as it took her to open the door, walk through the doorway, and close the door. How long would that take? Two seconds? As soon as the door was closed she was a shadow against a shadowed wall, with the light from the window acting towards me as footlights do to an actor—blinding me to all else but its own light. Observation is a habit with me these days, but I possess neither the eyes of a cat nor the power to polarize light. Sorry, Inspector, but there it is!"

Knollis shook the hand from his shoulder and turned back into the room. "A fulsome explanation, Mr. Highton, but you're right. I expected too much. One thing I must ask: are you prepared to say whether this woman did or did not resemble Mrs. Burke?"

"I can say that she did, Inspector," said Highton.

Knollis jumped at the admission. "You can?" he asked eagerly.

Highton gave his mocking smile again. "I can, Inspector, but I'd be drawing on my imagination instead of on observation and perception. Sorry, but I won't say it for you! I was in this room for less than a minute, and what we might call the Woman-Incident occupied a mere fraction of that time."

Knollis smiled wryly. "You're that almost mythical person, the intellectually honest witness. Now look, Mr. Highton; as an artist, and consequently as an observant person, what can you tell me about the general demeanour of Mrs. Burke as she sat with you in the waiting-room?"

"I did run my eye over her," Highton admitted. He added: "As an artist, of course. She's getting on!"

"You're horrible," snapped Knollis.

"Yes, I suppose I am. Actually, she's a well-preserved woman, and I admire women who don't let themselves run to seed. I don't profess to be a mind-reader, but I can tell you what she was doing. She was staring at the toe of her right shoe, and a frown appeared between her eyes once or twice. I saw nothing unusual in that, for most people attending a doctor's surgery have some worry or other on their minds."

"When did you first hear of the doctor's death?" Highton hesitated. "You'd better get my landlord to check that—if you want the identical second. I was talking to him across the bar when a fellow came in and said there were a lot of bobbies across the road, and that Dr. Challoner had been found murdered in his own surgery. It'd be about ten to eight."

"What did you do? Go out to see if there was anything to be seen?"

Highton shook his coppery head. "I froze!"

"Froze?"

Highton nodded. "Some people dash out, some people retreat—or escape, and some people pause and reflect. I reflected. I reflected alone, because everybody else in that bar ran to Kirkland Street."

"And having reflected?" said Knollis.

"I decided there was only one thing I could do that would be of assistance to anybody."

"That was?"

"Have another drink," said Highton. "The landlord was not present, so I went round the bar, pulled myself a tankard of mild, and had it on the house."

Knollis pulled his hat on his head. "I fancy that this is where we came in. You'll be prepared to sign a typed copy of your statement, Mr. Highton?"

"If it says no more than I've told you," said Highton. "Now, if you don't mind, I'll work. I want to see if I can imagine the scene in the surgery when Challoner lay dead. Perhaps we can compare it with your photographs at a later date?"

"It should be interesting," said Knollis.

"If you like it, I'll give it to you."

Knollis turned with a frown. "A morbid subject, surely?"

"Agreed," said Highton. He turned to Ellis, who was now putting away his note-book and pencil. "Sorry I didn't tell you what I was doing when you took me in the surgery. I don't like to consider a subject consciously, but prefer to get my conscious mind into a state of suspended animation and let my subconscious soak up the material. Thanks for showing me round."

"You're sticking around for a few days?" asked Knollis as he opened the door.

"For at least another week, Inspector."

Reaching the street, Knollis took Ellis's arm and led him away from the waiting car. "We're going for a little walk, Ellis. I'm curious about that lady."

"If it was Mrs. Burke, then why did she go back?" Ellis pondered.

"If it was Mrs. Burke, then *how* did she go back?" said Knollis. "She couldn't have repassed the constable, or he would have noticed her—and remember that he was by the kiosk until Lincoln fetched him to Challoner! He'd nothing else to do but watch the passers-by and listen for the 'phone bell."

He crossed the road to the corner of Kirkland Street and Bowden Street, and steered a diagonal course to the kiosk on the other side of Bowden Street, and about a hundred yards or so from the corner.

"Thus far we are going well," said Knollis. "She reached this point about twenty past seven, we'll say. It's only a minute from the surgery."

He glanced round, and said: "Ah!"

"I'm with you," said Ellis. "Let's cross the street. It looks like the entrance to an alley or a passageway."

"And about thirty yards on," said Knollis. "She could have crossed without being noticed by the constable."

He walked down the passage with Ellis in the rear, for there was barely room for them to walk side by side between the ten-feet high stone walls. Forty yards further on they came into another street.

"We now turn left," said Knollis.

"And come back into Kirkland Street," said Ellis.

They did get back into Kirkland Street, two doors below the Challoner house. Knollis consulted his watch. "Six minutes only, and we were ambling."

"So that's how it was done," said Ellis.

"Having settled my problem, let's consider yours, Ellis. Why did she go back?"

"And we've to prove that she didn't go straight home as she says in her statement! We've to prove that she returned. . . ."

Knollis narrowed his eyes. "What caused her to change her mind, Ellis? What thought caused her to return to the surgery? Was it something the doctor had said to her? Or a sudden impulse? And another thought occurs to me! The waiting-room is the room on the other side of the lounge wall; the waiting-room is between the lounge and the consulting-room—"

"I suppose Highton's reliable as a witness?" Ellis interrupted.

"Why shouldn't he be reliable?" demanded Knollis.

"Witnesses have been known to fake evidence!"

Knollis was loath to admit the possibility, but nodded glumly. "There is the laughing dog coincidence to take into account. I grant you that. And I suppose it would have been possible for Highton to slip back and put paid to the doctor, but why, Ellis? Tell me why? He'd known the doctor only for a few weeks, apart from the meeting in Algiers, which, on Highton's own admission, only lasted for the space of half a morning. Highton gains nothing by Challoner's death—in fact if he decides to stay in England he will lose by it, for it's certain that a fellow like Challoner must have had a certain amount of influence in Sturton Lacey, and could have introduced Highton to some worthwhile connections."

"Seems you're going to be right," muttered Ellis, "but he had the opportunity, and I can't dismiss him from my mind yet."

"No, we can't dismiss him," agreed Knollis. "Funny, but every time we move we come up against the enigma of the laughing dog! I wonder what the deuce it means?"

"I've searched my mind for any old thing that might link up with it," said Ellis, "and all I can think of is the old nursery rhyme where the little dog laughed to see such fun—you know the thing!"

"The little dog must be laughing his head off just now," said Knollis, "but I'll have the last laugh—and that's the best laugh of all."

VIII

THE SLAMMED DOOR

THE CONSULTING-ROOM looked like a village jumble sale when Knollis and Ellis walked in after their interview with Highton. Inspector Manson and Sergeant Johnson, aided and abetted by two detective-officers, were investigating in the grand manner, and a litter of Challoner's professional records were scattered round the room.

Manson came forward eagerly when he saw Knollis appear round the door. "Any news, Knollis?"

Knollis flung his hat into a chair. "You made the test?" he asked.

Manson's eager expression faded. He began to rumble deep in his belly. ". . . tried it with negative result. Not a ruddy sound!"

Knollis took him by the arm and led him towards the inner door, saying to Ellis as he went: "You know what to do!"

Then he took Manson through the hall to the lounge, and closed the door. "Listen!"

A dull thud was heard some seconds later, coming from somewhere beyond the dividing wall.

"I think that was what Lincoln heard," said Knollis. "Now Highton tells me . . ." He went on to repeat Aubrey Highton's story of having seen the woman leave by the waiting-room door.

"That makes a difference," nodded Manson. "What's the next move?"

"Get Lincoln here. Send one of your blokes for him. Perhaps Johnson will be the best man for the job."

"I'll fix that straight away," said Manson. "We seem to be moving at last."

They returned to the consulting-room, and Johnson was sent on his errand.

"We can't afford to suggest any ideas into Lincoln's mind," said Knollis. "This is the plan; you've two men here, plus the constable in the waiting-room. The constable will open and close the door leading into the street. One of your men will, one minute later, open and close the consulting-room door leading to the yard, and the other will attend to the door leading into the house."

He called in the constable, and explained their duties to all three men.

"I see," said Manson. "The idea is that Lincoln heard the door, and not the falling chair?"

"Lincoln himself said it was a door," Knollis re-minded him. "The other possibility was our own invention, and your test has proved it false."

"You'd think she'd have closed it quietly," said Manson.

"She would in the normal way, but she'd the latch-lock to cope with. You know how you have to force the catch against its springs."

"So you do," rumbled Manson. "Well, it all gets very inter-esting."

Some fifteen minutes later Lincoln was ushered into the room looking bewildered and uneasy. Knollis greeted him with a reassuring smile.

"We'd like you to help us in an experiment. Will you come with Inspector Manson and myself, please?"

They went to the lounge, where Knollis invited the young clerk to be seated. "Please don't speak," he said.

He snapped his fingers with sudden impatience and hurried back to the consulting-room, where he told the men to work the plan the opposite way round, leaving the waiting-room door until the last. He returned to the lounge and softly closed the door. A large question mark was evident on Lincoln's forehead, but Knollis made no attempt to answer it. He took a magazine from the table and made a pretence of reading it while surrep-titiously watching the hands of his wrist-watch. Two minutes sped by, and another minute, and yet another. There came a dull thud from beyond the wall of the lounge and waiting-room.

Lincoln looked up quickly. "That was it, sir!"

Knollis perched himself on the edge of the table. "That was the sound you heard on Tuesday evening?"

"Which door was it?" Lincoln replied.

"I can't tell you that at present," said Knollis. "You're fully satisfied that it was a similar sound you heard on Tuesday?"

"I'm certain of it—but of course it may have been any of the doors!"

"Three doors have been opened and slammed within the past few minutes," said Knollis. "The one you just heard was the last of the three. I arranged for it to be the first, and then realized that if you heard it you would make some remark, and thus miss either of the others if it was possible to hear them in here."

Lincoln smiled. "That was clever, Inspector!"

"I'm not susceptible to flattery," said Knollis. "Now you've no objection to answering a few more questions?"

"Why should I?"

"Why indeed," Knollis said quietly. "Here we go then. You're fully aware that Dr. Challoner intended to marry Mrs. Madeleine Burke?"

Lincoln looked from one to the other uneasily "Well—"

"I'm not asking you to break any confidences in regard to your employers," said Knollis, "but merely expecting you to admit, as a frequent visitor to this house, what you know to be the truth. You were aware of his intentions, weren't you?"

"Ye-es," Lincoln said with a reluctant nod.

"Which way do you go home from this house? In which direction does your home lie?"

"I turn left in Bowden Street, and turn right at the top."

"You got here about seven-twenty, or as near that time as makes no matter? And you came from home?"

"Why yes!" Lincoln said in a surprised tone.

Knollis slid from the table and walked the carpet until he stood over the young clerk. "Tell me, Mr. Lincoln: what did you say to Mrs. Burke when you met her on Tuesday evening a few yards beyond the telephone kiosk?"

Lincoln's mouth opened, and closed again.

Manson stared at Knollis in awe and said: "'Struth!"

"Well?" said Knollis grimly.

Lincoln's lips trembled. He sought to avoid the steely grey eyes that pierced into his mind. "I—I—"

Knollis bent lower over his witness. "Shall I tell *you*, Mr. Lincoln?"

He took his note-book from his pocket and flicked back the restraining elastic with a sharp snap. "Well?"

Lincoln licked his lips and glanced about the room as if seeking a way of escape.

Knollis glanced at Manson. "Will you please ask Miss Challoner to step this way, Manson?"

Manson ambled casually towards the door.

Lincoln was there before him, his back square against the panelled surface. "No! No! Don't bring Joan into this, for God's sake. I shouldn't have said it! I know I shouldn't, but I was anxious for Joan!"

Knollis walked to him and took him by the arm, leading him back to the settee. "Take a seat, Mr. Lincoln. I like my witnesses to be comfortable. Now tell me: what did you say to Mrs. Burke?"

Lincoln looked from Knollis to Manson and began to whimper like a whipped dog. "What would you have done! I can't afford to keep her in the way she's been brought up. I didn't want his money for myself, but I wanted to make sure that she'd got it to keep her going until I'd passed my finals and could begin to earn real money. I didn't want Mrs. Burke to get it, either. She's been working for it ever since her husband died, and she didn't care how she got it. She's shameless, and—and rotten!"

Something like a sob escaped him, and he glanced up at Knollis with a silent plea for mercy.

"Go on!" said Knollis in a grim voice.

"Well, I'd been filing his will that afternoon. It gave her seventy-five per cent of his estate if he'd died after marrying her, and two thousand pounds if he died before. It was a damnable thing, and I'd been boiling about it all afternoon, and I was going to the house to tell Joan so that we could both have it out with him. And then I met Mrs. Burke under the lamp just the other side of the kiosk—from here. She greeted me as if I was an old friend. She called me by my first name, and smiled. I—well—I got hold of her by the shoulders and shook her, and I told her she wasn't going to get a penny of his money; she wasn't going to rob Joan of what rightly belonged to her!"

He stared at the carpet and his jaw tightened. "I nearly killed her! She smiled at me and said: *'You silly, silly boy! Do you think you can fight me!'* And then she just walked on. If she'd stayed another minute I'd have had my hands round her throat and strangled her."

"Yes?" Knollis murmured gently, anxious to intrude no question or remark which might stem the emotional outburst.

Lincoln exhaled his breath in one deep sigh. "Well, I went to the house—came here, that is. When I heard that door slam I decided that his last patient had gone, and that it was time to go and have it out with him. He was dead when I got there, and it was too late. Mrs. Burke's got two thousand pounds of Joan's money!"

"It was perhaps as well that he was dead when you found him," said Knollis. "You see, Mr. Lincoln, you're young and impulsive, and if Dr. Challoner had flared up you might easily have laid your hands on his shoulders, and then round his throat, and you might have strangled him! Mrs. Burke escaped that fate by walking away. Dr. Challoner couldn't have got away, because he was seated in an arm-chair with his back against a wall! You see what I mean . . . ?"

Lincoln's eyes bulged from his head. He started up from his seat, and Knollis gently pushed him back again.

"I—I didn't strangle him, Inspector! I swear I didn't! I couldn't have strangled him!"

"Oh, and why?" asked Knollis.

"I'd no rope," Lincoln said with naive simplicity.

His remark broke the tension that had mounted in the room, Knollis's hands went limp, and he laughed.

Manson's belly-laugh filled the room. "That's an answer, Knollis!"

Knollis offered his cigarettes to Manson and Lincoln, and took one himself. He lit all three from his lighter, and grinned happily at Lincoln. "What's the extent of the doctor's estate?" he asked, and glanced at his note-book as if the information was already there as a check on Lincoln's statement.

"About eight thousand five hundred, Inspector."

"Investments?"

A degree of defiance appeared in Lincoln's manner. "I can't tell you that! I'm a *confidential* clerk."

"Hodson and Spender have promised to prepare a statement for us," said Manson, "so it's immaterial whether Lincoln tells us or not. The only thing is that it'll save time if he does."

"You see?" said Knollis.

"Well," sighed Lincoln, "that relieves me of the responsibility. Challoner had shares in a chemical manufacturing company. Two of the patent medicines which they prepare and sell were his own prescriptions. He also had a sleeping interest in his father's old firm—they import fruit and wines."

"So that his income was derived from his practice, plus the dividends from these two firms?"

"He gave a lot to charity," Lincoln said in a tone indicating that the doctor's generosity had been challenged.

"We may as well have that information as well," said Knollis; "not that it's likely to be of much assistance."

"He gave a hundred a year to the local hospital, and a similar sum to the county tubercular clinic, and then two hundred a year to the Deptford Foundation."

"Good enough," said Knollis. "Now tell me, Mr. Lincoln: how did Miss Challoner react to this remarrying notion of her father's?"

"Well, I mean, she obviously didn't like it. She thought it was a betrayal of her mother, and she told him he was not being true to her memory."

"And what did he say to that?"

"He said it was an outworn convention, and that a second marriage was never more than a marriage of convenience, and a companionate one. He said that Joan and I would want to be on our own when we got married and had a house, and that while Mrs. Burke would make an excellent housekeeper he had to regularize the arrangement to save scandal, and that he could repay her by educating young Leslie and looking after them both.”

“Yes?”

“Well, Joan asked him why not engage a house-keeper and leave it at that. The doc said somewhat cynically that the world had never looked on house-keepers in any Christian spirit, and the tougher the Christian the more intolerant they were.”

“He seemed to have a capacity for thinking,” said Knollis in a tone of admiration.

“Well yes, he had.”

“Miss Challoner and yourself hated the idea of all that good money going to Mrs. Burke, eh?”

“Who was the better entitled to it?” demanded Lincoln.

“I’m not acting as a judge of ethics,” said Knollis, “but it does seem to me that the doctor was entitled to do as he liked with his own money!”

“Well, that’s your opinion,” Lincoln sulked.

Knollis flicked a wink at Manson. “The doctor’s death has meant a considerable saving to you and Miss Joan, hasn’t it?”

“What the hell do you mean?” snapped Lincoln.

“If the doctor had stayed alive you would have lost seventy-five per cent of his money whereas now you’ve lost, say, about twenty-five per cent. A considerable gain!”

Lincoln jumped to his feet. “Look here! I didn’t kill him, see!”

Knollis waved his hands in a gesture of regret for any false impression he might have given. “I’m not saying you did, Mr. Lincoln, but I do wish Miss Joan’s evidence with respect to yourself was more solid. She admits being upstairs when you came, and staying upstairs, and not coming down until you called to tell her that something had happened to her father. By the way, she really was upstairs all the time?”

“Where else could she be?”

“Downstairs,” Knollis said laconically.

“I won’t put up with any more of this,” shouted Lincoln. “Third degree; that’s what it is! If you think I killed him, then arrest me and charge me!”

He stalked to the door. He turned to look at them both for a full minute, and then said wearily: "Oh, go to the devil!"

"Mr. Lincoln!" Knollis called softly as the door was closing.

The door re-opened slowly, although Lincoln stayed behind it, unseen.

"Please tell Miss Challoner I'd like to see her."

The door closed, very gently.

"Rattled him, by George!" boomed Manson with great satisfaction.

"I hated doing it," Knollis said apologetically, "but I had to find out what he knew. He's all right; just a hot-headed lad."

"Hot-headed lads have been known to kill!"

Knollis wiped his forehead with his handkerchief. "I know, Manson, but this was the work of a more experienced type. It was premediated, as witness the rope. No, there's a lot more behind Challoner's death than we know as yet. I still refuse to believe that the laughing dog sketch was innocent doodling—and if it was it revealed something that was disturbing Challoner's mind."

A quiet voice from the doorway said: "You wanted me?"

Joan Challoner came into the room, pretty, tastefully dressed, and on the defensive.

"We'd like to go through your father's private papers, Miss Challoner," Knollis said. "I hate upsetting you in this way, but I'm afraid it must be done, and we've left it longer than we should already."

She stared her lack of understanding. "But all his papers are in the consulting-room, Inspector!"

"I'm looking for his diaries, Miss Challoner."

"But they are private, Inspector!"

"I'm sorry, Miss Challoner," said Knollis on a note of finality.

"Oh well!" Her hands fell to her sides. "They are in a strong box in the attic. Do you want me to take you up?"

"It's immaterial, thank you. We can find our way." She turned to the door, paused, and over her shoulder asked a question. "Inspector Knollis, you don't really think that—that Eric had anything . . . to . . . do . . . with—well, with Father's death?"

"I sincerely hope not," Knollis replied.

"I see," she answered. "Thank you!"

"Bit ambiguous, weren't you?" said Manson. "Bit tough on her, too!"

Knollis led the way up the two flights of stairs to the attic. The brief-box was lying on the top of a pile of suit-cases. He laid it on the floor and squatted beside it.

"This is the devil's own profession, Manson. You know it as well as I do? Do you think I'm devoid of human feelings? Believe me when I say I'm a sensitive soul, but it's the grey matter under my scalp that has to function in these affairs, and I daren't let my heart rule my head. I have to be the grim inquisitor. You know, Highton was right when he told me that I'd fall down on a case some day. The internal conflict can play the very blazes with you, and I've never managed to get hardened. Still—here we are with a body on our hands, and all too little helpful evidence. If—and I do use that word; if Mrs. Burke did go back and strangle Challoner, then Lincoln is morally guilty."

Manson seated himself on a dusty cabin-trunk and looked into Knollis's grey eyes. "Why should she strangle him? What had she to gain?"

"Two thousand pounds," Knollis said dryly. "Half a loaf is better than no bread. Lincoln works with Challoner's solicitors, Mrs. Burke knows that. A remark passed to her by Lincoln is of more significance to her than the same remark passed by any other person. Lincoln said she was not going to get Joan's money. Mrs. Burke, as I see it, regards that as a threat that Lincoln can persuade Challoner to change his mind."

Manson frowned. "Well?"

"Assuming that Burke did kill Challoner, then she made sure of getting two thousand pounds."

"Yes, I see the point," said Manson. "If Lincoln killed him he sacrificed two thousand pounds to make six thousand. If Burke killed him she sacrificed a doubtful six thousand for a certain two thousand, and half a loaf is better than no bread."

Knollis snapped his fingers. "That's the whole point. Now let's have a look at these diaries. Quite a stack of 'em, too. You take that bundle, and I'll have a go at this."

There was silence for a considerable time, apart from the rustle of the thin sheets of india paper.

It was Manson who disturbed it. "Knollis," he said in a curious voice, "there's something queer here?"

"What is it?" Knollis asked absently.

"He apparently started keeping diaries when he was twenty-one, which was in Nineteen-twelve."

"Yes?" Knollis asked patiently.

"I've got 'em from Nineteen-twelve to twenty-seven—"

Knollis looked over his own collection. "That's all right. I've got all the others from twenty-eight to forty-six. You'll remember the current one was in the surgery."

"Yes, I know," Manson replied testily, "but I can't find Nineteen-fourteen!"

Knollis at once became interested. "Check 'em again."

"Sorry," Manson said two minutes later. "I haven't got it, old man!"

"Queer," murmured Knollis.

"You either keep diaries, or you don't," went on Manson. "This fellow kept 'em in no dilatory way. Now where is that diary?"

He leaned over towards Knollis to look in the brief-box. "Not there, anyway! What's that envelope in the bottom, Knollis?"

"I don't know, but I'll find out," replied Knollis. "I'm an inquisitive man."

He opened the envelope and drew out a small sheet of thin paper, blank except for the thin blue rulings and three printed dates.

"Twenty-fourth, fifth, and sixth of July, Nineteen-fourteen," he quoted.

"And no entries!" boomed Manson.

"Wait . . . a . . . minute," said Knollis.

He got to his feet and held the page from the diary under the skylight, twisting and turning it so that the light fell on it from various angles.

"Here," he said, handing the page to Manson. "Keep your fingers on the edges, and have a look at that. Something has been rubbed out. See what it is?"

Manson examined the page thoroughly, and whistled.

"What do you make of it?"

Manson looked up and blinked. "A blessed drawing of a laughing dog!"

IX

THE CROSSROADS OF SUSPICION

WITH THE COMING of evening, Knollis and Ellis retreated to the privacy of the otherwise empty writing-room of their hotel. Ellis threw himself into one of the hide-covered armchairs and charged his meerschaum with the foul blend he called Ellis's 'Eavenly Effluvium. Knollis, from the chair at the opposite side of the fireplace, immediately complained.

"Why the heck can't you smoke decent tobacco, like other people?"

"Other people smoke this," Ellis retorted.

"What other people?" demanded Knollis. "I've never met with it before."

"Lots of other people," said Ellis, "but no one person smokes all the brands at the same time—except me. It's a blend of Bishop's Brew, Copper Shag, and Thick Twist—"

"You've got the names wrong," Knollis interrupted innocently.

"Oh? How?"

"You mean Devil's Brew, Copper Beech, and Senna Pods!"

Ellis turned his gaze to the ceiling. "There are two possibilities. . . ."

"Like it, or lump it?"

"Eric Lincoln or Madeleine Burke," said Ellis.

The smile vanished from Knollis's lean features. In a second he was tense and earnest. "Yes, two possibilities, Ellis! The solution lies with one or the other of them."

"And the laughing dog?"

Knollis grimaced. "I'm inclined to say damn the laughing dog. It's omnipresent, I admit, but I can't think it had anything to do with Challoner's death. It is very obviously connected with some event in his past life, but I'm satisfied that the cause of his death lies somewhere in the Challoner-Burke-Lincoln tangle. There are, as you said, two possibilities. . . ."

He half-closed his eyes, and peered closely through the resulting slits.

"Visualize the thing, Ellis. Mrs. Burke leaves the surgery. Challoner was alive at that time, as the medical evidence proves. She meets Lincoln. They have words. She returns to the house via the passageway and Denver Street, this so that she can gain the house without being seen by Lincoln. She takes the rope, and strangles him. She leaves by the waiting-room door, and hurries home."

"There's a snag," said Ellis. "If she hurried home, then why wasn't she seen by the constable at the kiosk?"

Knollis winced. "Ugh! That's a stab in the back!"

"Anyway," said Ellis, "let's hear the other."

"Well, Lincoln hurries to the house, calls to Joan Challoner, and then goes straight to the consulting-room and strangles the doctor. He then returns to the lounge. Burke enters while Challoner is dying, realizes she may be involved in an affair that can prove disastrous to her, and makes a hurried exit by the said Kirkland Street door. Lincoln hears the door slam, wonders if Challoner has got free of the rope, and hurries to the consulting-room. Challoner is now dead, so Lincoln officially discovers the body, panics, and runs into the street."

He shuffled lower into the chair, balanced his slippered feet on the mantel, and sighed. "Now, which is it?"

Ellis sniffed, and sent another puff of smoke to intensify the smoke-screen he was raising between them. "You're slipping in your old age!"

Knollis looked round quickly. "In what respect?" Ellis puffed furiously and did not answer.

Knollis peered through the smoke. "Well, out with it!"

"The rope, of course!"

"The rope?"

"The rope!" Ellis repeated with irritating nonchalance.

Knollis lit a cigarette and stared at the oaken panels of the mantel. He suddenly said: "Oh Lord!"

"I thought you'd get it," murmured Ellis. "We've used the rope all the way along as proof that the job was premeditated. We've decided that the rope was brought by the killer, and we've done nothing about tracing its source. And I'd remind you, honourable sir, that this very theory cuts out both Lincoln and Burke. Your theories regarding those two insists that whichever of them snuffed Challoner did so with no more than five or ten minutes' notice!"

"I've made a horrible slip somewhere, Ellis!"

"The infallible sleuth exists only within the covers of a 'tec novel," said Ellis in an attempt to comfort the distracted Knollis. "But the truth must prevail! Burke was going home when she met Lincoln, and she could not have killed Challoner. Supposing she had gone to the surgery to kill him, then why didn't she? If she had the rope in her handbag, then there was nothing to prevent her putting her plan into action. She was the last patient. The Kirkland Street door was locked. There was no sound from the house."

"True enough!" Knollis admitted miserably.

"Now Lincoln could have done it," went on Ellis. "He'd been boiling up all afternoon, on his own admission. He was going to have it out with Challoner—and who's to say he wasn't also going to do him in? My notion is that he did the job, that Mrs. Burke went back and found Challoner dead or dying, and scarpered!"

"You're a wise old owl," Knollis grunted.

"To wit, to woo, and to woo, to kill—that was Lincoln," said Ellis. "One day I'm going to be an inspector."

"One day I'm going to be a chief-inspector," said Knollis, "but that day is a long way off. What was the length of the rope?"

"Six feet nine inches—"

"Of ordinary cotton rope, clothes-line stuff," mused Knollis. "An ordinary overhand loop knot was made in one end, and the other end passed through it. Both ends were knotted to prevent fraying, and the end that was tied to the chair had been cut with a knife, a good clean cut."

"And the knot was in the nape of the neck, and looked as if it had been under his left ear, and then pulled round as it was tightened. Right-handed bloke, too—but why go over all these points again? You know 'em off by heart?"

"I'm refreshing my memory," said Knollis. "I'm also making sure I've made no more obvious slips. Look, Ellis; please hop to the 'phone and make two appointments for to-morrow morning. Ask Mrs. Burke to see me at headquarters at ten o'clock, and Lincoln to see me there at eleven. You should find Lincoln at Challoner's house. I'll get to the bottom of this business before it sends me mad! A night's sleep on it should reduce the facts to something of a pattern. We'll let the whole thing have a holiday for the rest of the night when you've 'phoned. Oh, and you might leave the door open while you're away. A drop of fresh air won't hurt the room."

Ellis made a rude reply as he went.

By morning Knollis had his plan of action clearly outlined in his mind. He knew that the mental comfort of a witness was always disturbed by the official atmosphere of police headquarters, and by the strangeness of the setting, and he set the scene in Manson's office as carefully as if he were staging a play. He took the central position behind the desk, with Manson on his right, Ellis on his left, and a detective-officer in the corner of the room with instructions to report the proceedings as ostentatiously as possible.

Madeleine Burke was shown in as the clock struck ten, a chubby, koala-like figure in a heavy fur coat and fur hat and gloves. She bustled in complaining of the cold morning, and then came to a halt, looked around, and shot a suspicious glance at the three officers, sitting before her like a bench of magistrates.

Knollis made a great to-do of inviting her to be seated. She was to make herself comfortable. Perhaps she would like a cigarette? And a light? He set her chair at an angle to the table so that the full light from the window fell on her intelligent features. Then he sat back and folded his hands across his jacket.

"I do hope we haven't inconvenienced you this morning," he began, using his favourite gambit. "We're very busy, as you must realize; time is short, and we just can't find time to call on all our witnesses."

Madeleine Burke bowed, and waited—suspiciously.

Knollis leaned across the desk. "Certain information has come into our possession, Mrs. Burke, which makes it necessary for us to ask you to make a fuller statement regarding your movements on Tuesday night."

Her lips tightened almost imperceptibly, and she dipped her chin deeper into the collar of her fur coat.

"Can you tell us at what time, approximately, you arrived home from Dr. Challoner's surgery?"

Her chin came up. "I thought you'd asked me that, Inspector!"

Knollis laughed uncertainly. "If we did, then we've no record of it, Mrs. Burke. There are so many facts to deal with that we haven't got them correlated yet, and we may have missed some of them. Unfortunately, we're not infallible, and mistakes happen in the best-regulated offices." He drummed his finger-tips on the desk and smiled.

Mrs. Burke considered her well-manicured hands. "Well, I should say it was about twenty to eight, Inspector. I didn't take particular notice at the time. After all, why should I?"

"Quite so; why should you?" Knollis hastened to agree. "Tell me, Mrs. Burke; you did go straight home when you left the surgery?"

She stared at him, her vivid blue eyes innocent in the framework of fur. "But I most certainly remember telling you that I did, Inspector! Why yes, of course I went straight home!"

"Mrs. Burke," said Knollis patiently, "we've information to the effect that you returned to the surgery that night, and left again at half-past seven."

"But—but that's preposterous!" she protested.

Knollis wagged his head. "I'd like to believe you, Mrs. Burke, but the evidence is rather convincing. Can you prove that you went straight home?"

She bit her lip. "No-o, I can't, Inspector!"

"None of your neighbours likely to be able to help you?" asked Knollis, determined to give her every chance to clear herself.

"I'm afraid not. No, no one can help me . . ."

"You did meet young Lincoln on the way home?" Knollis shot the question at her in the hope of shocking her into confusion. To his own surprise she smiled and nodded.

"Oh yes, that is right!"

"On Bowden Street?"

"Yes, a few yards beyond the kiosk—but I can't see him coming forward to help me." She wrinkled her brows. "In any case, Inspector, what are you after?"

"Trying to learn whether you did or did not return to the surgery," Knollis said blandly.

"Oh!"

Knollis eyed her carefully. "Tell me, Mrs. Burke; do you keep a dog?"

"Do I—what a queer question, Inspector! Is it supposed to be relevant?"

Knollis's smile resolved into a thin tight line.

"Do you keep a dog, Mrs. Burke?"

"Well, I did!"

"Why don't you keep a dog now?"

"Hugh didn't like them, and so I got rid of it," she replied. Then, defiantly, she added: "Lord Roberts was also—he didn't like cats!"

"I see," said Knollis. "Tell me, Mrs. Burke; what happened when you met Lincoln on Bowden Street?"

Her eyebrows rose. It was evident from her expression that she thought he was unbalanced. She cleared her throat, licked her upper lip, and replied: "We had a few words."

"Would you mind detailing the nature of the row, Mrs. Burke?"

"Row? Then he's told you?"

"Just that."

She shrugged her shoulders. "He was abusive. He called me a scheming woman who'd wangled Hugh into a promise of marriage so that I could get his money. He said I wasn't going to get either Hugh or the money. That was all he could say, because I walked off."

"And went straight home!"

She sank back in the chair with a weary sigh. "I've already told you that I went straight home, Inspector!"

"Mrs. Burke," said Knollis softly, "who, in your opinion, killed Hugh Challoner?"

"Why—" she began, and then closed her lips and glared at Knollis for the trap he had laid.

"Yes, Mrs. Burke? You were saying . . . ?"

"I—I don't know! I can't think!"

"You've an opinion, surely, Mrs. Burke. You were on the point of speaking a name."

"I—I—" she said, dry-lipped.

"Yes, Mrs. Burke?"

"I, well, I think it was Eric. I can't prove it, but I think he went straight to the surgery and killed him when he left me. He was furious, and in such a temper that he didn't seem to know what he was saying or doing. I was afraid of him."

"He killed him in order to prevent the marriage?"

She lowered her head into the fur collar, and mumbled the affirmative in a low voice. "Yes."

"Where was your son on Tuesday evening, Mrs. Burke?"

Her head shot into view. "My son? Leslie? What has he to do with this?"

"He could perhaps verify the time at which you arrived home!"

"He can't, Inspector. He was at the Youth Club. He left home with me, and didn't get home until half-past nine."

Knollis scribbled a note and pushed it under Ellis's nose; then tore it into small pieces and put them in the ash tray. "Please see Mrs. Burke home, Ellis. Thank you, Mrs. Burke; that will be all."

Ellis escorted her from the office. The shorthand writer sat back to relax. Manson turned to Knollis with a quizzical expression, and one word: "Well?"

"I don't know, Manson," Knollis replied in a tired voice. "If she did go back, then she's no intention of admitting it. She's a determined woman. She's fighting for her cub, and doesn't mean being beaten. Ellis thinks she's innocent, and I place a lot of value on his opinions, but I still think she could have done it. I've sent Ellis to check the length and condition of the clothes-line at her house—a job your own men should have done on Wednesday morning!"

He paused to light a cigarette.

"Even then," he went on, "I'll be beaten by the thing. If she went in the first place with the intention of strangling him, why on earth didn't she do it? Ellis must be right! There's only one plain conclusion on which I can rely: the job was premeditated! Mrs. Burke couldn't have done it. It must be young Lincoln, and if it was he's pulled a fast one across me with his general air of *naïveté* and adolescence."

"Let's send Johnson to check the rope at his house," suggested Manson. "I'm sorry it didn't get done. I got all mussed up, what with the Chief Constable coming down, and the C.I.D. super, and then the decision to call in your people. . . ."

"Surgeon's report in yet?" asked Knollis.

"Some time to-day. He only did the p.m. last night." Manson pressed a switch on the intercom telephone and gave a message to be relayed to Sergeant Johnson. As he switched off a constable put his head round the door to announce the arrival of Eric Lincoln.

"Show him in," said Knollis.

Lincoln, looking hot round the collar, walked straight to the desk, planted the palms of his hands on it, and pushed his nose into Knollis's face. "How much longer does this persecution go on?"

Knollis looked round him towards the door. "Where's the dog?"

Lincoln blinked. "Dog? What dog?"

"Haven't you brought your dog?"

"Dog? I haven't got a dog!"

"Don't like 'em, eh?" said Knollis. "You've never had a dog as a pet?"

Lincoln was obviously thrown off-centre by this unusual treatment. He straightened himself, ran the palms of his hands up and down his trouser legs, and then eased his collar with a finger.

"Well, yes, I used to have a dog."

"What happened to it?"

"I sold it. Why?"

"That's my question," countered Knollis. "Why?"

"Why did I sell it? Well, I used to take it with me to see Joan at the house, and the doc didn't like it. As a matter of fact he was scared of it, so it became a case of love-my-daughter-get-rid-of-the-dog . . ."

He put his head askew, closed one eye, and regarded Knollis somewhat comically from the other. "I say, what is this? Dogs, dogs, dogs! Oh . . . ! That laughing dog, eh! Trying to pin something else on me, are you?"

"Pin something on you!" Knollis exclaimed in shocked tones. "Mr. Lincoln!"

"You take a statement, you question me on it, you requestion me, you examine me, cross-examine me. Why the devil don't you hang me? Don't you believe a word I say?"

"I believe every word you've told me," Knollis said soothingly. "The point is that you use too few words. You don't tell me everything I want to know, and so I have to keep fetching you back."

"You're getting me in bad books with my employers," snorted Lincoln. "They're beginning to wonder if I did the doc in!"

Well, I'm fed up with it, and at the end of my tether, and I'm going to—"

"Shut up and sit down!" snapped Knollis. "Take a pew!"

It was an order, and the immature Lincoln quailed beneath Knollis's manner and stern eye. He backed into the chair lately occupied by Madeleine Burke.

"Tell me," said Knollis in a milder voice. "Tell me; did you, like Lot's wife, look back when you left Mrs. Burke in Bowden Street?"

"No-o!"

"Pity," said Knollis. "You might have solved the enigma of Dr. Hugh Challoner's death."

"You mean it really *was* Mrs. Burke?" Lincoln whispered.

"So you do think she killed him?"

Lincoln was flustered by the direct question. "Well, I've wondered."

"Where were you in the year Nineteen-fourteen?" asked Manson in a pontifical voice.

"I wouldn't know that," said Lincoln. "I wasn't born until twenty-five."

"Which is a fair answer," said Knollis, suppressing a smile at Manson's discomfiture.

He turned to Lincoln. "So you thought that, eh? We're beginning to understand each other, Mr. Lincoln."

A weak smile came to Lincoln's pale face. "Who else could have done it, Inspector?"

"You," Knollis said with brutal candour.

Lincoln winced, and shrank back in his chair, biting his lip.

"Look at it from my angle," suggested Knollis. "You threaten Mrs. Burke, and tell her you can put a stop to her plans for marrying Hugh Challoner. You knew him well, and knew him as a man of strong will who could not easily be put off. Consequently, you knew he was practically immovable while still alive. . . ."

Lincoln nodded miserably.

"You were in a vile temper, by your own admission, and could quite easily have charged into the house and strangled Challoner while the mood was on you."

"I didn't kill him, Inspector!" Lincoln whimpered. "So help me, God, I didn't!"

"I'm not saying you did," said Knollis. "I'm saying you could have done."

"It must have been her," Lincoln said desperately. "Who else could have wanted to kill him?"

"How could she have killed him?" Knollis asked innocently.

"Oh, she either followed me back or slipped into Denver Street by Williamson's Passage—that's a narrow passage connecting the two streets."

"And then?"

"Well, I think she got behind him and slipped the loop over his head. I've been reading some strangulation cases, and it seems that the sudden shock as the loop is tightened is capable of incapacitating the victim almost instantaneously."

"Very interesting reconstruction, Mr. Lincoln. I must read those books some time. Are they your own property?"

"They're in the bosses' legal library at the office."

"You go to the Challoner house every night?"

"Oh yes. I have a light tea at home and then dine with them most nights when Joan isn't out."

"Bless your elastic tummy," smiled Knollis. "Hop it, my lad. I've done with you—and thanks for helping!"

Lincoln rose and made for the door. He turned with a sheepish smile. "Sorry I flew off the handle, sir! I guess my nerves aren't too good just now. You know how it is!"

"Don't I," said Knollis. "Good-bye!"

The door closed, and Knollis turned to Manson. "That damned laughing dog is exciting intense cerebral activity!"

"Doing what?" stammered Manson.

"Nuts!" said Knollis irritably.

X
The Rope Trick

It was an hour or so later when Ellis returned.

He laid two coils of white cotton rope on the desk. "Exhibits A and B," he said simply.

"Rope, eh?" rumbled Manson.

"Let's have the story," said Knollis.

Ellis took the chair, literally and metaphorically, marking each point as it was made by a long finger laid on the edge of the desk.

"Mrs. Burke is no fool. She asked me indoors when we reached the house. She removed her hat and coat, gave me a couple of fingers of Scotch against the wintry weather, and asked me where I'd like to look. I eyed her up and down, and decided to tell her the truth, that I was looking for a cotton clothes-line. I regret to say that I added the untruth that it was possible someone had tried to incriminate her. She smiled mysteriously, went into the kitchen, and came back with this—Exhibit A."

"The loosely wound one," said Manson.

"Yes, sir. She told me quite frankly that it was damaged. Someone cut a length from it during Monday night. Monday, according to her, was a bad drying day for the washing, so she left the line out all night in readiness for what we might call a re-hanging on Tuesday morning. She put her coat on again and took me out to the garden. The distance between the line-posts is roughly thirty-two feet. There is obviously a lot of spare rope, and it hangs below the cleat hook on the post at the top end of the garden and hard by the boundary wall—"

"Any back gate?" Knollis interrupted.

"No back gate. The two streets are back to back. The sole entrance to the house is by the front gate. You'll remember the path that curves to the left from the gate to the front door. There is also a four-foot space between the house wall and the dividing fence leading to the back door. The back wall is six feet high, and the top of the line-post is about six inches higher."

"We are now going to hear that someone climbed the wall during the night and sawed off six feet nine of Mrs. Burke's clothes-line," Manson snorted in a disbelieving tone.

"Not sawn off, sir," said Ellis. "About a foot below the top of the post, and on the side nearest to the wall, are marks suggesting that the rope was pressed against the post and cut with a razor blade."

He paused for Manson to comment, but Knollis urged him on. "Go on!"

"I asked her where she bought the rope, and when. She said she got it from the multiple provision shop at the corner of the street, and about three or four months ago. I next asked when she discovered the loss of part of her line, and she said it was Tuesday morning, when she went to hang out the washing. I further asked if she had since connected the missing length with Dr. Challoner's death, and she nodded. She repeated my suggestion; someone was trying to incriminate her."

"You'd a witness to the conversation?" Manson asked anxiously.

"I fetched the driver in when she produced the rope, sir," Ellis assured him. "He took down the conversation and is at present transcribing it."

"Good man!" boomed Manson.

"Exhibit B you bought on the way home?" asked Knollis.

"From the corner shop, a branch of the Maydew Provision Dealers. They sell food, and household equipment. I examined their stock, and this is the only type of cotton rope they sell. It's forty-eight feet long. All their others are brown manilla rope."

"Let's compare their lengths," said Knollis.

He called the detective-officer from his corner table, untied the two hanks, and handed one end of each to him. The detective-officer fed them through his hands until the end of Mrs. Burke's line was reached. Ellis took Manson's blue pencil from the desk, and marked the uncut line at that point. He then ran the inch-tape along the surplus length. "Six feet three inches!"

"That's wrong," said Manson.

"Not necessarily," said Knollis. "The used line will have stretched. This cotton stuff does so to an amazing extent, and again we can't expect every line to be exactly the same length—or can we?"

"Which means that Challoner was strangled with Burke's clothes-line," rumbled Manson with deep satisfaction. "Looks as if Lincoln tried to frame her!"

Knollis reached for the inter-office 'phone and depressed the switch. "Get me Hodson and Spender, please."

"What's the notion?" asked Manson.

Knollis waved him into silence. He waited until the buzzer sounded, and asked for Eric Lincoln.

"Hello, Mr. Lincoln," he said a moment later. "This is your *bête-noire*, Inspector Knollis. No, nothing serious! What type of razor do you use? Yes, razor—shaving. You do? Thank you!"

He replaced the receiver, and grinned. "The poor devil will be wondering what I'm trying to fix on him this time. Anyway, he uses an electric razor, and has done so since Miss Challoner bought it for his birthday eighteen months ago."

"That's queer," remarked Ellis. "I've a birthday every year!"

Knollis was turning on him with a scathing comment when Sergeant Johnson entered, smiling broadly.

He produced a coil of rope from under his coat, and brandished it with a triumphal cry. "We've got him!"

"Same stuff!" ejaculated Manson.

"Brand new last week," said Johnson. "A length of it is missing. I had a break-down outside Lincoln's house, and had to borrow this so that a baker's van could tow me round the corner, and then, queerly enough, the engine started up before I needed the rope!"

"How queer!" Knollis said with a sardonic smile.

"What are these ropes?" Johnson asked.

"Oh, they are all ropes with which the doctor was strangled," said Knollis. "Let's measure yours."

"It's short," said Johnson. He delved into a large pocket inside his jacket and produced a new rope. "I've got this to return to Mrs. Lincoln, and it seems longer to me, although I haven't measured it yet."

Ellis went to work with the inch-tape, to announce a minute later: "Six feet seven inches short."

"And a nice clean cut," said Manson. "Y'know, Knollis, this is mad!"

"Looks as if mine isn't the one," said Johnson in a deflated tone.

"I like mad cases," smiled Knollis. "The madder they are, the easier they are to solve. The more trouble our man goes to, the more we have to work on. Now, who looked over the Challoner house for the rope?"

"Detective-officer Davis," said Manson. "Want him?"

He nodded to Johnson, who spoke into the inter-office telephone. Davis appeared a few minutes later.

"You went over the Challoner premises for the remainder of the rope with which the doctor was strangled?"

Davis nodded. "I did, sir."

"You found no rope?"

"Only a brand-new one in the wash-house, sir. It hadn't been untied, and still bore the price ticket."

Knollis's head went forward on his neck. "What!"

"It was a brand-new one, sir."

"Is there a lock on the wash-house door?"

Davis blinked, and stammered his reply. "I—I didn't notice, sir."

"Didn't notice!" Knollis snapped. "Johnson! Get Miss Challoner on the 'phone for me."

He turned on Davis furiously. "If this is the best you can do for the crime bureau you'll soon be walking a beat again. Only a new rope! My God!"

There was an awkward silence in the office until Sergeant Johnson announced that Miss Challoner was on the line. Knollis dismissed Davis, and took over the telephone.

"Inspector Knollis speaking, Miss Challoner. Can you say whether there is a lock on your wash-house door? Yes, that is right; l.o.c.k. on the wash-house door! There isn't! Thank you.

Now the next point. Can you remember buying a new clothes-line within recent weeks? You can't, and don't think you did, but you'll check your order book. You didn't need a new line because the washing goes to the laundry? You won't mind if I send a man down to check the order-book? Thank you very much!"

He replaced the receiver. "So that's that! Ellis, get down to the Challoner house, check her grocery orders for the past six months. Also confiscate the rope, and have a good look round those back premises while you're there. Now this afternoon you'll do a spot of surveying. Mrs. Lincoln will know Johnson by now, and we mustn't take any risks."

"Manson! Have you any new men not very well known in the town?"

"In the uniformed department, yes; we've several straight from training school."

"Then Ellis will take one of 'em this afternoon. Can you get surveying tackle?"

"We can borrow a theodolite from Wainwright, across the street."

"And look for a cut on the line-post," said Ellis.

He left for the Challoner house.

Knollis issued further instructions. "Johnson, I'd like you to spend a few hours trying to find out what Lincoln was doing on Monday evening and during Monday night. Don't forget to check the reports of the constables on beat! Now, Manson, I'd like you to come with me to the Green Dragon to see Highton, and then we'll lunch; afterwards we visit Hodson and Spender. I then intend to spend the rest of the day considering the evidence and writing up my reports."

Aubrey Highton was about to go down for lunch when they arrived, but obligingly placed himself at their disposal, albeit the old mocking smile was evident on his lips.

"What are you looking for this time, Inspectors?" he asked. "Finger-prints, or bloodstains?"

"Neither," said Knollis shortly. "We're looking for a length of cotton rope. Can you oblige?"

Highton's mouth dropped at the corner. "How irritating! If you had asked me last week I could have obliged you. I had a lovely piece round my cabin trunk. I cut it sooner than be bothered with the knots. I chucked it under the bed, and the chambermaid kept slinging it on the bed, and after the game had gone on for several days I threw it in the fire! Now isn't that a nuisance!"

"I don't suppose it happened to be manilla rope?" Knollis said caustically.

Highton shook his head. "That white stuff, Inspector. I bought it from a shop in the Rue d'Isley, the Monoprix—the Algerian Woolworths. By the way, I don't suppose this inquiry has anything whatsoever to do with Challoner's death? I mean, your braces have just collapsed as you walked along the street, and you said to yourself: '*Ha! Mr. Aubrey Highton will have a piece of white cotton rope just the right size!*' That, really, is the truth, isn't it?" he asked earnestly.

Knollis restrained himself with difficulty. "One of these days . . ." he muttered.

"I never liked having rope round the place," said Highton. "They always say that if you give a man enough rope—but you know the saying. I was afraid of being tempted into taking my life!"

"Not you," snapped Knollis. "You're too fond of life!"

"By the way," called Highton as they made for the stairs. "I realize that you wouldn't want it for the holding up of trousers. How silly of me not to think of the real reason straight away. You needed it for tying up a dog—a laughing dog! Well, I really must eat, so if you gentlemen will excuse me. . . ."

He pushed past them and entered the bathroom, bolting the door. Knollis stamped down the stairs with Manson on his heels, and sought out the landlord. "I want to speak to the chambermaid who turns out Mr. Highton's room."

She was fetched from the licensed side of the house, where she was doing duty as the barmaid. She blinked as she recognized Manson. "I haven't done anything, have I?" she giggled.

"Remember clearing away a piece of rope from Mr. Highton's room?" said Knollis.

"I didn't clear it away, sir. He kept chucking it under the bed, and I kept chucking it on the bed. I thought I could tire him out, and I did. I saw bits of it on the fire one morning when I went in to clean out the ashes."

"What morning?" Knollis asked sharply.

She poised a finger on her over-rouged lips. "It'd be Wednesday morning, sir."

Knollis slipped half a crown into her hand, and led Manson to the street.

"Not going to lunch here?" Manson asked in a disappointed voice.

"What? With his mocking smile facing me through the meal! Find somewhere different, Manson."

At two o'clock they presented themselves at the offices of Hodson and Spender, and Manson introduced Knollis to Mr. Frank Hodson, a tall, fair man of scholarly appearance and serious manner.

"I have all the facts you required, gentlemen," he said. "If there are any questions relating to them I'll do my best to answer them."

"With regard to the will," said Knollis. "Mrs. Burke receives two thousand pounds, and the residue goes to the daughter? That correct?"

"Correct, Inspector. There are no minor bequests."

"Not even to his favourite charities?"

"Not even to them," said Hodson. "I was surprised when he gave me the draft of the new will, but a client has a right to do as he likes with his own money."

"The will was drawn up this summer," said Knollis. "What was the date of the previous one?"

"There was no previous will, Inspector. I tried to persuade him to regularize his affairs on many occasions, but he said there was no need for it. If he—er—snuffed it the law would see that his daughter received his estate. It was late in July when he came to see me with regard to the drafting of a will. He gave me a pencilled draft in the rough, and asked me to prepare it for him. I queried the bequest to Mrs. Burke, and I'm afraid he told me to mind my own business."

"His charities?" murmured Knollis.

"Paid direct by cheque on the first of January each year, Inspector."

"This Deptford Foundation; what can you tell me about it? I've never heard of it before."

Hodson shrugged his thin shoulders. "Neither have I, Inspector. I must admit that I've inquired, but have failed to trace it. The cheque was paid by Challoner to Empson and Sloane of Warwick Square, London, and that is all I know about it."

"You've failed to trace it?" repeated Manson.

Hodson nodded. "To the best of my knowledge there is no charity or non-profit-making association of that name in the country."

"Did you ever see the cheques, or receipts?" asked Knollis.

Hodson shook his head.

"I see," Knollis said slowly. "Tell me, Mr. Hodson, have you ever heard Dr. Challoner refer to a laughing dog?"

"A—what?"

"Young Lincoln has said nothing to you?"

Hodson grimaced. "Lincoln has gone into his shell since Tuesday, Inspector, and apart from saying that you suspect him of killing his prospective father-in-law, he has said nothing."

"The point is this," said Knollis. "A drawing of a laughing dog was found on the current page of Dr. Challoner's desk-diary. We're trying to establish whether or not it has any significance."

Hodson waved his hands vaguely. "It sounds like nonsense to me, Inspector. Whoever heard of a dog that laughs?"

"You've heard of things making a cat laugh?"

Hodson's legal mind was apparently unable to match the imaginative quality of Knollis's own. "A common saying, a colloquialism, Inspector."

"Yet you'll remember that the little dog laughed to see such fun and the dish ran away with the spoon!"

"The—the notion is in the realm of fantasy, Inspector? Are you seriously thinking that a pencilled drawing of a dog can have any bearing on a man's death? Mind you, I don't know whether it was pencilled, or drawn with pen and ink, or even in chalk, but the matter is irrelevant."

"Mr. Hodson," Knollis said quickly, "Dr. Challoner had interests in two firms . . ."

Hodson opened the file that lay before him. "Challoner was responsible for two prescriptions made and sold by the Eesal Chemical Company, and on which he drew royalties."

"They don't happen to have a Laughing Dog Brand among their products?"

"Releef Cough Cure, and Challenge Rheumatic Salts," Hodson said dryly. "R.e.l.e.e.f.—Releef, since it is impossible to register a proper word as a trade name. The other firm in which he had an interest is Pierre Leblanc et Cie of Marseilles. Challoner lost a packet on them during the war, but the firm are operating again now, and he expected his first post-war dividend at the end of the present financial year."

"No Laughing Dog brands?" Knollis asked hopefully.

"They export fresh fruits, dried fruits, and local wines from Algeria, Inspector, but beyond that . . ."

"Mr. Hodson, what can you tell me about the projected marriage between Challoner and Mrs. Madeleine Burke?"

"Only that they were to be married!"

"You know that Lincoln and Challoner's daughter are to be married?"

"Obviously."

"What is Lincoln's salary? May I ask that?"

Hodson hesitated. "I don't know whether I should answer that, Inspector, but I pay him five pounds ten shillings a week, and he earns it! A very conscientious young man is Eric!"

"That's what I'm afraid of," said Knollis.

"Eh?" demanded the startled solicitor.

"We'll let it pass," smiled Knollis.

"Look here," rumbled Manson. "You and I have known each other for a good number of years now, Hodson, and we can talk without the reins or bit, can't we?"

"I hope so, Manson," replied Hodson.

"You're a shrewd fellow," went on Manson. "Like we fellows, you have to learn to use your wits."

"Modestly, I think I can allow that," bowed Hodson.

"Then who the devil killed Challoner, and why did they do it? You knew all about Challoner, and you must have your suspicions!"

Hodson tipped back his fair head until it rested on the back of the high chair. He looked Manson straight in the eye. "Manson, I haven't the faintest suspicion. I've practically all his papers here, and the man was sound financially, sound morally, and I should say he was sound physically. I've puzzled over his death since it was first announced, and I can't think of a solitary reason why anyone should desire his death."

Knollis slapped a hand on the table. "There must be a reason, Mr. Hodson! Men aren't murdered just because some fanatic happens to feel like doing a fellow creature to death—not often, anyway," he allowed reluctantly. "In any case, this tragedy bears none of the marks of the fanatic, and all the marks of a well-planned murder by some intelligent person."

"I'm sorry. I can't help you," said Hodson.

"Lincoln objected to his marriage to the Burke woman," said Manson.

Hodson shot him a quiet glance of contempt. "I don't know about that, Manson. Eric was obviously aware of the arrangements, inasmuch as he had to handle most of the documents, but I still fail to see why he should be suspected of bringing Challoner to his death!"

He looked down at his desk, and looked up again with set features. "Gentlemen, I tell you both frankly that if you should go so far as to arrest Eric Lincoln and charge him with Challoner's death, then my partner and I will back him with every cent we possess!"

Knollis rose and pushed his hat on the back of his head. "I hope your faith is justified, Mr. Hodson."

"It will be, Inspector! It will be!"

Knollis and Manson took their leave, both somewhat disgruntled, and returned to police headquarters, there to attend to the routine office work until Ellis broke the spell shortly after half-past four. He skimmed his bowler hat to the peg, and flopped into a chair.

"Any joy?" asked Knollis.

"Some afternoon!" Ellis replied.

"Result?"

"As before. Someone scaled the wall and cut the line from the post. My man, a washing-powder traveller just then, learned that Mrs. Lincoln left her whites out until supper-time. I understand that frost and cold air tend to bleach 'em."

"Interesting," murmured Knollis.

"More to come," Ellis replied imperturbably. "We loaded our tackle into the car and went to look at the street behind La Burke's. The house over the wall is empty."

"Meaning that our man could walk down the garden, climb the wall, and help himself without any difficulty!"

"There's a rustic seat under the wall," Ellis continued, "and it shows signs of having been walked on."

"Six feet nine inches of white cotton rope," boomed Manson, "and all this trouble to find it."

"No, we've got the six feet nine," Knollis corrected him. "It's the remainder we need, and the headache at the moment is not so much where that length has gone, but where the two lengths from Burke's and Lincoln's have gone!"

"Will we ever see a way through the ruddy case?" asked Manson. "It seems to get more complicated every time we take a step."

"An idea is playing round inside my head," said Knollis. "I think I'm beginning to see daylight. . . ."

"A new lead?"

Knollis nodded. "It's merely floating at the moment, Manson. I'll tell you about it when it comes to rest."

"A session at the flicks; that's what he needs now," said Ellis, charging his meerschaum and puffing furiously until the office was fog-bound.

Manson coughed through the smoke. "The—the flicks!"

"A Donald Duck, or a Pop-Eye," Ellis nodded.

"A Donald—are you going crazy, Sergeant?" asked Manson.

Ellis smiled mysteriously through his heavy walrus moustache, obviously pleased that he was puzzling the Inspector. "It's the piebald horse, sir."

Manson was beyond words by now. He grunted, and waited.

"It's lucky to see a piebald horse—if you don't think of its tail," Ellis explained. "The more you try not to look at its tail, the more persistent the tail becomes. Similarly, it's sometimes wise not to think about a problem that is occupying your mind, and the best way to solve it is not to think about it. See what I mean, sir?"

Manson swallowed hard. "One of us is batty!"

"Now the best way for him not to think about the tail is to occupy him with something else, and this way leave his mind free to work on the case," went on Ellis with twitching lips. "Donald Duck has solved one case for him, and Mickey Mouse helped with another."

Manson shook his head sadly. "I dunno!"

"Where's a cinema with at least two cartoon films showing?" asked Ellis.

"Down—down the street, on the left," stammered Manson.

Ellis then shook his disciplinary ideas to their roots by tapping the oblivious Knollis on the shoulder and saying: "Come on, Cock! It's two one-and-nines for us!"

XI
THE THREAD OF THOUGHT

ELLIS LED his chief's thoughts into comparatively trivial channels as they left the cinema. He had known Knollis for upwards of five years, and worked with him on practically every one of his cases. In that time he had learned not a little about him, and some aspects of creative psychology never mentioned in the lecture rooms. The Knollis method was to cram the brain with facts, and then retire, as it were, leaving the demon of the inner brain to classify and correlate them. Knollis never fully understood the operations of his own mind, and was inclined to hark back, dragging fact after fact from his mental reservoir and subjecting them to the cold light of reason. It was this phase which Ellis wished him to avoid, and so, as he fell in step beside him, and as his eyes sought for a café or restaurant, he began to question him about his early days.

"Y'know," he said in a thoughtful strain, "I've often wondered about you."

"Oh? In what respect?" Knollis asked absently. "You joined the Force in twenty-two, didn't you?"

"March, twenty-two; yes."

"When did you leave school?"

"School?" said Knollis. "See, it would be September, Nineteen-eighteen."

Then, dragging himself back into Ellis's company, he asked: "Why this sudden interest in my life, Ellis?"

"You'd be sixteen when you left school, and too young for the remaining months of the war."

"Er—yes, that's right."

"That's what I mean," Ellis explained. "What did you do for a living for the four years before you joined the Force?"

Knollis chuckled. "You'd never guess in a week of Sundays. I was learning to be a mechanical engineer. Those were the days! Working from seven in the morning until five in the evening, and attending technical classes four nights a week. There wasn't much spare time now I come to think back!"

Ellis fingered his black moustaches. "It doesn't make sense. Why the dickens did you turn thief-taker?"

"If you'll cast your mind back you'll remember that the engineering trade wasn't in a healthy state at that time, and so I got out. It isn't such a great change when you come to think about it. I merely turned a flair or a bent into another channel. I always liked taking things to pieces, finding out how they worked, and putting them together again. Joining the Force was an experiment. I didn't know whether I was going to like it or not. I wasn't worried about the monetary side, because I've always maintained that doing the thing one wants to do is more important than making money at some job you don't care for. The first few months in the Force were deadly, and then I began to realize that people could be as interesting as machines, and more so. I began to take them to pieces to see how they ticked, and then I began to study mentality, and behaviour, and all the subjects generally classed under the one term psychology. Coincident with my interest in people I began to find a curious sense of satisfaction in the unravelling of problems. It was a short step to the detective department as probationer—and here I am, a detective!"

"So that was it," said Ellis. "Funny how differing motives can lead people into the same job. I joined to get my own back. My old man kept a grocer's shop in Clerkenwell, and was badly bashed about by some roughs who demanded protection money from him. The old man, being what he was, told 'em to go to blazes, and he spent two months in hospital. He never really recovered, and died two and a half years later. As soon as I was old enough I got into uniform with the idea of having the Force behind me while I broke 'em. And then, queerly enough, I began to realize that there was something else behind this business, and that the laws we were upholding were based on fair play and not revenge. Funny I should tell you this, because I've never opened my mouth about it before. Y'know, they ain't bad laws, taking 'em all round!"

"The laws are sound," said Knollis; "it's the system of punishment that's at fault. We're a Christian people working on the Mosaic law of an eye for an eye and a tooth for a tooth. The country's beginning to see daylight, but it's going to be a good many years before we learn the real truth, that there's a law of compensation and that we reap as we sow. I mean, you throw a ray of light at a mirror, or a rubber ball at a wooden fence, and it comes back at you. Action is like that, or so I see it. And that is why I think that in the long run we'll suffer for dealing out capital punishment. Are we justified in killing a second person because he's killed someone else? It worries me at times. I enjoy the problem, and I enjoy the chase, and I hate murder so much that I hunt the murderer down—and then hand him over to death. It's a paradox, Ellis, and I can't solve it. My mind is split in halves, and I can't balance one against the other nor yet find a compromise."

He was silent for a moment, and then mused: "How do we solve it?"

"Cream cakes and eclairs," said Ellis. "Utility buns, but I love 'em. Look, a window full, and it's a café! Let's go in for tea. This feed's on me!"

Knollis grinned. "Perhaps that is the answer, Ellis, after all. I'll accept your hospitality, old man, knowing that the cakes will eventually feature as bus fares on your expenses account."

"So help me!" exclaimed Ellis, and turned into the doorway.

Three-quarters of an hour later he stood on the doorstep, patting his stomach. "Quite good for peace-time! Now back to the hotel for a rest. I put a new Western in my bag when we came down, and I haven't even had time to read the blurb!"

"You've had that," said Knollis. "We're going to the Challoner house. I've got an idea."

"Can't it wait until morning?" grunted Ellis. He looked into Knollis's face, lit by the light from an open shop doorway. "No, it can't. What's the notion this time?"

Knollis did not answer, but strode through the town to Kirkland Street, entered the premises via the surgery, and sought out Joan Challoner. She looked drawn and tired, and her restless eyes betrayed the bewildered state of her mind.

"You've no news?" she faltered.

"At the moment, no," Knollis said softly. "I wonder, Miss Challoner; could I see your father's sketches again? I'd like them in the consulting-room for half an hour."

"I'll fetch them," she said with a listless nod.

"Afterwards I'd like to see the attic again."

"You may go where you like in the house, Inspector. Eric is taking me out to-night; he says I need a change. The house is yours."

With the sketch books under his arm, Knollis went back to the consulting-room and Ellis, who had waited for him.

"Take pencil and paper, Ellis."

"Ready," said Ellis. "If it takes one man a week to sweep the main road from Edinburgh to Doncaster . . ."

"You're a fool," commented Knollis.

"And therefore a wise man," replied Ellis.

Knollis thumbed his way through the sketches. "They're a bit higgledy-piggledy since they've been removed from the books, but we can classify them later. Ready? The Mouse-Tower; that's Germany for Nineteen-twenty-four. La Scala, Milan, twenty-six. Acropolis, twenty-three and apparently in twenty-seven. Lake Geneva, twenty-five . . ."

Ten minutes later he asked: "Any blanks?"

"Nineteen-fourteen missing. So what?"

Knollis stood with his hand to his brow for a moment, and then strode to the door. "The attic, Ellis."

Ellis chased behind him up the two flights of stairs. "Take the cabin trunk, and I'll do the suit-cases in the corner yonder. And yet this place hardly seems to be a suitable place in which to hide a diary. Oh well, on with it, Ellis!"

"Nothing doing," Ellis said almost immediately. "The thing is empty. I'll take this other case. Also empty unless there's any-thing under this sheet of newspaper. Oh-oh!"

"What is it?"

"Look!"

Ellis held up a sheet of buff-coloured cartridge paper on which was drawn a recognizable caricature of Hugh Challoner, represented as a laughing dog.

"Highton's drawing, eh?" Knollis said in a low tone. "Give it to me. Quick! Before Joan Challoner goes out!"

He grabbed it and chased down the stairs with Ellis follow-ing at a more leisurely pace.

"Miss Challoner!" he called. "Miss Challoner!" She appeared on the landing above him. "What is it? Anything wrong?"

"Can you come down?" called Knollis.

She descended the stairs quickly.

"Ever seen this before?"

She stared in amazement at the grotesque caricature. "My—my father! The—the laughing dog!"

"Drawn in Algiers by Aubrey Highton," said Knollis. "You've never seen it before? You're sure of that?"

She shook her head, and her eyes were still fixed on the drawing. "I swear it, Inspector!"

She forced her eyes to meet his own. "What in heaven's name does it all mean?"

"Now listen," Knollis said tersely. "Highton says the idea just came to him. Whether it did or whether it did not is beside the point. The idea of the laughing dog suggested something disagreeable to your father, and in some way the secret is connected with his death. *We have to find out what that secret was—or is!*"

"But how?"

The outer door opened, and Eric Lincoln joined them. He caught sight of the caricature and stared at it for a few seconds before he recovered his wits and said his good-evenings.

"That is the idea," said Knollis. "How far are you prepared to go to discover your father's murderer? I don't want you to go dramatic, or melodramatic, or do anything sensational."

"I—well, need you ask how far I'll go?" she challenged him.

"No, I needn't," said Knollis. "You'll do it, but your boyfriend won't be so keen."

"I'm game for anything," Lincoln said in a voice that was far from convincing.

"Highton may know the secret behind your father's death, and he may know nothing at all," said Knollis. "Your job is to find out which! Now, has he attempted to pay any attention to you since your father brought him into the house, Miss Challoner?"

"Why—yes!"

"Good enough. Then fall out with Lincoln, and seek solace in Highton's company."

"Here, I say—!" protested Lincoln.

Knollis ignored the protest. "You go to Mrs. Burke, and apologize for insulting her on Tuesday evening. Tell her that your girl has thrown you over because the police suspect you of being concerned in her father's death. Ask her advice as an experienced woman; flatter her, take her out, and find out whether the laughing dog means anything to her or not. I'm going to London on the early train to-morrow, so report direct to Sergeant Ellis if and when you discover anything—and that means whether your report is affirmative or negative. Now can I rely on the pair of you?"

Joan Challoner nodded with emphasis, and Lincoln somewhat reluctantly.

"Where were you going to-night?" asked Knollis.

"I was taking her to the flicks," replied Lincoln.

"Then take her to the flicks. You'll part on the way home. Miss Challoner will return home, and you'll go and sulk in the bar of the Green Dragon where Highton can see you. Let him drag the story out of you, and don't go half-way to meet him! By the way, Miss Challoner, you're not staying in the house alone, are you?"

"No, Inspector. My day-girl is coming back each night to sleep in."

"That protects you if Highton gets too devoted. Now hop it. We're going to look over the house again."

Knollis and Ellis simply hung around until the front door closed behind the young couple, when Knollis led the way to the sitting-room, and made for the bureau.

"Done a risky trick, haven't you?" Ellis protested.

"It's the way the thread of thought suggested it, Ellis. It is a risk, I admit, but I've got to take a risk."

"And how do you think it will turn out?"

Knollis shrugged. "By Burke coming across to make a fuss of Joan Challoner in the hope of chiselling her way into the house for keeps. You know the idea; we two women have both suffered, and we should comfort each other. Highton and Lincoln will probably get thick while Highton is trying to grab Joan, and the law of opposites should do the rest."

"You hope!" said Ellis.

"I hope," repeated Knollis. "Now this bureau; you take the drawers to the table and work there. I'm looking for secret cavities. I refuse to believe that Challoner destroyed the diary."

After a time Ellis asked: "What do the letters *L.C.Q.R.* stand for? They're on an envelope in this second drawer that's got a photograph of a girl in it, and boy, is she purty!" He whistled, and straightened his tie.

"Let me see," said Knollis, striding to his side. "Heart-shaped face, small ears, *retroussé* nose, mop of dark hair, and an English type. There's something familiar about her face, Ellis! Who does she look like? Joan Challoner?"

Ellis brushed his moustache. "Yes and no," he said after due consideration. "What about the initials?"

"Haven't a clue. I must think about them. Meanwhile I can report that the bureau is innocent of secret cavities, priests' holes, and hidden passages. The diary isn't here!"

"Someone coming in," said Ellis.

Manson's deep voice came from the hall, and Knollis replied. Manson entered the room. "Thought I'd find you here! What's this? Pretty girl, eh?"

"These initials mean anything to you, Manson?"

"No-o! I know S.P.Q.R. They were the insignia on the banners of the Roman Legions."

"They mean Small Profits and Quick Returns, don't they, sir?" Ellis asked very innocently.

"They—" began Manson, and then looked down his nose at Ellis. "Nearly bought it, didn't I! I forget the exact interpretation, Sergeant! My Latin isn't as good as it used to be—but I used to be very good at school!"

Knollis was doing his usual trick of staring into space and ignoring his companions. He suddenly slapped a hand on the table. "You're going to say that I'm mad!"

"Probably," retorted Ellis, "but in what respect?"

"Mrs. Burke told us that Challoner drew the laughing dog while she watched him, and while, presumably, they were talking. In short, he was doodling!"

"That's logical," rumbled Manson.

"The best authorities assure us that patterns drawn while doodling are symbols outcropping from the sub-conscious mind!"

"Pretty common knowledge these days," said Ellis.

"I've studied myself in this respect," went on Knollis. "I always draw four perpendicular lines, and then draw four horizontal and parallel lines through them, making a sort of grid. I then begin at the bottom corner and connect the first vertical line with the first horizontal line, and continue the process with each other pair of lines until I've produced what looks like four figure eights drawn inside each other. In brief, I draw the warp and woof of a problem and then connect them so that they form the finished pattern. I tie up all the ends, exactly as I attempt to do when working on an investigation like this present one. You see the point?"

"Clear up to now," said Ellis, charging his pipe.

"I follow you," said Manson doubtfully.

"Dr. Challoner was talking rationally to Mrs. Burke; we can safely assume that. His subconscious mind was busy with another very different subject, a subject symbolized by the laughing dog that he was drawing. Now what I want to know is this: which of his patients was the most likely to disturb his mind? What do we know about his patients, the ones who attended the Tuesday evening surgery?"

"I came to tell you about them," said Manson. "Our chaps have examined his case-books and medical diaries, and each of his Tuesday evening patients was a regular client he'd seen on a good many occasions before—with the sole exception of Aubrey Highton!"

"Good lord, yes!" exclaimed Ellis.

"That's the point," said Knollis earnestly. "My theory is that Highton was the patient who disturbed his mind—and remember that he'd only just seen him when he admitted Mrs. Burke. Now you know my opinion of coincidence! I refuse to believe that Highton's caricature of Challoner, portraying him as a laughing dog, was a coincidence! I believe that Highton knew Challoner, and knew his secret. I believe that he insinuated himself into Challoner's good graces for the purpose of being invited to England. . . ."

"And now where do we stand?" asked Manson.

"Let's assume that Highton really did come to England to kill Challoner. Like all killers, he had to study his man and his habits. Any murderer risks his life when he commits the capital crime. Being an intelligent man he didn't intend taking any more risks than were absolutely necessary, so he took a room in the hotel directly opposite Challoner's house—"

"Challoner put him there," interposed Manson, "and Miss Joan will corroborate the fact."

"Damn, yes!"

Knollis stalked about the room, his lean fingers pinching his chin. He came back to Manson and nodded.

"I'm taking the line of least resistance for the sake of argument. Challoner put him there for purposes of his own."

"Weak," said Ellis. "In any case, it doesn't matter how he got there. The point you're trying to make is that the situation of the bedroom was ideal from the point of view of a killer!"

"Ye-es," said Knollis. "Highton was the patient before Burke. Highton watched the surgery from his darkened bedroom, saw Burke leave, and then slipped back and killed Challoner."

"So that when he says a woman left at half-past seven he was lying?" suggested Manson.

"Not necessarily, although it could be. It's an old dodge, and you've seen it crop up in innumerable cases—the mysterious stranger who's never found, and whose existence, even if granted, provides no motive, satisfactory or otherwise. The Wallace murder at Liverpool was a case in point."

"Which would bring Mrs. Burke into the clear?"

"It would seem so, Manson, although we must tax her on the point."

"Vastly interesting," said the puzzled Manson, "but where do we go from here?"

"Back to Dr. Hugh Challoner. He made three donations to charity each year: one direct to the local hospital, one direct to the county tubercular clinic, and one to a seemingly legendary charity called the Deptford Foundation which was paid through a Warwick Square firm of solicitors by the name of Empson and Sloane—whom I intend to visit tomorrow."

He had picked up his pencil and was scrawling idly on the envelope that had contained the photograph. "I hope to be coming back on the eight-ten, Sunday night, or an early train next day."

Manson glanced at his scrawl. "You're doing it now!"

Knollis looked at the envelope. "I shouldn't have done. The envelope might have to be produced in court yet. Heigh—wait a minute!"

He had drawn a laughing dog, not too well, but still recognizable as such. Under it he had written the word *chien*, and over it the letters L.C.Q.R.

"That was the word the doc said to Mrs. Burke," muttered Manson. "French for dog."

"French is spoken in Algiers—where Highton came from," said Knollis reflectively. "L.C.Q.R.? How's your French, Manson? Or yours, Ellis?"

"Mine's horribly rusty," grumbled Manson.

"Non compree," said Ellis. "I'm elementary school."

"The idiom has to be taken into account," said Manson. "I seem to remember that laughs is *rit*."

"Yes, the idiom!" exclaimed Knollis. "The laughing dog becomes the dog who laughs, or the dog that laughs. *Le chien qui rit*—L.C.Q.R.! And that was how Challoner explained the dog to Mrs. Burke! Therefore it has a French association." He laughed. "Now for the anti-climax. We don't know what it meant to Hugh Challoner!"

XII

THE DEPTFORD FOUNDATION

MR. JONATHAN SLOANE was a short little man with bowed legs, and a long bald head lightly fringed with curly blond hair that made him look like an Easter egg. He received Gordon Knollis with due courtesy and little enthusiasm.

"Take a seat," he said in a snuffly voice. "I hope you're not going to smoke in my office, for tobacco smoke is anathema to me. Now, what can I do for you?"

"I'm investigating the death of Dr. Hugh Challoner of Sturton Lacey. You handled some business of his."

Sloane drew in his lips, pondered, and sniffed. "We did," he said bluntly.

"I happen to be interested in the Deptford Foundation," said Knollis, looking hopefully at the little lawyer.

Sloane's head fell over almost on to his shoulder. "I don't dispute it, Inspector, but what is it?"

Knollis stared his unbelief. "You mean to say you don't know? That you've never heard of it?"

"Never heard of it," Sloane repeated. "Is it some private institution?"

Knollis gave a barely perceptible shrug, and a dry smile came to his thin lips. "Come, Mr. Sloane! Your firm passed Challoner's cheque to this charity every January!"

Sloane sniffed. "You are sadly mistaken, Inspector. I admit we've handled a certain transaction for Dr. Challoner for a good many years, but I can assure you we've never dealt with any Deptford Foundation. I venture to suggest there is no charitable organization of that name."

"You did receive a cheque from Challoner every year?"

"We did, Inspector. I've admitted it."

"What happened to it?"

"We deducted two-and-a-half per cent commission and sent on the balance to a pair of initials in the care of a Mr. Sam Bradley of 43 Dunwell Street, E.C.4."

Knollis made a note of the address. "The initials?"

"L.D., Inspector."

"The laughing dog again, eh?" murmured Knollis.

"The—er—what?" sniffed Sloane.

"Let it pass," said Knollis. "I take it that the cheque was made payable to bearer, and not to any specific person?"

"We sent cash—bank notes and treasury notes. It made a bulky package, but that was the instruction."

"When did you last see Dr. Challoner?"

"We've never seen him. The money was sent by District Messenger. May I ask a question?"

"You may," said Knollis.

"Where did you pick up this—er—Deptford Foundation idea?"

"From the solicitors who handled the rest of his affairs, Hodson and Spender of Sturton Lacey. They informed me that he contributed to three charities every year; the local hospital, the county tubercular clinic, and this alleged foundation."

"Very queer," mused Sloane. "We've wondered about the business from time to time, but there was no reason to suspect it was anything but legal and above-board, and consequently had no reason to refuse it. Er—Inspector, this is a question I shouldn't ask: we haven't been assisting, say, blackmail!"

Knollis scratched his head before answering. "Well, to be honest, I don't know what's behind it, Mr. Sloane. It may be blackmail within the legal meaning of the word, or it may be what the Irish call a whisht-me-dear, or it may be just a straightforward payment for services rendered. I was hoping that you might be able to give me a clue."

"I know less than you do yourself, Inspector."

"Ever met this Bradley?"

"No. The occasion has not arisen when it seemed either necessary or desirable."

"Thanks," said Knollis, and left.

Mr. Sam Bradley was a retailer of newspapers, magazines, tobacco, comic postcards, string, brown paper, and cheap toys. Several customers were in the shop when Knollis walked in, and so he stood aside until they were served. Bradley, a broad, squat man with a happy face, nodded affably. "Afternoon, sir. What can I get for you?"

"A word in private," said Knollis. "I'm from the Yard."

"The Yard! I haven't done anything wrong!"

"I didn't say you had," said Knollis. "I want to ask a few questions about someone else."

"I don't know anything about anybody else!" Bradley protested in an anxious voice.

"Do we talk here, or in your house?" asked Knollis. Bradley eyed him with suspicion, but led him through to the living-room and sent his wife to tend the counter.

Knollis produced his warrant-card to satisfy the newsagent, and began his questioning. "The matter is a simple one, Mr. Bradley. You've provided an accommodation address for a person known as L.D."

"Well yes," Bradley admitted, "but there's nothing wrong in that, surely!"

"I can't say yet," said Knollis. "What can you tell me about the affair?"

"I've done nothing wrong," grumbled Bradley.

"What was L.D.'s name, Mr. Bradley?" Knollis asked in his best official manner.

"Durand. Louis Durand—and a very pleasant gentleman he is."

"I don't doubt it," said Knollis, "but I want to get in touch with him. The man who posted those letters has died."

"Died!" exclaimed Bradley, his features betraying his thoughts so clearly that it was almost possible to read them before they became spoken words. "Died—and the Yard's interested. That means he was—murdered! There's only that Dr. Challoner case in the papers just now!"

"That's right," said Knollis, and shot in a question while Bradley was off his guard. "Where can we find the laughing dog?"

Bradley blinked. "You know that an' all!"

"Don't you think you'd better tell me the whole story?" suggested Knollis.

Bradley was still in a semi-trance. "Dead, eh? That's an easy two quid a year gone west—for just handing a letter over the counter to him."

"How did it start, Mr. Bradley?"

"Must have been about Nineteen-thirty-two, or perhaps the year before that. That's right, it was thirty-two! He was no more than a lad when he came in and asked if I could supply an accommodation address for letters. He said there'd only be one a year, and it was worth two quid to me. I'd have been a fool to turn it down."

"A deuce of a fool," agreed Knollis, anxious to encourage his man.

"Came in nice and handy, as all money does. He said he'd pick it up himself, and if he didn't come I was to save the letters, even if he didn't come for years. In case he ever had to send for it his messenger would give a password. He was to say: *'I'm from the Laughing Dog'*, and then I was to hand over, and the messenger would give me the two quid."

"What's Durand like?"

"Smallish fellow with a queer sort of smile."

"Red-haired?" Knollis asked anxiously.

"Red?" laughed Bradley. "He's as black as a tom-cat—a black tom-cat." He paused and added: "He's a Frenchy, but a gent."

"Black, eh?" murmured Knollis in a disappointed tone. "Oh well! Anyway, did he ever send a messenger?"

"No, sir. He didn't. He came himself when he did come."

"I expect so," Knollis said dryly. "How old do you think Durand is?"

Bradley scratched his head. "Oh, I'll give him between thirty and thirty-five. Bit difficult with foreigners; you can't tell very well."

"He called every year?" asked Knollis, and again the note of anxiety was apparent in his voice.

"Thirty-eight was the last time he came in until this year. April it was, and I'd had the letters saved up right through the war. Eight of them there were, and they made a bulky parcel. He'd altered a lot, but I knew him straight away. *'Remember me, Mr. Bradley?'* he asked. *'God help me if it isn't Monsewer Durand!'* I said. *'You look as if you've been through it all right.'* He gives that funny sort of smile and *'God help me but I have, Mr. Bradley,'* he says, *'and I'm broke to the wide.'* He asks me if I've anything for him and I gives him the bundle of letters. He opens one of 'em and it's full of notes. *'Eight two's are sixteen,'* he says, *'and here's twenty quid for you, Mr. Brad-*

ley. Loyalty's about the only thing I've any respect for.' Then he says there won't be any more letters because his friend that sent them's going away, and won't be coming back. *'I don't forget good friends, Mr. B.,'* he says, *'and if everything goes well with a plan I'm working on you'll get a hundred quid for yourself.'* He bought a packet of cigs from me, chucked a quid on the counter, and walked out. That was the last time I saw him."

Knollis whistled softly. "So he told you it would be the last letter. Now listen, Bradley, if you hear any more of him you're to contact me at the Yard. No more pretending you know nothing!"

Bradley grinned. "I was careful when you first came in. All the bobbies aren't as polite as you."

"I'm not susceptible to flattery," said Knollis, suppressing a smile. "He came in thirty-eight, and not again until April this year."

"That's right, sir."

"Where can I find Durand?"

Bradley shook his head. "So help me, Inspector, but I don't know. I could have sent the letters on to him if I'd known where he lived, couldn't I?" he asked naively.

"That's true," said Knollis. "You'd recognize him again?"

"If I knew him after eight years I reckon I'd know him after seven months, sir."

"Also true," said Knollis. "How much money do you think was in the envelope?"

"Oh, going on for two hundred quid!"

"You never knew that the envelopes contained cash?"

"I'd no idea, and it wouldn't have made any difference if I had known. I'm honest. I told you I'd done nothing wrong."

"True enough," Knollis admitted. "Tell me: how did you know Durand was French—apart from his name?"

"His accent, sir. It sticks out a mile."

"Oh well . . . !" said Knollis, thanked Bradley, and returned to the Yard, where he went into conference with Chief-Inspector Burnell and Superintendent Lawson and discussed the case thoroughly.

"A collection of cul-de-sacs, that's what you've got," said Burnell. He rubbed his large hands backwards and forwards over his baggy trouser knees. "This Highton fellow's mixed up in the case, but I'm hanged if I see how you're going to prove it. Seems to be one of the wily sort. This laughing dog motif; does it convey anything at all to you?"

"Not a darned thing," said Knollis, "and yet it crops up at every twist and turn." He narrowed his eyes. "If Durand is Highton, then it means that Highton dyed his hair and moustache while he was Louis Durand. If he came over in April to draw the money he'd time to get his colouring right before the time when he and Challoner got together."

"And his passport photo?" murmured the Superintendent.

"Red photographs black, sir," Knollis reminded him.

"That's true! He'd have no difficulty there. Neat point, that!"

"The name of the tourist agency through which he booked his holidays?" suggested Burnell.

"I have that," said Knollis, patting his pocket. "Duval of Ludgate Hill in conjunction with the Cosmos Shipping Line of Cockspur Street."

Burnell spread his hands. "Well then!"

"Yes, you're right," said Knollis. "I'll see them."

He went to Cockspur Street first, to meet with disappointment when he learned that copies of past passenger lists were not kept. "As for Duvals," said the clerk, "they're in Queen Victoria Street now. The premises and all their documents were destroyed in the fire-blitz."

Knollis checked on that information and returned to the Yard, from where he held a long telephonic conversation with Manson. After reporting his activities, he said: "I'd like you to check Challoner's bank account and see whether any unaccountable sums were paid out by him before thirty-two. Then find out where he spent his holidays in thirty-one. Next item is to ask Miss Joan to pump Highton about his past. Got those down?"

Manson replied that he had. "I'll have the answers ready for when you get back."

"I want 'em in the office on Monday, please," said Knollis. "Ring me at noon. Now, anything happened with regard to Miss Joan and Highton?"

"I saw him out shopping with her this morning. Lincoln's as sour as little apples about it, and I've threatened to turn the sulky little bull over my knee if he doesn't grow up."

"Two other items," said Knollis. "I want Highton's age, and the year in which Burke was married."

"What on earth for?" demanded Manson.

Knollis replied lamely: "I really don't know, but I want 'em."

He could almost see Manson shrug. "Oh well, if you want 'em, you want 'em. Ring you at noon then. 'Bye!"

Knollis spent Sunday in his own home, but was out and about by half-past eight on the Monday morning. He made his way to Gray's Inn Road and had to wait an hour before Highton's agent arrived for the day's work.

Darby, an earnest fellow with grey hair, gave him a shrewd glance as he asked for information about Highton.

"Highton? A good man, Inspector. No genius, but a fair talent. Good commercial artist."

"How did you get in touch with each other?"

"He wrote to me from Algiers, and called a few weeks later with samples of his work. That was in April. He said he would be making a home in England later in the year, and he called on me again about three weeks ago. That's all I know of him, and all I need to know of him. He produces the work, and I sell it and draw commission on sales. What's he done wrong, anyway?"

"Nothing," said Knollis. "He happens to be a vital witness in a case I'm investigating, and I wanted to check on his reliability."

"He's all right, Inspector," Darby assured him. "Artistic integrity and all that, you know! He'll tell you what he saw, and do it without adding trimmings. I can tell that by his stuff. He's a good draughtsman, but, strictly in confidence, he's inclined to be too photographic and not sufficiently imaginative. He'd do well in a job like designing. He's all right from your point of view, of course, and should be an ideal witness. Well, I'm busy, Inspector. Pleased to have been of assistance to you. . . ."

Knollis was out on the pavement before he was aware of what had happened, a rueful smile on his face. He turned into a teashop to drink coffee and munch a bun, then sauntered aimlessly along the streets deep in thought. At eleven o'clock he descended to the Underground, and came up again at Westminster to amble round the corner to his office at The Yard. He drew a sheet of paper from the tray, found a pencil, and drew four vertical lines, parallel to each other. Through them he drew four horizontal lines, equidistant and also parallel. Starting at the bottom left-hand corner he drew a loop connecting the first horizontal line with the first vertical one. He connected the second pair in a similar way, and so on until he had converted the grid into a fourfold figure-eight.

He threw the pencil aside, leaned back in the chair, and clasped his hands across his waistcoat. The answer lay somewhere within that pattern. Let the first horizontal line represent Hugh Challoner, and the next Madeleine Burke, and the third Eric Lincoln, and the fourth Aubrey Highton. Now let the vertical lines represent motive, method, opportunity, and psychological capability, and then observe the correspondences. By changing the order of the characters it was possible to regard each in turn in a logical manner.

He frowned. It was specialized advice that he needed. He'd been trying to work out the case as an individual, while the triumphs of the Yard had been achieved mainly as the result of brilliant teamwork. No man ever got anywhere worthwhile without help and advice from at least one other person, which was the basic truth behind the old advice never to forget the people you passed on the way up because you might meet them again on the way down.

He rose and went to Burnell's office. "Got a few minutes to spare?" he asked.

"Come in," Burnell greeted him. "What's on your mind?"

"The brain temporarily refuses to function. I'm experiencing one of those damned psychological plateaux. Know 'em?" said Knollis.

"I know 'em, and they can be plain hell!" said Burnell. "What's the major worry?"

"This laughing dog," said Knollis. "I can't get a single clue to what it is!"

"Perhaps you haven't asked the right question," replied Burnell. "The bloke outside the ring sees more of the game than the protagonists, and that's how I see your worry. There are six primary questions you can ask, and you've only asked one. What is it, you've asked! Then how about having a go at the other five?"

"Who is it? Which is it? Why is it? How is it? Where is it?" chanted Knollis, as if repeating a lesson.

He suddenly looked up at the grinning Burnell. "Holy smoke, yes! Who in this building knows Algiers?"

Burnell pondered. "Sergeant Lindley in the photo department. He did some useful work for M.I.5 during the war. Why?"

But Knollis was on his way, tearing round the building as if there was not a second to spare. Burnell followed in his own dilatory style, his long arms swinging by his sides, and his heavy cheeks sagging towards his collar.

Knollis charged into the photographic department and blurted out a demand for Sergeant Lindley, now and immediately. He was fetched from a dark room, and blinked as he faced the anxious Knollis in the full light of day.

"You were in Algiers!" said Knollis as if he were accusing him.

"Why yes, sir!"

"What is the laughing dog?"

"Why, it's kept by Henri Brogard and his wife!"

"Where is it?"

"On the Rue de Constantine, sir!"

"But *what* is it?" snapped the exasperated Knollis.

"A café, sir. *Le Chien Qui Rit.*"

"Darn queer name," said Burnell from the doorway, "but no more stupid than the names of many English pubs!"

"Le Chien Qui Rit!" said Knollis. "The Dog who Laughs! What sort of a place is it?"

"Oh, very respectable, sir! A Bohemian sort of place patronized by artists, and writers, and musicians."

"They take in guests?"

"Why yes! They did while I was there, anyway, sir."

"A café on the Rue de Constantine," mused Knollis. "Like to go again, Lindley?"

"Give me the chance, sir!"

"You may get it, Lindley."

Burnell laid a huge paw on Knollis's shoulder. "Now what, my friend? What do you do now?"

"Go straight back to Sturton Lacey," said Knollis. There was a new and keener light in his eyes, and he had completely forgotten his appointment on the telephone with Manson at noon.

XIII

THE RETURN CALL

MANSON NODDED when Knollis finished the recital of his investigations in London. "Thought something must have happened when I rang at twelve o clock and they said you were on the way back. I got all the stuff you wanted, with the exception of Highton's age. Mrs. Burke was married on Easter Sunday, Nineteen-thirty; Challoner's bank-book is clear of any 'Deptford Foundation' payments before Nineteen-thirty-two, and his holiday for that year was spent in Denmark."

"What about Miss Joan's inquiry into Highton's past life?"

"What about it!" rumbled Manson. "I saw her early this, morning, and got chalked off! Mr. Highton is a very nice man, let me tell you! He had nothing to do with her father's death— she says it was Mrs. Burke. Highton has told her all! His past is an open book, and he's as innocent as a new-born lamb. Looks as if your crazy idea has gone the wrong way, doesn't it?"

"Does it?" Knollis murmured in a tone that might have meant anything.

"What do we do now?" asked Manson.

"Where's Ellis?"

"Messing about in the sergeants' room. Why?"

Knollis shrugged. "I merely want to let him know I'm back. See you later."

He went to find Ellis, and found him completely at his ease; his boots were under the table, his feet were balanced on the edge of it, and he was well down in the chair, while the room was a fog of smoke from the meerschaum. "How's the game of cops and robbers?" he threw casually over his shoulder.

"You'll be surprised," said Knollis.

"I am," said Ellis when the tale was done. "Nothing's happened at this end, although Lincoln may commit mayhem on Highton before many hours have passed. It looks to me as if Mr. Highton is much practised in the art of wooing a girl, and is a fast worker. Either that or she's a far better actress than I give her credit for being. She walks about Sturton Lacey with her arm hooked through his and looks happy—which is more than she has done in Lincoln's company! Did I say nothing had happened? Highton left something for you this morning."

He opened a drawer and took from it a flat package ten inches square. "I haven't opened it."

Knollis did so, and produced a pencil drawing.

"What is it?" asked Ellis.

"Highton's imaginative reconstruction of the scene in the surgery as Challoner lay dead. Darby, his agent, said he'd no imagination. I beg leave to differ. This is darned good work. Grim, grisly, and morbid, but still good work."

It might have been drawn from one of the official photographs taken before Challoner's body was moved, with the exception of one or two small items. The room was photographically portrayed. The tall cabinet of instruments, the bookshelves with their worn bindings, the electric fire in the corner opposite the waiting-room door, the dispensary door ajar, the table-desk with its litter of paper and books, and the desk-diary and small red diary lying on the morocco-bound blotting-pad, while from behind the desk projected the head and shoulders of the dead man.

He turned it over, to find written on the back: *"To Inspector Knollis, with the compliments of Aubrey Highton."*

He stood it on the mantelpiece, and regarded it with admiration through the fog of Ellis's 'Eavenly Effluvium. "Wish I could draw as well. Still, on with your boots, Ellis. We've work to do."

"At this time of the day? Where are we going?"

"Mrs. Burke's."

"Whaffor?" asked Ellis as he bent to tie his laces.

"To tell her a fairy story."

"Why not a bedtime story?"

"Bedtime stories are intended to lull people to sleep. Mine is to wake her up," Knollis said grimly.

"Putting the cat among the pigeons?" Ellis asked curiously.

Knollis clicked his tongue. "This is more like presenting the pigeons to the cat. Ready yet?"

"Gimme time!" protested Ellis. "That's one, and this is two. Now my hat."

Mrs. Burke answered the door with a novel in her hand. She invited them inside with perfunctory politeness and took them through to the sitting-room, where a good fire was burning.

"Alone?" asked Knollis.

She heaved a sigh. "I hardly see my boy these days. He spends all his spare time at the youth club. Still, I do know where he is! Now, is there anything I can do for you? There must be, or you would not be here."

"No," said Knollis. "The boot is on the other foot tonight. You don't mind if we take seats?"

"Oh, I'm sorry. By all means," she said. She fluttered round to shake the cushions of the chesterfield. "Do make yourselves comfortable. You'd like a drink?"

"No, thank you, Mrs. Burke. We're here to give you some news. We've learned what happened last Tuesday night."

She sought her chair, made a fuss of settling herself, and then looked up with casual indifference. "Then you've found who—who killed Hugh Challoner?"

Knollis leaned forward, one finger wagging at her as he made his points. "You went to the surgery last Tuesday, saw Dr. Challoner, left in the normal way, and started for home. You met Eric Lincoln, had the row with him, and—"

"And came home," she interrupted with an inclination of her head.

"And did nothing of the kind!" Knollis retorted. "You crossed Bowden Street, and went via Williamson's Passage and Denver Street to the surgery, letting yourself in by what is normally the exit door in the consulting-room, and leaving by the waiting-room door shortly after half-past seven. . . ."

"I—I came home," she persisted in an unconvincing voice.

"Dr. Challoner was alive when you left the first time," said Knollis. "He was dead when you left on the second occasion."

She stared dully at the blazing fire, and when she looked up there was fear in her eyes. "I'm scared, Inspector."

"Of what, Mrs. Burke?"

"Of—of being the next!"

"What makes you think you might be the next, or that there is likely to be a next?"

Her voice sank to a whisper. "Hugh was murdered for money, and he left me two thousand pounds."

"You did go back to the surgery, Mrs. Burke!"

"Yes," she said with a long-drawn sigh. "Yes, I went back, Inspector. That's why I'm afraid. There was someone in the dispensary."

"Tell me all about it, Mrs. Burke. It will be better that way. A fear loses its intensity when shared."

"Perhaps that will be the better way," she said. "I did go back. I don't know who saw me, but I went along Williamson's Passage into Denver Street, and round into Kirkland Street to the consulting-room door. There was someone moving about inside, and so I knocked instead of going in, just in case he had a late patient whom he might be examining. There was no answer, and so I knocked again. There was still no answer, so I turned the knob and opened the door a few inches. Then I pushed it wide open and went in. . . ."

"Yes, Mrs. Burke?"

"Hugh was lying on the floor with the chair tumbled beside him. I ran to him and fell on my knees and tried to raise his head. It rolled heavily on his neck, and I knew he was dead. I was going to run into the house and telephone the police, and then I caught sight of a shadow in the dispensary. The door was about half open, and the shadow fell across the outer wall. I was paralysed for a moment, and then I suddenly got up and ran into the waiting-room and into the street. I turned into Bowden Street and crossed the road, and stood watching the house. Only a minute or so seemed to elapse before Eric Lincoln ran from the house, looked both ways, and ran to the constable at the kiosk. The two of them hurried to the house, and then I came straight home. I got the door closed, and fainted across the hall. I was in a state of collapse when I came round. I got myself a drink, came in here, and tried to think what to do for the best. I couldn't decide, and so I—well, I did nothing and said nothing. Next morning it seemed to be wiser to deny all knowledge of Hugh's death, and that was what I did when Inspector Manson called."

Knollis narrowed his eyes. "Tell me, Mrs. Burke: was the door leading to the house open or closed?"

"Closed, Inspector."

"And the door leading to the waiting-room?"

"Also closed."

"Tell me: was the light still on in the waiting-room when you entered?"

"Why, yes!"

"And the light in the consulting-room? I mean, you didn't switch on that light as you entered?"

"Oh no, it was already on."

"I see," said Knollis.

She was staring into the fire again. Twice she glanced up, and each time lowered her gaze.

"Yes, Mrs. Burke?" Knollis said gently.

"It was Eric Lincoln, wasn't it?"

"I don't know, Mrs. Burke. Do you think that?"

"I don't know, Inspector, but he so badly wanted Hugh's money."

Knollis rose and prepared to leave. He caught sight of a heap of parcels on one of the dining chairs. "Getting ready for Christmas, Mrs. Burke?"

She smiled wanly. "It's Leslie's birthday tomorrow, Inspector. One of the parcels was given me by Hugh a few days before his death. I don't quite know whether to give it to him or not."

"I would, Mrs. Burke. I think I would. Well, we'll bid you good night."

He and Ellis went to the Challoner house. The police guard having been removed from the surgery, Knollis had to ring the front-door bell. It was answered by Joan Challoner.

"Oh! It's you!"

"We'd like to go through to the surgery, Miss Challoner. Sorry if we're disturbing you!"

She closed the door and walked slowly before them to the lounge. "Mr. Highton is with me. Care to come in?"

Knollis followed her into the room. Highton was occupying a fireside chair, his legs sprawled across the hearth. "Come in here, Inspector. You should spend an hour with us."

"Too busy, thanks," Knollis replied. "By the way, I must thank you for the sketch you left, and congratulate you on its excellence. Nice work, if I might say so."

"Nothing much," said Highton. "Just an imaginative reconstruction."

Joan Challoner looked inquiringly from one to the other.

"I've done the Inspector an Algerian scene," lied Highton with a wink at Knollis. "You must get him to show it to you some time."

Knollis blinked as an idea came to him. "Suppose you'll manage to celebrate your birthday in a mild way, Mr. Highton?"

Highton looked puzzled. "My birthday?"

"It is your birthday tomorrow, surely," said Knollis. "I know someone told me they had a birthday!"

"Mine's in April," said Highton. "You've got mixed, Inspector."

"It's Leslie Burke's," Joan Challoner said disinterestedly. "He's thirteen."

"Which makes my forty-five feel like a hundred," smiled Knollis. "You're a long way from that middle-age feeling, Mr. Highton! How old are you? May I guess you to be thirty?"

Highton bowed mockingly. "Thanks for the compliment, Inspector. You've given me two years I've already had!"

"Thirty-two, eh? You don't look it, and that isn't flattery."

Joan Challoner grimaced. "You both make me feel an infant. Twenty isn't very old really, is it?"

"Old enough," said Knollis.

"Just nice," said Highton with an admiring glance.

She flushed under his gaze, and Knollis excused himself. He picked up Ellis in the hall, and together they went to the consulting-room.

"What's the object of this here visit?" asked Ellis.

"To look into this here shadow in the dispensary story of Madeleine Burke's," answered Knollis with a light smile. "Hop inside and switch on the light. Then hide behind the door."

He got down on his knees behind the table as Ellis retired to the tiny annexe, and squinted over his shoulder.

"Where's the light now in relation to yourself?"

"Slightly behind me, and to my right."

"Take a peep behind the door, and dodge back as you see me looking round. Right! That's it, Ellis!"

He got to his feet and dusted his knees. "Want to try it? Come out then, and I'll go in."

Two minutes later Ellis called: "Looks as if her yarn might be true. Now what's bitten you?" he asked as Knollis planted his hands on his hips and stared at the window in the outer wall.

"Got an idea, Ellis. See this window? Double casement. Each sash one large sheet of hammered glass, with two small panes of clear glass. Switch off the light. Yes, we can see the lights in the bedroom on the backs of Denver Street. Now that's interesting!"

Ellis brushed his moustache with the back of his hand. "I'm dense, or you're mad. Which is it?"

"Come on," said Knollis with a sudden burst of energy. He returned to the lounge, entering only after knocking discreetly on the door. Joan Challoner and Highton were sitting on either side of the hearth in the deep fireside chairs.

"Where can I find Eric Lincoln?" Knollis asked abruptly.

A pout of annoyance was his answer from Joan Challoner. It was answered by Highton. "You'll probably find him in the saloon bar across at the Dragon. Found him out at last?"

"If he isn't there I'll find him out," snapped Knollis, and slammed the door behind him as he left.

With Ellis tagging on behind he almost ran across the street to the hotel, and found Lincoln leaning against the bar looking slightly the worse for wear. The landlord showed him a private room in which he could interview Lincoln, and Knollis steered him into it and pushed him into a chair while Ellis put his broad back against the door and produced note-book and pen.

"Wha's all this?" Lincoln demanded hazily.

"That door! The one that slammed! Come on now! Wake yourself! I want to ask you some questions."

"I'm a'right!" protested Lincoln. "I know wha' you're tal'ing abou'. Door slammed! A'right! So wha'?"

"Where were you when you heard the waiting-room door slam, Lincoln?"

A cunning look came into Lincoln's eyes. "I was in the lounsh—so there!"

"You know the position of the dispensary?" said Knollis. "There are two windows in the outer wall, overlooking the garden and rear premises. The lower panes are opaque. The upper panes are clear glass. From the back bedrooms in Denver Street it is possible to see straight down into the dispensary!"

Lincoln made a desperate effort and pulled himself together to some degree.

"Back be'rooms i' Denver S'reet!" He blinked, swayed in his chair, and gulped. "Oh, my Gaw'!"

"Well?" demanded Knollis. "Do you still insist that you were in the lounge?"

Lincoln struggled out of the chair. "Le' me go! You can' keep me here. I know the law, and I'm going!"

"Open the door for him, Ellis."

When Lincoln was out of sight, Knollis said: "'Phone for a police car, and see him home. On the way out, ask the landlord to see me in here. I'll wait for you in the saloon bar."

Ellis looked at his wrist-watch. "Half-nine. Just time for a pint or so if I hurry!"

He hurried.

The landlord joined Knollis a couple of minutes or so later. "I'm afraid the lad was more stewed than I realized, Inspector. I should have refused to supply him much earlier."

Knollis waved the explanation away. "Look, Mr.—er—?"

"George Camden."

"Look, Mr. Camden, your guest Highton has placed a fair amount of valuable information in our hands. Unfortunately, we can't do much with it unless his times are corroborated, and I think you can do that."

"Well . . ." Camden said uncertainly.

"Can you remember at what time Mr. Highton entered the bar on last Tuesday evening?"

"Why, yes. It was just on a quarter-past seven. He ordered a drink and stood against the bar."

"He left the bar shortly afterwards?"

Camden nodded. "He seemed to be a bit like the Cheshire Cat that night, sort of coming and going all the time. He does that, though. Wanders in and out of the other rooms looking for interesting folk to talk to. I expect it's with him being an artist, and he's looking for subjects!"

"I expect so," said Knollis. "You can't give me an idea of his comings and goings, can you?"

"Well, about twenty-past he pushed his empty tankard and two bob across the counter and said he'd have to run out to the back. I refilled him and put his change beside the tankard. I can't say what time he came back. I was pretty busy, and the room was filling, and I obviously wasn't taking account of what any customer in particular was doing."

"Quite so!" said Knollis. "He vanished again later?"

"Be about twenty-five past the hour, I should think. He was gone a fairly long time, and it must have been ten minutes before I noticed him again."

Knollis made a pretence of consulting his note-book. "That about covers his story," he said. "I wouldn't mention this interview to him. He might think we questioned his truthfulness, and you know how temperamental these artists are!"

"Oh, he's a queer bloke to have around," said Camden. "If he hadn't told me he'd served in the Foreign Legion I might have thought he was a sissy, what with his peroxide for his hands, and his rubber gloves—"

"Rubber gloves?" Knollis asked quickly.

"Ay, he used to leave them about the bedroom according to the girl that cleans the room. Probably uses 'em when he's painting so's he won't soil his hands. Still, I know he was in the Legion because he showed me his papers. Funny fellow!"

"An artist!" said Knollis.

"Very clean, mind you," went on Camden. "He has a bath most days, and what we call his super-bath once a week. Spends an hour or more in the bathroom, and cleans down the bath and the wash-bowl before he comes out—and that's a thing that's appreciated by the missus and the girls. Flushes no end of water down the bath."

"He does, does he?" murmured Knollis, and a happy smile broke over his face. "Well, well, well!"

"Now I've had some very different guests," began Camden, but Knollis urged him back to his bar and asked him to have a drink. Ellis joined them some time later, and cocked an eye as he noticed his chief's unusual state of contentment. He said nothing until they were walking back to their own hotel, and then he put a pertinent question.

"Why the happiness? Good beer or good news?"

"Highton wears rubber gloves and uses peroxide," smiled Knollis. "I won't be going to bed before midnight. I've some paper and pencil work to do."

XIV
The Lincoln Story

At half-past eight the next morning, the eleventh of November, Knollis rang police headquarters from his hotel. "I want Eric Lincoln in my office for questioning at nine sharp."

At a quarter to nine he was speaking to Chief-Inspector Burnell at the Yard from police headquarters. "I want Lindley to go to Marseilles and interview anybody and everybody on the staff of Leblanc's firm and try to bring back somebody who knew Challoner during the same year. Can that be done, sir?"

"Will be," said Burnell shortly. "Means air travel, but I think we can afford it if we cut down our drinking and smoking. Anything else, Knollis?"

"Not at the moment, thanks," replied Knollis, and rang off.

At nine o'clock sharp Eric Lincoln was shown into the office, but this time he was in no blustering mood. Knollis took one long look at him and gave a secret smile. Lincoln was badly scared.

"We've finished bluffing, Lincoln," he said sternly. "You are going to tell me the truth, the whole truth, and nothing but the truth this time. I still don't think you murdered Challoner, and so the usual caution will not be necessary. Now tell me: what were you doing in the dispensary?"

Lincoln scowled down on him. "I haven't said I was in the dispensary!"

"But you were, weren't you?" said Knollis. "Remember those bedroom windows in Denver Street, and how they overlook the dispensary windows!"

Lincoln licked his lips, and avoided Knollis's eyes.

"We know you lied to us earlier," said Knollis, "but we can scrap the previous statements if you care to tell us the truth—or do I have to tell you the truth?"

Lincoln looked up without moving his head, his eyes furtive and suspicious. "You're trying to fix me."

"I'm trying to clear you," Knollis said angrily, "and like the adolescent young pup you are you can't discriminate between the truth and lies." He slapped his palm on the desk. "Now do you intend to help, or hinder? I don't mind, just so long as I'm aware of your intentions. I don't care if the newspaper men notice how many times you're interviewed, and start to hint in their papers. It's your own reputation!"

"You can't damage my reputation any more than you have done," snapped Lincoln. "My name's mud in the town already, and even Joan won't have anything to do with me!"

"Wasn't that arranged?" demanded Knollis.

"It was arranged, but it's got out of hand. Highton's convinced her that I killed the doc while I was supposed to be waiting for her, and she believes him."

"Who did kill him?" asked Knollis.

Lincoln lowered his eyes again. Then his head came up defiantly. "It was Mrs. Burke—and I can prove it!"

Knollis gave a deep sigh. "Then why the devil don't you? What's holding you back?"

Lincoln put his hands to his head and took a frenzied turn round the room. "Oh, how can I? It's better for it to go unsolved. If I tell you what I know, then the whole story will be in the papers, dragging Joan down and making a public holiday of the doc's affair with Mrs. Burke. I've got to protect Joan! You must see that, Inspector! You've got to see it!"

Knollis pointed with his pencil to a chair. "Take a pew, Lincoln. Go on, sit down! You're making me dizzy, and yourself into a neurotic. Good. Have a cigarette, and a light. Now relax."

He waited for a time, and then leaned across his desk and in a quiet voice explained his point of view.

"If you know anything of the history of Scotland Yard, you must realize that we've very few failures on our books. I can break this case, Lincoln, and I'm going to break it. You can help me, or you can hinder, but you won't prevent me getting at the truth. All you'll do is make it take me longer. The story is bound to come out, and there's nothing you can do to prevent it. You can prove that Mrs. Burke murdered Dr. Challoner. You were hiding in the dispensary when Mrs. Burke returned to the surgery. You saw what she did. She's your enemy, and she's Joan's enemy. I quite appreciate your chivalrous attitude towards Joan, but it's all wrong in the present situation. You won't spare her a single moment's worry or anxiety. In fact all you're doing is intensifying her mental agony. Highton may have acted the lout and made love to her, but if he's made any headway with her it's only temporary. Highton is a type she hasn't met before. He's temperamental and unstable, and what she feels for him is no more than fascination, and I repeat it's only temporary. Women always go for security, and you represent security to her. Highton is a fly-by-night, and she'll lose interest in him faster than she found it. Do you honestly think she likes suspecting you of being responsible for her father's death? And can you blame her if she does? You've done nothing to help either her or us."

Lincoln stirred uneasily, his mental discomfort betrayed in his unsophisticated features. "Well," he murmured, "if you put it like that!"

Knollis flopped back in his chair, and folded his hands across his waistcoat. He took a glance at the shorthand writer in the corner of the room, and winked. "Now let's have the story," he said to Lincoln. "You went straight to the surgery—the consulting-room—when you reached the house?"

Yes, Lincoln nodded. "I called upstairs to Joan and she said she'd be quite a few minutes before she was down. She told me about the new magazines in the lounge, and I said I'd wait in there. I slammed the door to make her believe I'd gone in, and tiptoed to the consulting-room. I didn't knock, but turned the knob slowly and opened the door. I didn't see the doc at first, so closed the door and looked round. The light was over the table and slightly in front of it, so that the back of the desk was in the shadow. Then I saw him, and I went faint for a few seconds. I pulled myself together and took another look at him. He looked dead, but his hand was opening and closing as if he was trying to grasp something. I was just going to chase out to the 'phone when I heard footsteps in the yard outside, and they were coming to the door. I skipped inside the dispensary to hide, and half-closed the door. . . ."

"Go on," urged Knollis, trying to restrain his impatience.

"Well, it was her—Mrs. Burke. There was a dead silence for a minute after she came in, and then she gave a long *'O-h-h!'* and *'Hugh!'* I squinted through the crack between the door and the frame, and she was on her knees at his side. She wasn't looking at him, but at the surface of his desk. There was a small red book on it that looked like a diary. She looked towards the house door and then towards my door, and grabbed the book and put it in her handbag. She put her hand inside the doc's waistcoat and I think she was feeling his heart. I was going cross-eyed with squinting through the crack, so I moved a foot or so to peer round the door. I think she must have heard me, because she glanced round, and then got to her feet and almost ran to the waiting-room door and after that I heard the door slam."

"And then?" asked Knollis.

"I got back to the lounge as quickly as I could," said Lincoln. "I was scared, and don't mind admitting it. I didn't know what to do. I opened a magazine and laid it on the settee, and then opened the door with as much noise as I could and went back to the consulting-room. I took one more look at him, and I honestly did panic. I wanted air, and I ran outside into the street after I'd called Joan."

He lowered a shamed face. "I'm—I'm not used to facing violent death like you are, sir."

"No blame on you for that," said Knollis. "Now tell me: what did you think about Mrs. Burke's visit?"

"Well, after the row we'd had on the street I thought she'd guess that I should go in to play up with the doc, and that I'd find the book she'd forgot—I think it was a diary, sir!"

"It was," Knollis agreed.

"I mean," went on Lincoln, "she'd be in such a hurry to get away that she'd forget it after she'd strangled him, and not remember it until afterwards. Then, when we had those words on the street she'd rush back to collect it before I went in the consulting-room."

"I see," said Knollis. "Having satisfied yourself that Mrs. Burke strangled Dr. Challoner, can you suggest why she did it?"

"Money," said Lincoln, now confident in manner. "It's my opinion that she knew something about him, and that it was in that diary. She'd been blackmailing him, and he'd refused to do anything else for her. He was perhaps thinking that Joan and I were right, and he shouldn't marry Mrs. Burke. She knew how his will stood, so she killed him so that she'd get the two thousand and not lose everything. Another week or so and we might have got him to execute a new will—and then where would she have been?"

"You tell me," suggested Knollis.

"On the rocks."

"I see," Knollis said meekly. "Tell me, Mr. Lincoln: where does this laughing dog come into the picture?"

Lincoln shook his head earnestly. "It represented whatever it was that Mrs. Burke held over him. He didn't like dogs, and that was what they call a repression. He pushed down the incident that troubled him, and because a dog was connected with it he repressed the idea of dogs as well. I read about that kind of thing. There was a case the other day, in a book, reading about a woman whose husband died when the radio was playing a popular waltz. After that she couldn't bear to hear the music because unconsciously it connected with her husband's death."

"Really!" said Knollis. "And you think this laughing dog might have something to do with somebody's death?"

"Well, I mean . . ." faltered Lincoln. "The doc didn't get really interested in her until her husband was ill!"

"And might have fallen in love with her, and bumped off her husband so that he could marry her in due time?"

"I didn't want to say that," said Lincoln.

"Thanks for everything," said Knollis. "I'll bear in mind what you've told me. I'm sure I'm grateful. Now I must let you get back to business. . . ."

The detective-officer in the corner turned to grin at Knollis as the door closed behind Eric Lincoln. "Bit buzz-headed, isn't he, sir?"

Knollis wagged his head. "What a thing it is to be young! Impulsive, wuzzy-minded, and wishful thinking. He'd be really pleased if we hanged Mrs. Burke for him. Still, he's cleared himself without knowing it—and solved the mystery of the diary. The next problem is how to get hold of the diary without Mrs. Burke's suspicions being aroused."

Manson and Ellis entered the room, and the three stood discussing the case for some minutes, until a constable announced that Mr. Aubrey Highton would like to speak to Inspector Knollis.

"Show him in," said Knollis, with a glance at Manson. "I wonder what he wants!"

"See you in a while," Ellis said suddenly, and left the office as Highton was being shown in.

Highton lounged into the room, looked all round as if making a mental inventory, and smiled at Knollis.

"Didn't know whether you'd be out of bed yet. Look, Inspector, I want to go to London in three days. Have you done with me? Got all I can give you? Have I signed all the statements I've made, and all that?"

"Coming back to Sturton Lacey?" asked Knollis, stalling for time in which to think.

"Dunno for sure," replied Highton. He opened his coat in order to get at his inside pocket, from which he took a wallet and a handful of letters. "Darby wants to see me within the next few days, and I've also had a letter from old Ferry who says he would like to discuss business at his Paris address within the near future. I need a discussion badly! My prospects have vanished since Challoner decided to get himself murdered."

He cocked an eyebrow. "Further to the point, I'm getting too fond of his daughter, and I think it's time I removed myself to a safe distance. She's in love with that Cuthbert that's just gone out, and she intends to marry him. I couldn't marry her in any case. . . ."

"Why not?" asked Knollis.

Highton gave him a mocking smile. "There are some things that just aren't done, Inspector, and taking a kitten from its warm hearthrug and trying to turn it into a fox of the fields is one of them, so if you've done with me I'd like to get away. It's Tuesday to-day, and I want to leave Saturday. I'll be at the

Dragon until Saturday morning, so give old Camden a ring if you need me for anything. I think I've told you all I can, and there shouldn't be any impediment, but I thought I'd ask you, if only in the sacred name of courtesy."

Knollis didn't appear to be listening. He was leaning forward, regarding Highton's tie intently.

"What's up?" asked Highton. "Egg on it?"

Knollis laughed. "No! I thought it was identical with my own at first. It isn't, although very similar."

Highton looked down at his own tie, and then at Knollis's. "Colour-blind, eh? Mine's strawberry jam with two stripes of vanilla ice across it. Yours is dandelion on a field of grass."

"Not the one I'm wearing," said Knollis. "I mean my school tie—Burnham Grammar School."

"Not this one," replied Highton. "This's good old St. Bertrand's!"

"Liverpool?" Knollis asked at random.

"Apples, cherries, hops, and women," laughed Highton. "I don't go much on apples. Well, must get along. Got a coffee date with Miss Joan—oh pleasant company! She's far too good for that puritanical swipe. Morning all!"

He marched out, leaving the door wide open. Knollis walked to it and closed it, then returned to Manson, his eyes narrowed into mere slits. "Apples, cherries, hops, and women!"

He swung round to the detective-officer who was still in attendance. "Go down to the reference room and find out whether there's a St. Bertrand's School in Kent!"

"Why Kent?" asked Manson as the officer hurried away.

"Read your *Pickwick Papers*?"

"Ye-es! What's that got to do with it?"

"Mr. Jingle described Kent as *Apples, cherries, hops, and women*. This is the break I've been looking for, Manson!"

"Now what?" rumbled Manson.

"Will the funds stand an air trip to Kent?"

"I suppose so. What's on your mind?"

"Where's the nearest airfield with a charter service?"

"Swinnerton. Eight miles away. Blue Vine people."

Knollis waited until the detective-officer returned with the confirmation, and then asked Manson to book him to the nearest airfield to St. Bertrand's School.

"The school is right out in the country, sir," interposed the officer. "The nearest airfield is the R.A.F. station at Manston."

"A landing there can be arranged," said Knollis. "Get a signal to the Yard, and book the aircraft. I'll be ready in half an hour. Where's Ellis?"

Ellis was nowhere to be found, and Knollis left for Kent without seeing him.

XV

THE HIGHTON STORY

KNOLLIS STEPPED OUT of the Anson at Manston and into the waiting police car. At half-past three he was walking through the wrought-iron gateway of St. Bertrand's to the lodge, from where he was escorted to the Principal's study. The Principal, a rotund man of fifty, with greying hair and easy smile, looked askance at Knollis's warrant card.

"Scotland Yard," he murmured. "I don't think we've ever had a detective within the walls before, and I can't imagine what your business can be!"

"I'm delving into the past," said Knollis, "and require all the information you can give me regarding an old scholar."

The Principal's eyebrows shot up. "One of our old boys! Which one, Inspector?"

"Aubrey Highton."

"He's in trouble?"

"Merely a matter of checking information," Knollis said ambiguously, and crossed his fingers behind the cover of the table.

"Can you give me an approximate date, Inspector? I've only been here five years, and can't recall a boy of that name during my time."

"Probably left in thirty-one or thirty-two."

The Principal rang a bell, and had the appropriate file brought to him. "Highton, you said? Highbury, Higham, Highland, Highton . . . Here we are. Highton, Aubrey, entered Nineteen-twenty-six, and left us at term-end in thirty-two, Inspector. Age on admission, eleven years."

"Physical description given?" Knollis asked anxiously.

"Brown hair, brown eyes, medium complexion. Require any more of that?"

"Seems like the same lad," said Knollis. "Any mention of special abilities?"

The Principal laughed. "Here's the file, Inspector. You'd better read it for yourself."

"Not too good at maths, eh?" smiled Knollis. "Promising artist, and has dramatic ability. Yes, this is the same Highton. Parents dead. Guardian, Mr. Wilson York, The Broadway, Healdswood."

If levitation had been possible Knollis would have floated from the Principal's study to Healdswood Broadway with the speed of thought. As it was, he went by the more prosaic police car, and had himself dropped at the end of the street. He walked along to the village post office, where he introduced himself as an old friend of the Yorks, and the garrulous sub-postmistress told him how to reach the house, repeating the information three times to make sure that it had penetrated.

"Where is Mrs. York's sister these days?" asked Knollis.

"Oh, she went off again a good many years ago, sir. Mrs. York never thought she'd get over her first husband getting killed, and there you are! But you never know, do you?"

"Torpedoed, wasn't he?" murmured Knollis. "Or am I getting confused with someone else?"

"You must be, sir. They were married in some foreign place in the month before the first war, and he got killed in France in the second week in August! Shocking thing for a bride, wasn't it—and her carrying his baby!"

"Terrible," muttered Knollis. "Well, thank you! The third house past the County Library! I really should have remembered!"

Mrs. Wilson York didn't seem to know Knollis at all, and she seemed less eager to meet him when he presented his warrant card. Reluctantly, she invited him indoors, and presented him to her husband. Knollis looked them over and mentally named them Mr. and Mrs. Jack Spratt.

"I'm interested in the whereabouts of Aubrey Highton," he said bluntly. "His benefactor has died."

"We saw it in the papers," said Mrs. York, "but we didn't know the family secret was such an open one."

"Tell me," said Knollis; "where did his mother go after Aubrey was born?"

"She stayed with us, of course."

"Until when?"

"My husband found her a secretarial job at his office—he's an architect, and she stayed until the boy was five."

"Nineteen-twenty?"

"That's right," said York, pushing his way between his wife and Knollis. "Look here, Inspector. What are you after? As man to man, let's have it?"

Knollis gave a cat-like smile, secret and content. "There's nothing to it, really. Challoner's accounts show a sum of nearly two hundred pounds paid out every January. The money apparently went to Highton, and it's my job to check it. No more, no less."

"Ye-es," muttered York. "She was in her rights, but she shouldn't have done it. Too much like blackmail for my fancy. I'd paid Aubrey's school-fees—and everything else—ever since he was born. When it was time for him to leave school Sylvia put her foot down, and said it was time Challoner contributed to the upkeep of his own boy. She wrote to him—traced him through the medical directory, y'know—and put the proposition to him. For some queer reason she didn't want him to see her own writing, and got Madge here to copy the letter and sign it. Challoner came clean, either through dam' good sportsmanship or sheer fright—God knows which—and said he'd pay two hundred pounds a year through a London solicitor. That wouldn't do for Sylvia, and she looked round until she found some London tradesman who would provide an accommodation address, and then wrote Aubrey, told him the truth—that he was illegitimate, and told him to fix up with this tradesman. For some queer reason, she'd never come to see him, and the lad never saw her at all after his fifth birthday."

"Where is she now?"

"Can't say, old man. She apparently made up her mind to disappear. She didn't mean Challoner tracing her through us, and she didn't mean him tracing the lad through the solicitors, so she made everything as complicated as possible."

"I see," nodded Knollis. "Tell me, Mr. York; did she ever mention the affair in Algiers?"

"Why, yes! That is, she told my wife the whole thing."

Knollis looked at Mrs. York.

"He was a young doctor, taking a holiday in Algiers with his father, a fruit and wine exporter of Marseilles and London. His father had to go back home, and left him to sow his wild oats. Sylvia was nineteen, and had a secretarial job at the consulate. She and Hugh Challoner fell in love, and didn't bother about the parson, I'm afraid. They spent a week at a café—"

"Le Chien Qui Rit?" asked Knollis.

"That's the one," said York. "Can remember the queer name. Anyway, Challoner skipped off home without saying good-bye to her. She came home as soon as she knew, and although she'd traced him and knew where he lived she refused to let us contact him, so I, in modern parlance, carried the can financially!"

"Tell me," said Knollis; "how did she manage to retain the name of Highton in a village like this, where conventions are so rigid?"

"Conventions and necks," York said grimly. "She shot the yarn that she'd married her second cousin. I say! Aubrey isn't in trouble, is he?"

"Well," said Knollis, "I saw him this morning, and I hope I look as happy if I get into trouble!"

"That's a blessing!" sighed Madge York. She put a hand on Knollis's arm. "Do tell the dear boy to come and see us!"

"I'll persuade him to do so if he's free," said Knollis. Knollis flew back through the darkness to Swinnerton, arriving at his hotel shortly after ten o'clock. A lady's handbag was lying in the middle of his bed. He picked it up, turned it over, and finally opened it. Inside, among the various feminine paraphernalia, lay a small red diary. He rapidly skimmed the pages, found that one was missing, and then, still clutching it firmly, hurried from the room to find Ellis.

Ellis was sitting up in his bed, the electric fire burning, a dressing-gown round his shoulders, and the fiery meerschaum creating a smoke-screen round him. It was just possible to see that he was engrossed in his Western novel. He shook himself back from the prairie to Sturton Lacey as Knollis charged into the room and sat on his bed.

"Where did this come from?"

"Hello, Cock?" returned Ellis. "Had a good day—flipping about the country like a blinking sparrow? You can keep those flying contraptions for me! Give me a bike with two good brakes. I can always get off and walk if anything goes wrong!"

"Flying's as safe as your bike!" snapped Knollis.

"Then heaven help it!" retorted Ellis. "Anyway, what have you been a-doing of?"

"Where did this diary come from?" persisted Knollis.

Ellis laid his pipe on the bedside table and folded his hands across his chest, while a too-serious expression came over his features.

"Rotten story, old man! I feel put out over it. Mrs. Burke went to church this morning—Remembrance Day in case you didn't know. After church she and some of her fellow-workers at St. Aidan's Church repaired or went to a local restaurant for lunch. Some time between entering and leaving the restaurant, she lost her handbag, and reported its loss to the uniformed department. An hour afterwards it was handed in by some fellow who had found it. The sergeant in the lost property office thought we might be interested, and sent it up to Inspector Manson. He happened to look inside, and there was the diary!"

"Well, well, well!" murmured Knollis. "And of course all these happenings were purely coincidental! You didn't have anything to do with her handbag being lifted, did you? Nor with the sergeant thinking we might be interested? Nor for that matter with the bag-lifter handing it in to us instead of keeping it? What a remarkably lucky string of coincidences!"

"Lucky, wasn't it?" Ellis said innocently. "Does the bloke who found it get a reward?"

"The usual ten per cent of the total value."

He grinned at his sergeant. "IIow many ounces of Devil's Brew, Copper Beech, and Senna Pods will that provide?"

"The finder wished to remain anonymous, so it will cost Mrs. Burke narry a single penny."

"It was a stroke of genius!"

Ellis began to twist the ends of his moustaches into a smarter pattern, and then brushed his hand sharply across his mouth. "Now why do I do that? Am I the genius referred to in the testimonial?"

"We'll have the vital pages photographed in the morning, and then return it to the L.P. office, who can let her know that it has been found. I don't think she'll have any suspicions if it comes from the uniformed blokes. Now for my day!"

Ellis listened eagerly as Knollis told his story, and afterwards asked: "Going to see Highton in the morning?"

"I'll be at his hotel by half-past eight, my lad. So will you!"

"Not me! There's a shock coming to you."

"Regarding Highton?"

"Or Joan Challoner, whichever you think fit. Highton has left his hotel and moved into the Challoner house."

Knollis stared, and then whistled softly. "Then she must know! He must have told her!"

"That he's her brother?"

"Of course."

"But with what darned object?" demanded Ellis. "Surely it was all to his benefit to keep quiet."

"Surely it was all to his benefit to tell her," said Knollis. "Are you falling asleep? You've summed up Joan's character by now, and should realize that she'll feel obliged to share the old boy's estate with Highton, whether he's her half-brother and illegitimate or not!" He paused, and then said: "You know, Ellis, our young friend Eric is not going to like this one little bit. He's down by about three thousand pounds now. Mrs. Burke's share knocked it from eight thousand odd to six thousand, and you can bet your pipe that Highton'll get half of the remainder. Highton seems to have a brain on him. Well, so have I!"

He proceeded to use it when he called on Highton, with Ellis as witness, on the following morning. Highton and Joan Challoner were breakfasting and the artist seemed to be quite at home. Joan Challoner tried to encourage Knollis to call later in the day, but he was persistent, and Highton sauntered into the hall in dressing-gown and pyjamas to see what was happening.

"Ah, my old friends the Inspector and Sergeant. Let 'em come in, Joan, my dear! Get two more cups. Sorry we can't offer you anything to eat unless you like toast."

He gave Joan a playful smack between the shoulder-blades. "Two cups, saucers, and spoons. We'll have tea for four, although I suspect the Inspector's errand of being more concerned with swords for two. But come in, both of you! There's a devil of a draught round my legs. That's better! Doors were made to shut, you know."

He led them into the breakfast-room, saw them seated, and took his own place at the table. Joan Challoner bustled in, somewhat uneasily, with the extra crockery, and handed Knollis and Ellis a cup of tea each.

"Perhaps you men would sooner be alone?" she murmured, edging towards the door.

Highton waved her back. "Resume your seat, fair lady. What the Inspector has to say can be heard by all the world. What's the trouble, Mr. Knollis?"

Knollis sipped his tea before answering.

"Enough arsenic in it, Inspector?" mocked Highton. "We gave you all we had."

"It's a nice cup," said Knollis, "but then I've tasted Miss Challoner's tea before."

"And you never told me," Highton said reproachfully.

"I've been down into Kent," said Knollis.

Highton nodded as if it was no news to him. "How was the dear old school? I thought your interest in my tie was more than friendly. And Aunt Madge and Uncle Wilson? In the pink, I hope?"

"Aunt Madge would like you to visit her," said Knollis. "She asked me to convey the message. I said I would—if you were free."

Highton extended his arms and fluttered his fingers. "Free as the birds of the air. Well, now you know my horrid secret, where does it fit into your schemes?"

"Before I can tell you that, I should like to hear the full story from your own lips. I know most of it. Oh, and I have a man busy at the offices of Leblanc in Marseilles!"

"Then you'll soon know the rest," Highton said grimly. "Have another cup of tea, both of you, and I'll tell you the story. Using your note-book, Sergeant? Perhaps as well, because I may contradict myself. Joan knows most of the story, and she isn't shocked."

He gave a sardonic laugh. "I'm afraid we can't say the same for the respectable Sturtonians, who now think we're living in sin."

"Can we have the story?" Knollis asked wearily.

"I bore you? Then on with the dance. Hugh Challoner accompanied his father to Marseilles and thence to Algiers in the summer of Nineteen-fourteen. Early in July it became obvious that war with Germany was inevitable, and his father rushed back to Marseilles to confer with his firm, leaving Hugh to continue his holiday. He'd made friends with a Sylvia Highton then working at the Consulate. The result of that—er—friendship was me. They spent a week at—care to guess where?"

"*Le Chien Qui Rit*, Rue de Constantine," said Knollis.

"Correct," said Highton. "My mother skipped back to England in the October of that year, and cooked up a yarn about having married a second cousin who had just been killed in action in France. She sported widow's weeds, and thus avoided the gossips. She left me with Uncle Wilson when I was five, and I haven't seen her from that day to this. Uncle Wilson was a great scout. He did everything for me, and eventually sent me to St. Bertrand's. I stayed there until I was sixteen, and then did a year as an art student, after which I earned some sort of a living in an advertising agency. It was too dull for me, so I took myself for a holiday, found myself at Sousse in the Gulf of Tunis, and got talking to some Legionnaires. Later, I joined the Legion, as I've already told you, and you know the rest of that side of the life-history."

"Suppose we go back to the age of sixteen, and start again," suggested Knollis.

"Yes! Well, it seems my mother wasn't content to let Uncle Wilson spend his money on me. She wrote me a letter in which she told me the whole story, and said I was to see a man called Bradley in London and arrange for him to accept a letter or package for me once a year. I was to insert a message just saying *Arranged* in the *Times*, after which I could bank on two hundred pounds a year less two-and-a-half per cent solicitor's commission every January. I drew it up to joining the Legion, and knew the rest would be mounting up for me when I got out. It was after I got out that I became curious about the old man, and I made up my mind to meet him in due course. I was in no hurry, and I wanted to learn all about him if I could. I got a London firm of booksellers to send me a copy of the *Sturton Lacey Courier* every week, and from time to time there were spasms about his doings. Twice there were photographs of him, once at a Masonic dinner, and once opening something or other at the church. Then came the interesting news. Dr. Hugh Challoner, the much-travelled Sturtonian, was arranging his first holiday abroad since before the war, and would visit Algiers and the North African coast."

He broke off to hand round his cigarettes and lighter.

"I was soon organized. I haunted the shipping offices to study the passenger lists, and lo, Dr. Hugh Challoner duly arrived. A spot of spying is cheaply arranged in Algy, and I learned within an hour of his landing that he'd taken rooms at the Bretagne. A spot of backsheesh here and there provided for his interest being aroused in the droll artist who worked at the corner of the Rue Michelet and the Rue Jean Mace, and he sent a message insisting on an appointment."

"I said you had brains," murmured Knollis.

"Thanks for that," bowed Highton, "but wait a minute! I made a mistake, a very great one, and it nearly cost me my life. My twisted brand of humour encouraged me to draw him as a laughing dog. I wanted to see how he would react after thirty-three years. Well, he reacted! He looked as if all the blood had been drawn from his body. We'd had a break for drinks during the sitting, and I'd taken him to a little place I knew round the corner. It wasn't a nice place, but it was colourful, and I reckoned that he'd want atmosphere and all that while on holiday. Unfortunately, a gentleman possessing too much live-stock passed some of it on to me without telling me. I discovered it just as my father was leaving me, and put my hand inside my shirt to remove it. That was the mistake!"

"Very dramatically told, and the pause comes in the right place," said the matter-of-fact Knollis, "but what was the mistake?"

Highton opened his dressing-gown and unbuttoned his pyjama jacket. "This!"

Over his heart was tattooed a laughing dog.

"A damned silly thing to have done," said Highton. "My sense of the dramatic to which you've just drawn attention was the cause. The old man saw it, tried to pretend he hadn't, and hurried away. I closed shop that night, flew to Paris under an assumed name, saw my French agent, and then flew to England and had a good look round Sturton Lacey while the old boy was still away. I went back to London and lay low until he was back and settled."

"Wearing black hair, a French accent, and drawing on the accumulated money from Bradley to keep you going?"

"Exactly. How did you guess I'd dyed my hair?"

"I won't tell you that," said Knollis. "As an artist you should know. But why did you go ginger in Algiers?"

"I hoped the old boy wouldn't spot the family resemblance if I was red," said Highton. "Coloration can make the deuce of a difference to one's appearance, you know!"

"Look," said Knollis. "What was the object of this masquerade? Why didn't you go to him openly, and—er—well, claim your birthright?"

"Couldn't do it," said Highton. "Too prosaic. In any case, I didn't want to sponge on him more than I had done. If he could find me a job, well and good. To tell you the truth, my plan went awry after he'd spotted my tattoo. I just came to England, and hoped that something would happen. It did! He tried to murder me!"

"He—what!" exclaimed the startled Knollis.

"Not—not my father!" protested Joan Challoner.

"Your father and my father. He tried to finish me. I can't prove it was him, but who else could have done it? I didn't know another soul in town. It was a fortnight after I arrived. I was going in the Dragon yard when somebody stepped from behind the gates and coshed me with something heavy. Camden found me lying unconscious in the yard, with a bruise like a goose egg behind my left ear. I swore him to secrecy with five quid, told him a yarn about somebody throwing a stone at somebody else and catching me, and then went across to the surgery to have it treated. I wanted to see how the old boy would react when he saw me alive. He didn't like it one little bit. He said it didn't look as if Sturton was healthy for me."

"Are you sure it was Father?" Joan Challoner asked anxiously.

Highton shrugged. "It was either your father or your boyfriend—and you can take your pick, my sweet."

"What night was it?"

"A Thursday, and I'll get you the date from my diary if you really need it."

"I—I don't see Eric on Thursdays, as a rule," she stammered.

"One other point," said Knollis. "What happened on the night of his death, when you attended surgery?"

"Oh well, nothing much. He tapped me, ignored the tattoo mark, and said we should have to have our pipes X-rayed. It was evident that the climate was no good to me."

"And is it?"

"There's conflicting evidence," said Highton. "He said there was congestion of the left lung. I went to the clinic off my own bat, and they say my bellows are in A1 condition. You just take your choice!"

The telephone bell rang out in the hall, and Joan Challoner excused herself. On her return she stood in the doorway, trembling. "Inspector Manson would like you to go to police headquarters straight away, Mr. Knollis."

"Yes . . . ?" murmured Knollis, waiting for the news that quavered on her lips.

She suddenly pressed her hands over her eyes and began to weep bitterly. "Eric's—run away!"

Highton was with her before Knollis could collect his thoughts, his arms round her, comforting her. "You've nothing to worry about, darling. Eric didn't kill Father!"

Knollis blinked. "Who did kill him, Highton!"

Highton swung Joan Challoner round so that he was now looking over her shoulder into the room. A smile, half mocking, half bitter, crept over his features.

"I've already given you the solution, Inspector. Verily it has been said: *The eyes of a fool are in the ends of the earth!*"

<h1 style="text-align:center">XVI</h1>

THE AMATEUR DETECTIVE

INSPECTOR MANSON looked worried. "Lincoln's mother came in about three-quarters of an hour ago. Her Eric hadn't been home all night. She hadn't seen him since tea-time. She'd 'phoned his office, and he hadn't turned up there. I rang Hodson, and he merely answered that Lincoln was not yet at the office—and hung up on me! By the way, there's a message in from your Sergeant

Lindley. He's established the fact that Challoner was in Marseilles in Nineteen-fourteen, and went from there to Algiers."

"Lindley can be recalled," said Knollis. "The outer circle of the problem is now complete. We've got the whole of the Challoner story. All that remains for us to do is prove which of the three murdered Challoner. Burke and Lincoln had sound motives; Highton—well, several motives can be ascribed to him, and yet none of them seem to justify murder. Highton says he's given me the solution, so while you interview Hodson and see whether he knows where Lincoln is, I'm going through the evidence once more. There's a catch somewhere in this case. Highton knows where it is, and I'm not going to let him beat me!"

"Then I'll find Lincoln for you," sighed Manson. "I've got three men working the railway stations and bus station, and I don't think we'll be long in picking him up."

"Don't pick him," said Knollis. "Find him, and watch him."

The telephone rang, and Manson picked up the receiver. He listened for a minute or so, and turned to Knollis. "He caught the seven-ten to London, carrying an attaché-case. . . ."

"See his mother, and Hodson, and find out whether he has any relatives in town. If not, contact the Yard, and have them check the hotels, hostels, and boarding-houses. Where does his train pull in?"

"St. Pancras."

"Then they can concentrate on that area. He hasn't travelled a great deal, and isn't likely to move very far from his point of arrival—especially as he wouldn't get into town until late."

Manson instructed the sergeant to interview Lincoln's mother, and replaced the receiver. "I'll have a heart-to-heart talk with Hodson. See you later."

Knollis bent over the desk, and for the next two hours put fact against fact, statement against statement, and theory against theory in an attempt to break down the problem. Seen superficially, it was a simple case. Three people, each with a grudge against Challoner, had entered the consulting-room on the evening of his death. Their movements could be tabulated like a railway time-table, and although the time of Challoner's death could be fixed within a few minutes it was still impossible to lay a finger on any one of the three suspects and say: This person strangled Hugh Challoner.

Considering the method, he had to admit that any one of them could have used it. Lincoln had been right when he called attention to the mental shock, and the consequent temporary paralysis which followed the unexpected tightening of a noose round a human neck. Either Highton or Lincoln could have killed Challoner in that way—and so could Madeleine Burke!

Highton had rope to hand, the lashings of his cabin trunk. Madeleine Burke could have brought the rope with her, have changed her mind about murdering Challoner, and then exercised the feminine prerogative by changing her mind again—in which case she must have been back twice; once to kill him, and again to collect the diary when Lincoln was hiding in the dispensary. This hardly seemed possible, for while Lincoln had but a few yards to walk to the house and the consulting-room, Madeleine Burke had perforce to hurry down Williamson's Passage, along Denver Street, and the few yards along Kirkland Street to the rear entrance. On the other hand she might have killed Challoner before she left on the first occasion, and then have gone back for the diary, making but two visits to the consulting-room.

Lincoln? Knollis shook his head. It was reasonable to believe that Lincoln might have killed Challoner in hot blood, but to suggest premeditation on his part was to ignore his adolescent reactions.

Whoever killed Challoner had gone prepared, and later cut the Lincoln and Burke clothes-lines in order to confuse the issue. That is, Lincoln had tried to incriminate Mrs. Burke, or *vice versa*. It could be assumed without any shadow of doubt that the lengths of rope involved had been destroyed. Highton had admitted burning rope in his bedroom, but no great emphasis need be placed on that point, for Highton was the possessor of a mischievous mind, and seemed to gain satisfaction from his police-baiting tactics. He could be ignored.

Knollis drew Highton's sketch of the consulting-room towards him and considered it thoughtfully. Highton had been in the room for no more than a few minutes, and yet his brown eyes had garnered every detail. Darby was right to some extent with regard to Highton's photographic mind, and yet did him an injustice by failing to pay tribute to his imagination. Knollis had a picture in his mind of the room as it had been photographed shortly after the discovery of Challoner's dead body, and Highton's sketch might have been drawn from it with the exception of one or two minute items. The tall cabinet of instruments, the bookshelves with their worn books, the electric fire in the corner opposite the waiting-room door, the dispensary door ajar, the table desk with its litter of papers and books and the desk-diary and the small red diary laying across the morocco-bound blotting-pad, while from behind the desk projected the head and shoulders of the dead man; Highton had apparently chosen the open doorway of the waiting-room from which to sketch the room.

Knollis pushed the sketch aside, and rose to stalk about the room, one hand in his pocket, the other stroking the nape of his neck. Until Lincoln was found, and the reason for his flight revealed there was little to be done. He took his hat from the stand and went to have another chat with Highton, more to pass the time than anything else.

"Heard anything of young Lincoln?" Highton asked with the old mockery in his voice.

Knollis shook his head.

"Probably on his way to Africa," suggested Highton. "They go big-game hunting when they're crossed in love, don't they? It's Joan's fault he's gone, of course. I wanted to tell the truth to the young man, but she was trying to find a way round the problem. She didn't want to lose him—heaven knows why!—and neither did she want to tell him that her father had dumped an illegitimate child on the world. The old feminine ambivalence! Swing this way, swing that way, and never come to rest at any point. So the lad thinks she's given her heart to me, and he's done a bunk, with the result that you people will have jumped to the conclusion that he was responsible for the old man's death."

"No, I don't think that," said Knollis. "He wasn't capable of it. The job was premeditated."

Highton flicked his ash over the carpet and smiled. "I'm glad you realize that point, Inspector. Y'know, this can't have been a very nice case for you; I mean, you've had to dig up such a lot of mud!"

"My last three cases have been like this one," said Knollis. "I'd like a nice clean case without a sexual interest in it—and yet I suppose I'm indulging in wishful thinking."

"Why so?"

Knollis looked up with a faint smile. "Wasn't it our old friend Aristotle who said there were only three motives—the passionate, the monetary, and the ethical? I've never experienced a murder case founded on an ethical motive, and I doubt if I shall. Where there's a monetary motive there's always the feminine interest, and where the motive is passionate you find money as the secondary if not the primary object."

"That applies to this case, of course," nodded Highton.

"You mean?" Knollis asked sharply.

Highton lit a new cigarette from the stub of his old one, and threw the fag-end in the fire. He considered Knollis quietly for a few moments, and shrugged. "It's obvious to me, and it must be to you, only you're stalling. It was Madeleine Burke."

"Now why do you say that?" Knollis murmured.

"I've said it's obvious, and it is. She knew Joan and Eric were trying to wean the old man from the idea of marrying her, and it seems to me that he was holding her off while he had another think. She went round that evening to get a straight answer from him—or else. I knew little enough of him despite the fact that he was my father, but I should say he'd an excellent bedside manner—a manner calculated to sooth the most rambunctious. He used that skill to calm her, and she started for home like a good little woman. Then she met Eric. I know what happened because Joan pumped the story out of him, and has since told me. Eric tried to bluff her in his usual unsophisticated way. She boiled up, and back she went. She probably challenged the old man, telling him that she knew now that he had no intention of marrying her. She knew she'd lose everything if he lived and changed his will, and so she—well, you know what she did! I wondered at first whether it would be possible for a woman to kill him in that way, but I've looked up similar cases at the public library, and it has been done before! And that means it must have been her I saw leaving by the waiting-room door!"

He leaned back and stared at the ceiling. "I'm afraid it's a clear-cut case, Inspector! I know you've suspected me, but let me put it to you straight, and as if I was some other person. What had Aubrey Highton to gain by murdering his father? Financially, he's worse off. He was promised good contacts, and he's lost them. The family skeleton's been slung from the cupboard, and nobody likes to have his dirty linen washed in public. Aubrey Highton is branded as illegitimate, and that's not a nice thing! The mud will stick to Joan's name, and young Eric shares the said mud. What did Aubrey Highton stand to gain?"

"Well," said Knollis, "if your story of being coshed was true, you had a fairly good reason for killing your father!"

Highton shrugged. "It was true within limits. He did sock me, and nobody will make me believe it was anybody else, but he wasn't trying to kill me. He was trying to scare me into leaving the town. I was too dangerous to have about, especially as I was visiting the house and being seen in his company. There is a resemblance between me and the old boy, y'know, and it's quite pronounced when my hair's wearing its original colour. No, the old man wanted me to leave."

"And yet he invited you to visit him!"

"That was before he'd seen my laughing dog caricature and before he'd spotted the tattoo."

"I see," said Knollis. "By the way, you said you'd given me the solution to the problem. What was it?"

Highton rose and flung his cigarette into the fire. "That's where you came in, Inspector. I think I've given you a vital clue, but I'm not at all sure now, and I'd hate to make an ass of myself. You're on the right track, so why worry about it? What's preventing you from arresting the woman, anyway?"

Knollis reached for his hat. "That's where you came in, Mr. Highton! Good day!"

He returned to police headquarters.

Manson joined him in his office shortly afterwards.

"We're moving, Knollis. Lincoln's been found in a small commercial hotel on Euston Road. He took a taxi from there early this morning and went—well, guess where he went!"

"I give up," said Knollis.

"Somerset House!"

"So that's it. Well, he's wasted a lot of time and money, because if he'd stayed at home he'd have learned the truth from Joan and Highton within a few hours. Been to check up on Highton, eh?"

A buzzer sounded. Manson depressed the switch on the inter-office telephone. "Inspector Manson."

"Mrs. Burke to see yourself and Inspector Knollis, sir. She says it's important."

"Send her in."

"Wonder what she's trying to work across us this time," muttered Knollis.

Madeleine Burke almost ran into the room, a small face and neat ankles in a bundle of fur. "This came by post this morning," she panted. "I brought it straight to you—the parcel post doesn't come until mid-morning!"

She laid a disarranged brown paper parcel on the desk, and unrolled it.

"Rope!" exclaimed Manson. "Then it wasn't destroyed!"

"Where's the inch-tape?" Knollis asked calmly. "Hold this end. Six feet three inches! Let's look at the postmark. London, W.C.1. St. Pancras area!"

"So that's another reason why Lincoln went to London!" Manson blurted out.

Madeleine Burke turned and stared at him. "Then it was Eric who—who—!"

"Why?" Knollis asked quietly. "Did you suspect him?"

"Who else could it have been in the dispensary?"

"That's quite a question," said Knollis.

Madeleine Burke thumped her tiny fist on the table. "He's tried to put the blame on me all the way through. He hates me! The silly, silly boy! We could all have been so happy together if he hadn't been so avaricious!"

"You never suspected Mr. Highton?" murmured Knollis.

"Mr. Highton?" She gave a short laugh. "He'd no reason to kill Dr. Challoner, had he?"

"You know who he was—or is?"

"I do now, and I know what Hugh meant when he said the past had caught up with him. He invited Mr. Highton to Sturton not knowing it was his own son, and then he must have learned somehow or other. Even if his son was blackmailing him it wasn't that he was worrying over so much as—well, his conscience."

"Or his reputation," suggested Knollis.

She nodded reluctantly. "Well yes, that might have had something to do with his state of mind. He'd have been ruined in Sturton if the truth had got out—you know how narrow-minded these small provincial towns can be!"

"And are!" added Manson.

"Tell me, Mrs. Burke," said Knollis. "Would you still have married him if you had known the truth about Highton?"

"Why not?" she countered. "I believe in letting the one without sin cast the first stone."

"That's a Christian attitude, anyway," said Knollis.

"Very well, Mrs. Burke, you may leave the parcel with us. We'll give you a receipt for it."

He opened the door for her, and returned to Manson's side as the buzzer sounded again.

"There's a message from Mrs. Lincoln, sir. She's speaking from a kiosk. A parcel containing a short length of rope has been received by her husband this morning. She wants to know if you want to see it."

"Tell her to come straight here," said Manson.

He grimaced as he raised the switch. "The young fool seems to be putting his neck in the noose. If his brains were cordite he wouldn't have enough to blow his hat off."

Knollis said nothing, but waited until Mrs. Lincoln arrived with a similar parcel to that received by Madeleine Burke.

"Do you recognize the handwriting, Mrs. Lincoln," he then asked.

"I've never seen it before, sir. Have you heard anything of my boy?"

"He's all right," Knollis assured her. "He's in town on business, and staying at a respectable hotel. You can expect him home tomorrow at the latest. Now do you recognize this rope?"

"Well, it looks like the same stuff I lent the gentleman whose car broke down outside the house."

Knollis coughed, having temporarily forgotten the subterfuge used to get her clothes-line. "I see," he murmured. "Well, you can leave it with us, Mrs. Lincoln. It will be quite safe in our hands!"

"I don't want it," she said, "and thank you for telling me about my boy! I was so worried!"

"I'm sure you were," said Knollis, seeing her out.

"Now what?" demanded Manson when the door was closed.

"Have him picked up and brought back here. See you after lunch."

It was nine o'clock when Knollis was informed that Lincoln was back in town with his escort from the Yard. He parted Ellis from his Western novel, and they went to police headquarters. Manson was waiting in his office.

"He's here," he said, jerking his thumb towards the ante-room. "Darn nasty temper he's in, too. Refused to say a word unless his boss was present, so I've sent for him. The sergeant's in a temper, too. Lincoln chucked a large and bulky envelope into the river as they came through Bedford. The sergeant sent a signal back to the Bedford police from the next station. Perhaps you'd like his own story."

He pressed a bell-push.

The sergeant, a lean and hungry-looking individual, was still scowling as he entered the office. "I could have kicked myself, sir," he said to Knollis. "I reckoned I'd rubbed him over without him knowing it, and he didn't seem to have anything worth noticing."

"You'd no authority to search him," said Knollis, "so it can't be held against you. How did he manage it?"

"Made the usual excuse to go down the train. I knew he couldn't get off, so let him go alone. A minute later it struck me that I'd taken a risk, so I followed him down the corridor. He was leaning out of the window when I caught up with him. He looked round, saw me, put his hand in his inside pocket and brought out a bulky foolscap envelope. We were just going over the bridge—you know where it is!—and all at once he flung the thing into the river, closed the window, and walked towards me with a grin on his face. *You can ask the fishes for the clue to Dr. Challoner's death,*' he said. *'I'm tired of trying to help the detectives.'* And he pushed past me and went back to the compartment. We'd got it to ourselves, of course, and he grabbed a magazine, put his feet up on the opposite seat, and wouldn't say another word—and hadn't done when I bundled him into the car outside Sturton Lacey railway station!"

"Getting tough, is he?" grinned Knollis. "We'd better have him in, Manson."

A subtle change had come over Lincoln. He looked older, more sure of himself, and there was neither defiance nor servility in his attitude. Knollis sensed the change immediately, and dealt with him accordingly.

"Mr. Lincoln," he said. "We've no right to keep you here, and we'd no right to bring you back from London against your will. Do you wish to go?"

"I'm sure I don't care whether you keep me or not," replied Lincoln in a quiet voice. "I think Mr. Hodson is quite capable of protecting my interests. At the same time I should tell you that I have no intention of answering any questions until he is present."

"That's good enough," said Knollis. "We'll wait."

Hodson arrived ten minutes later, fussing round Lincoln, and glaring at Knollis and Manson. "Now what's been going on, gentlemen? Why did you fetch the man from London? What is the charge?"

"We haven't charged him with anything," said Knollis suavely. "We need his assistance."

"That's an old one," retorted Hodson. "You policemen are unbelievably naive! You issue a statement to the Press stating you're anxious to interview So-and-So, who you believe can give valuable information. Poppycock! Do you think the public are fools? Yes, you do! Well, they aren't, and they know quite well that you're silently accusing the wanted man of murder. The story's round Sturton already and isn't doing Eric much good. Now, what do you want with him?"

"Why did you go to London?" Knollis asked Lincoln.

"I went to help you."

"In what direction?"

"That's my business now, Inspector. If you're too dull to see any further than the end of your nose, that's your misfortune. The evidence is in the river at Bedford. If you care to dive for it, that's your affair. Me, I'm going home now. Any objections?"

"Surely you could have posted the two parcels without going all the way to London?" challenged Knollis.

Lincoln turned back from the door, a frown between his eyes. "Two parcels?"

Manson took them from a drawer and held them out.

Lincoln walked back to look at them. "What are they? I've never seen them before!"

"Recognize the writing?" asked Knollis, taking the Burke one from Manson and pushing it under Lincoln's nose.

"It's vaguely familiar. It looks a bit like Mrs. Burke's!"

"And where might you have seen Mrs. Burke's writing?" asked Manson in a deep rumble.

Hodson interrupted. "We squared up her affairs after her husband's death. Eric handled most of the papers. We had them from the strong room the other day and went through them to see if there was anything that might help the case."

"I see," said Knollis. "You, too, think the writing is Mrs. Burke's, Mr. Hodson?"

"I wouldn't say that without a sample by me. I'll take Eric's line—that it's vaguely familiar."

"It does resemble her writing, Inspector," said Lincoln. "What's in the parcel?"

Knollis unrolled the paper.

"Rope!"

"Enough to strangle a man with," said Knollis. "Who sent it?"

"It was posted in London, presumably last night. That's the worst of the G.P.O.'s parcels frank, it doesn't show the date and time of posting. Nevertheless, since it was delivered to Mrs. Burke this morning we can assume it was posted late yesterday. Posted, I repeat, in London!"

"Not by me!" Lincoln retorted quickly. "I can prove where I was during every hour of the short time I was in London."

"How?"

"I don't know London, so took a taxi from Euston. The driver found the hotel for me—recommended it, I should say. I took his number. I didn't go out again until half-past nine this morning—as they will prove at the hotel, and since I was followed about all morning by a so-called detective you shouldn't have any trouble in proving my alibi!"

"Why did you go to Somerset House?"

Lincoln sniffed. "I went to get certain evidence. Joan and her father have been the victim of a conspiracy, and I've all the information needed to expose it."

Knollis perched himself on the corner of the desk and brought a winning smile into operation. "Now we're really getting somewhere. Where's the evidence?"

Lincoln flashed a glance of pitying contempt on Knollis and Manson. "I've told you where it is! In the Ouse at Bedford!" He turned to Hodson. "Ready, sir?"

Knollis watched them go.

"That's two of my suspects who profess to have solved the case for me. I'm developing an inferiority complex!"

Then he laughed.

XVII
THE FINAL CLUE

KNOLLIS AWOKE the next morning with several questions in his mind. He sat up in bed, his chin on his fist, and stared through the window. Sergeant Handley, who escorted Lincoln from London, said it was a bulky envelope which Lincoln had thrown in the Ouse, and it was certain that a single birth certificate was not capable of making a bulky package. It was also certain that Lincoln had gone nowhere else but Somerset House while in London, so for what other evidence had he been seeking—and found? Sylvia Highton had obviously given false information when registering Aubrey, for he had retained the name of Highton; the story told him by Wilson and Madge was therefore true, and Sylvia had invented a second cousin of the same name as herself.

Lincoln might have obtained a copy of Challoner's marriage certificate, but for what purpose? There was no doubt about the validity of his marriage to the wife who had predeceased him, and consequently no doubt about the legitimacy of Joan Challoner. It was all very puzzling.

Knollis reached his note-book from the bedside table, and turned to the page dealing with Hugh Challoner. The sum total of his knowledge of Challoner read:

Hugh Challoner, the deceased.
Born 1891, Beverley, Yorks.
Married 3rd June, 1922. Then aged 31 years.
Daughter Joan born 31st August, 1927.
Wife died 10th July, 1942. Malignant tumour.
Self murdered 4th November, 1947.
Note: affair with Sylvia Highton in Algiers in June-July, 1914.

He grunted and turned the page:

Aubrey Highton, doubtful suspect.
Born 1915, Healdswood, Kent.
Educated St. Bertrand's School, Kent. 1926-1931.

Foreign Legion from 1938 to 1945? (Highton a bit contradictory on this point, not that it matters.)
Rue Michelet period, 1945-1947. Also doubtful.
Arrival in Sturton, mid-October. Was obviously in England during April.
Saw Challoner from 7.0 p.m. to 7.10 p.m. on night of C's death. Asserts he never went back. Neither his own nor Camden's evidence at all reassuring.
Doesn't seem to have any financial motive, and vengeance motive doesn't seem feasible since he loses a great deal by his father's death. Queer character, difficult to analyse.

And on the next page:

Madeleine Burke, potential suspect.
Born 1893, Redhill, Surrey. Now 54 years of age.
Married Easter Sunday, 1930.
Son Leslie born 1st November, 1934. Now 13.
Husband died 27th September, 1945. Pneumonia.

Following this there came:

Eric Lincoln, remote suspect.
Born 1925 in Sturton Lacey, and never been anywhere or seen anything or done anything. Courting Joan Challoner, whom he met at tennis club. Badly needs marriage to stabilize his character.

Knollis turned the page, and took his pen. He first used the butt of it to scratch his head. Sylvia Highton: now what did he know about her. Little or nothing. She was nineteen years of age when she had the affair with Challoner at *Le Chien Qui Rit*, and that placed her birth in the year 1893. If she were still alive she would be—er—see—yes, fifty-four years of age, and both Wilson and Madge York believed her to be alive. Queer that she hadn't come to the fore since Challoner's death! Was she still alive? Was she in the vicinity? Was it she who had killed Challoner? Had she waited all these years for her vengeance? Was it because she had been overlooked, and because Challoner had taken first one wife and then contemplated taking another? The feminine mind was a tortuous one, and its workings could not be ascertained by regarding the male mind.

The suggestion raised a whole host of possibilities, not the least disquieting was the possibility that he had been chasing his own tail for nine days, and had overlooked the obvious. It meant starting all over again, but it was a bad general who was afraid to change his plans. He entered the deduced facts regarding Sylvia Highton in his note-book, got dressed, and went down to the breakfast-room.

Ellis was already at the table, scowling contemptuously at the strip of bacon that lay on his plate. "The price of freedom," he growled. "There's more meat in my moustache!"

"We're taking a new line," Knollis said earnestly.

"Not another clothes-line, surely!" protested Ellis. "I never want to see another rope as long as I live!"

"Sylvia Highton," said Knollis. "I'm certain young Lincoln knows the truth about this case, and I could almost wish for the days of the rack and thumbscrews! He'll stand on his little dignity and see us working like devils before he'll come forward and help us. I imagine Hodson put him up to it."

"What about Sylvia Highton?" asked Ellis.

"Where is she?" demanded Knollis.

"Search me!"

"We've nothing but circumstantial evidence against Madeleine Burke. The same goes for Highton and Lincoln. Now suppose this Highton woman was living somewhere near, right under our noses . . ."

He explained his new theory thoroughly, enlarging on it as the association of ideas rushed to his assistance.

"And you think Lincoln knows the truth, eh?" said Ellis. "Well, that bulkiness you mention must have an explanation. What's the next move?"

"Down to headquarters as soon as we've finished breakfast, and get a string of messages across the country. Meanwhile, I'll take another cup of tea if you don't mind pouring it for me."

He retired behind the morning paper, but not to read it, for the print was a blur; his mind was occupied with the problem of Sylvia Highton.

At police headquarters he had a chat with Manson, and wrote out a string of questions for which he needed answers.

"This first one," he said to Manson, "asking where she was born, isn't as foolish as it may appear. People have a tendency to return to their old homes, and if she isn't still in Sturton I think we'll find her near her birthplace—in which case we'll have the job of breaking down an alibi. She may have come here to kill Challoner, and have returned straight away. Anyway, the Yorks will answer that question without being suspicious, and then we can get to work.

"The second question asks whether she married, and if so, whom. The third question asks for a description of her when last seen by them, and photographs if available."

"Should do something," answered Manson. "I'll send 'em down to the section straight away. And now what?"

"I'm going for a walk round the town," said Knollis. "There's little I can do until the answers arrive, and we can't expect them this side of lunch-time."

He collected Ellis from the sergeants' room, and together they walked the town until Ellis protested.

"Must we patrol the place in a cold east wind? Haven't we done enough pavement-pounding in our time? There's a snug little café over there, and I'm sure they make the most delightful coffee—and they've eclairs and eccles cakes in the window."

"All right," Knollis said absently. "Anything you say. We're as well in there as anywhere else until those messages come through."

He allowed Ellis to steer him into the café, and there took out his note-book and consulted the accumulation of facts and figures. He suddenly pushed back and got to his feet. "Holy smoke!"

"What's up, Cock?" asked Ellis.

Knollis slowly sank back into his chair, and stared keenly at Ellis. "I nearly yielded to an impulse. Here, take my note-book. The answer's in there. It's been there since early this morning."

"This makes about the fourth time we've had the solution," Ellis replied ironically. "Well, where do we find the answer? I can't see it."

"Compare some of the dates, Ellis! Compare the dates!"

Ellis shook his head. "The penny hasn't dropped."

Knollis wrapped his scarf round his throat and buttoned his coat. "Come on! Where are the local council offices?"

"Hanged if I know. I'll ask the waitress."

He sauntered across the café.

"Three streets away, first right and second left. Ugly red brick building in its own grounds. Used to be a private house."

"Then let's go."

Knollis hurried through the streets, disregarding the icy wind that was sweeping the town.

"It's the Clerk to the Council I want," he muttered.

Ellis came to a halt. "Then you don't want the council offices! Wait a minute!"

He crossed the street and asked a direction of the only person to be seen, a street-sweeper.

"Roundabout turn, Cock," he ordered as he rejoined Knollis. "His place is straight opposite the hotel!"

The abruptness of Knollis's manner sent the solicitor back in his chair.

"What can you tell me about the late Rating Officer, Mr. Edmund Burke?"

"Burke? Well, I mean, what do you want to know? He was a good man at his job, an excellent accountant, and I believe he was very happily married, and had one son."

"No, no, no!" exclaimed Knollis. "How long was he with your council? Where did he come from? Is he a townsman born, or did he come from away?"

"Oh well, I seem to remember that he came to us some-where round about late twenty-nine—as senior rating clerk. The Rating Officer died, and Burke stepped into his shoes. He came from Surrey."

"What town?" Knollis asked quickly.

"Let me think! Don't rush me, Inspector! Why, he came from Redhill!"

"Was he married when he came?"

"Why, no, I seem to remember that he wasn't. He went in lodgings until he found a house, and got married after that."

"Where? In Redhill or Sturton?"

"Sturton—at St. Aidan's. I know that is correct, because I had the pleasure of making the usual presentation on behalf of the council and the staff."

"Can you remember the bride's maiden name?"

The solicitor put a hand to his lips. "It was—it was—no, I can't remember it, Inspector. You're expecting too much of me!"

"I suppose I am," Knollis sighed. "Well, thanks for that. Come on, Ellis!"

Outside on the pavement he said: "Now do you see the thing? Which way do we go for St. Aidan's?"

"I don't see a thing yet," said Ellis, "and the way to the church is to the right."

And then he stood in the middle of the pavement and opened his eyes and his mouth. "Crikey!"

Knollis strode on, leaving Ellis to catch him up.

The Vicar of St. Aidan's was on the point of leaving the church when they arrived. Knollis introduced himself, and asked permission to inspect the registers.

"I know you, Inspector," said the Vicar. "I've seen you about the town during the past week. It's a horrible thing to have happened to us!"

"I didn't choose to come," Knollis said dryly.

"I was referring to the murder, Inspector! Dr. Challoner was a valued member of my church. The registers! For what year?"

"Nineteen-thirty—Easter Sunday, please."

The Vicar produced it from the wall safe. "I hope you are not seeking information that will bring more trouble to the town!"

"Merely checking information," said Knollis. He ran a finger along the entry. "Edmund Burke and Madeleine York, by licence. Yes, that's all right, sir. Thanks for your co-operation! Good morning."

He hurried Ellis from the church.

"We've still got to prove that she wasn't, and isn't, and never was Madeleine York. We must wait, Ellis."

Back at headquarters, Knollis had a talk with Chief-Inspector Burnell on the telephone. "There's a little bloke by the name of Bradley, a newsagent, at 43 Dunwell Street. Will you get someone to find out whether he's posted two parcels to Sturton Lacey within the past twenty-four hours?"

"Straight away," said Burnell. "Well, I think I'll be able to congratulate you again within a few hours. Good luck, Knollis!"

"That's all it's been," grunted Knollis. "Blindness on my part, and good luck on the part of Providence."

He rang off, and went to lunch.

The information began to come in at half-past one.

The message from Bradley was the first from the tele-printer, and read:

Bradley received large parcel postmarked Sturton Lacey with note requesting posting of two parcels contained. Note signed The Laughing Dog. Bradley says it must have come from woman, that being the password.

"That's fair enough," commented Knollis. "The whole case is becoming crystal clear, and I'm afraid Mrs. Burke will have an appointment with Teddy Jessop early one morning."

"And here's the rest, by the look of it," said Manson as another sheet of paper was laid on his table. "Sylvia Highton, when last seen by York, was short, dark, plump. She was born in Redhill, as was Madge York. No information on whether or not she was married. No idea where she is now, and no photograph of her since she was nineteen, copy of which is being wired to County Headquarters."

"For which we'll wait," said Knollis.

It arrived half an hour later, and Knollis nodded. "Copy of the same photograph Ellis and I found in Challoner's house. All right, Manson, please pick up Lincoln and get him to the Challoner house for two-thirty. I'll 'phone Mrs. Burke and ask her to meet us there, and I'll ask Highton if he can see me at that time. There's one doubt left in my mind which prevents me having a warrant sworn, so we'll have to sort out that detail and pick up the culprit without one."

He telephoned Aubrey Highton and asked if he would see him, and Highton agreed. "Don't be any later than half-past two, Inspector. I've a spot of important business to do on the 'phone at three o'clock."

"I'll be there," promised Knollis.

He next got in touch with Mrs. Burke, and although reluctant to go to the house, promised she would be there.

Manson went out, and Ellis came in and sat opposite Knollis, who was now scrutinizing the sketch Highton had made of the consulting-room.

"You'll pardon me if I call myself a fool, won't you?" asked Knollis. "I've been as blind as a bat all the way through this case, but can I see now! Highton told me he'd given me the solution to the case, and he has. Well, this is the last time his Puckish sense of humour plays with me. I'll quieten him for a long, long time!"

He threw the sketch across to Ellis. "Here, solve the puzzle for yourself. You've as many brains as I have!"

Ellis looked at the sketch for a long time. He made several pencilled notes on the blotting-pad, and then looked up with a quizzical expression. "The red diary?"

"That's it, Ellis. Now let's get going. The time is quarter-past two, and we haven't time to swear a warrant, anyway."

They met Manson as they were leaving the building.

"Lincoln's in court with Hodson. They've promised to send him down as soon as he gets back."

"Damn!" said Knollis. "We can't very well drag him out of there, or we'll have the magistrates on our track. Oh well, I hope he doesn't waste any time when he gets the message. We'll all go together in your car now."

As they settled themselves in their seats Knollis took the sketch from his despatch-case and handed it to Manson.

"Picture puzzle for you. The first prize is a murderer's neck. It only tumbled to me a few minutes ago."

Manson furrowed his brows. "I'm about sick of looking at the thing," he boomed. "Are all murder cases like this one has been?"

Knollis shook his head. "This has been the most tiresome I've been connected with. I didn't say anything, but a few days ago I was beginning to think I should have to declare a draw. It looked hopeless—and yet, when it's untangled, and all the evidence laid in a straight line it makes what you'd expect, a simple story!"

"Well, that's your opinion," rumbled Manson. "It's still a mess to me. Y'know, I hate the idea of a woman being hanged."

"I hate the idea of anybody being hanged," replied Knollis. "It's a primitive method of punishment based on revenge, and no deterrent to other would-be murderers. Still, you and I are paid to catch law-breakers, and not either judge or sentence them, so all we can do is think and carry on working."

Manson held out the sketch. "Perhaps I'm denser than usual, but where is the solution to the puzzle, Knollis. In fact, what is it? A clue, or what?"

"Highton is a clever fellow," said Knollis. "Notice how all the lines in the picture converge? Mind you, I know they do in every picture, but Highton's cleverness is in his choice of viewpoint."

"From the open doorway of the waiting-room!"

"To which point are your eyes led, Manson?"

"Why, see, to the centre of the table, to the red diary!"

"That," said Knollis, "is the final clue."

XVIII

THE LONG DROP

AUBREY HIGHTON chose the breakfast-room as the scene of the interview. "The lounge is all right," he explained, "but horribly noisy at this time of the day as a result of being on Kirkland Street. By the way, you've no objection to Joan being present?"

"I'd rather she wasn't," said Knollis.

"I'm afraid she'll insist, Inspector," Highton said airily, "and after all it's her house."

"In that case . . ."

Highton went into the hall and called his half-sister. "The Inspector's here with another quiz programme. I'd hate you to miss it, darling!"

He returned to the breakfast-room, his hands deep in his pockets, a mocking smile on his lips.

"I'm beginning to favour the idea of having a witness at these interviews. After all this time you must be getting hard up for a scapegoat, and I've no fancy for such roles."

"Mrs. Burke murdered Challoner—your father—didn't she, Highton?"

"We think so," said Joan Challoner from the door-way. "We know she did, because Aubrey has proof!"

Knollis, Manson, and Ellis all turned back to Highton as if governed by synchronized motors. "You mean that?"

Highton nodded. He seated himself on the corner of the table, and closed the blade of a large clasp knife that lay beside a fruit dish. "Yes, I mean that, Inspector. I suppose I'll have to tell you what I know. You see, I'm a curious sort of cuss, and I was intrigued that night when she asked me to take her place in the surgery queue so that she could be the last person to be interviewed by my father. If you've seen Camden he'll have told you I was dodging back and forth for half an hour or more on a variety of excuses. Well, I was watching Mrs. Burke! When I left the consulting-room I was so bad-mannered as to stand outside the door and listen, and she started giving him the works as soon as she entered the room. He'd promised her marriage, and she was going to see that he carried out the promise. He tried to quieten her, and said she couldn't force him, that nobody could force him, and that he was going to marry her—but he was choosing his own time. He added that he wasn't going to be dictated to by anybody, and least of all by his future wife, so she might as well get the idea into her head before as after! Proper bad-tempered he got!"

"Go on!" said Knollis as Highton paused to light a cigarette.

"I slipped back to the Dragon, straightened my clothes, and went into the bar and ordered a drink. I dodged back again and had to dodge out twice as quick two minutes later. When I got to the door Mrs. Burke was still talking, and she seemed to be just the other side of the door. *'You thought I didn't know about your earlier affair,'* she said. *'You thought I didn't know you had a grown-up son with no name but his mother's. Well, Hugh, you've left it too late! Good night!'* I skipped back on tiptoe, turned right towards the corner of Denver Street, and then turned and made a diagonal course for the yard of the Dragon. Mrs. Burke was leaving in a devil of a hurry as I was crossing the street. It suddenly struck me that there'd been dirty work at the crossroads, but I daren't go back! You must realize my position! I daren't go back in case anything had happened to him, so I returned to the bar, finished my drink, and ordered another. I was half-way down it when I had to go up to my room. I've already told you how I saw her leaving by the waiting-room door. When the news came into the pub, I stayed when everybody else rushed out. I was uncertain of myself for once in my life."

"Circumstantial evidence," rumbled Manson from his diaphragm. "We can't do much with that, Knollis."

"I can do a great deal with it," Knollis replied calmly. "Was that the front door bell, Miss Challoner?"

She went to answer. There were sounds suggesting an altercation from the hall, and then Madeleine Burke hustled into the room, followed by an indignant Joan Challoner.

"I've an appointment with Inspector Knollis, Joan, and I intend to keep it. Good afternoon, Inspector! And Inspector Manson! Hello, Mr. Highton! All right, Sergeant?"

She plumped down in a chair and unbuttoned her fur coat, then pulled off her fur hat and shook her hair free. "Looks like a church council. What's happening this time?"

Knollis took the floor. "Mr. Highton has just been explaining how you killed Dr. Hugh Challoner. Perhaps you'd like a résumé of the evidence?"

She touched her breast with a well-manicured finger.

"Me? How I killed Hugh? I'd certainly like to hear how I did it."

Knollis turned towards Highton. "Well, how about it? It's a challenge, y'know, and your father never refused a dare!"

"That's true," said Madeleine Burke.

"This is going to be damnably embarrassing, Inspector!" protested Highton.

"No more than it will be when you give the evidence in the assize court. Either get on with it or declare the story to be fictitious!"

"Well," said Highton dubiously. He lit another cigarette with unsteady fingers. "It's just this way, Mrs. Burke. You'll remember that while in the waiting-room . . ."

She regarded him earnestly as he rendered a somewhat less dramatic version of the story he had told before her arrival. When his voice trailed away in apologetic silence she nodded vigorously. "Yes, that was the way of it. Now what happens, Inspector?"

"I congratulate Mr. Highton," said Knollis.

Highton shrugged. "It was sheer coincidence. If she hadn't asked me to take her turn I wouldn't have been suspicious, I wouldn't have listened at the door, and I wouldn't have gone back. There's nothing to congratulate me on, Inspector."

"I think there is," Knollis said quietly.

Highton was regarding the tip of his cigarette. He looked up at Knollis's tone.

"You've broken what is probably a record," said Knollis. "I can't remember another case in which a man provided the evidence for the conviction of his mother!"

"His—mother!" exclaimed Joan Challoner.

Highton's cigarette slipped from his fingers and rolled across the floor. Ellis retrieved it and stubbed it in an ash tray.

Highton stared at Madeleine Burke. "My—my mother!"

"Sylvia Highton, or Madeleine York, or Madeleine Burke. The necessary documents are on their way, but there's no doubt about her identity. Care to refute that, Mrs. Burke?"

She shook her head. "No, I'm Sylvia Madeleine Highton."

"You caused the two parcels of rope to be posted by Bradley while Lincoln was in London?"

"I caused them to be sent, but I didn't even know Eric had been in London."

"With what object?"

She sighed. "There's no point in telling any more lies and half-truths. I was responsible for cutting them from my own and Mrs. Lincoln's clothes-lines. I hid them, hoping you would waste time looking for them. Then I had them posted to you hoping that the London postmark would take you away from Sturton."

Highton looked at his mother. He slid from the table, started towards her, and then moved away again. "Then he was alive when you left?"

She gave him a very curious look and did not reply.

"The sketch, Ellis!" snapped Knollis.

Ellis took it from the despatch-case and handed it to him. Knollis passed it to Madeleine Burke.

"Take a good look at it, Mrs. Burke."

She regarded it steadily, and then looked at her son with horrified eyes. "You—you did this!" she whispered.

Highton nodded mutely.

"Tell me, Mrs. Burke," said Knollis, "tell me, would you regard that sketch as an accurate reconstruction of the consulting-room as you saw it?"

"When I went back, yes," she said in a low voice.

"The diary was in the middle of the table, lying on the blotting-pad?"

She lowered her head. "Yes!"

"The same diary that was in your handbag when it was found and handed to the police?"

"Yes, Inspector."

"There is a page missing?"

"There is, Inspector."

"Tell me, Mrs. Burke: where did Dr. Challoner keep that diary?"

"I—I don't know, Inspector. I hadn't seen it since Nineteen-fourteen until that—that night!"

"And you recognized it straight away?"

"I helped him to fill some parts of it in," she whispered. "He's erased most of our entries since then, but one page he'd torn out."

"What was on that page, Mrs. Burke?"

"Must I . . . ?" she pleaded.

"You know what's at stake," Knollis replied simply.

"There were three days to a page, and the two sides of the page covered the six days we spent together at *Le Chien Qui Rit*. He drew a laughing dog on the first side of the sheet—the first page."

Knollis turned. "The photo, Ellis. Now, Mrs. Burke, this was found among Dr. Challoner's possessions. Do you recognize the girl?"

"It is myself, Inspector. It was taken before I left England for Algiers."

"Tell me, Mrs. Burke: you knew that Aubrey was your son?"

"Of course."

"Did Hugh Challoner know that you were Sylvia Highton?"

"He did not, Inspector. I never told him, and never intended that he should know. All I wanted of him was marriage—you must see that!"

"I see your point," Knollis said in a solemn tone. "You regarded yourself as married to him morally, and even if you had to wait forty years you intended that he should marry you legally?"

"Yes, but I didn't expect you to understand."

"Now tell me something else, Mrs. Burke: is your son's account of the conversation between yourself and Hugh Challoner substantially correct?"

"It is correct, Inspector."

"Tell me, Mrs. Burke: was the diary in evidence before you left the consulting-room on the first occasion?"

She paused, looked from Knollis to Highton, and at each face in the room in turn.

"Was the diary in evidence, Mrs. Burke?"

She buried her face in her hands, and her dark hair fell over her shoulders as she leaned forward. "Oh, my God! Must I answer! Must I answer?"

"You must, Mrs. Burke. Was the diary there when you left?"

"No-o, it wasn't! Oh, what have I done?"

"Told the truth," said Knollis.

He turned on Highton. "Shall I tell you what happened that night? You went back to the surgery after your mother left."

The mockery was absent from Highton's eyes as he turned them on his mother. "I didn't go inside, Inspector!"

"You must have done!"

"Can you prove that?"

"What was the clue you sketched into your picture?"

Highton grabbed the sketch from his mother's knee.

"It was an attempt to cast suspicion on her. I didn't know she was my mother. See this shadow? What the devil do you think that is but the shadow of a woman's form?"

"To be quite truthful, I hadn't noticed it," said Knollis.

Highton flung the sketch across the table. "I told you that the eyes of a fool are in the ends of the earth! Detective indeed! You've tried to foist the blame on me, and you've tried to foist it on my mother—if you hadn't found out that she was my mother you'd have condemned her out of hand. Can't you see yet what I was playing at?"

He looked at Joan. "I'm sorry, darling. I was trying to save you, and I wouldn't hurt you now, but blood is thicker than— well, half-blood and half-water! I was trying to divert your attention from Eric, Inspector! His guilt sticks out a mile. *He* was the only person to enter the surgery after my mother left, and before she returned. I was watching from across the street, and no one else entered or left the surgery from the street. But I couldn't see who entered from the house! Now do you see it?"

There was a commotion outside the house, the noise of running feet on the front path. Then hurrying feet in the tiled hall. The door was thrust open, and Lincoln stood in the doorway, breathless.

"I—I hurried!" he panted.

"It wasn't so urgent," Knollis smiled. "Tell me, Mr. Lincoln, what was in the package you threw into the Ouse at Bedford?"

"Proof . . ." panted Lincoln. "Proof that she's his—mother! They were in it together. But that isn't why I've hurried. We've just had a message from the Blue Vine Airways at Swinnerton to say that the aircraft will be standing by for Mr. Hodson's journey to Paris at three o'clock!"

Manson began to rumble deep in his belly, and in due course recognizable words came from his mouth. "What's that to do with us? He's capable of doing his own business, surely!"

Lincoln took a deep breath. "But you don't under-stand! He isn't going to Paris! He hasn't chartered an aircraft!"

"Why didn't you 'phone this?" snapped Knollis.

"We couldn't get a reply—or the exchange couldn't!"

Knollis's eyes narrowed to mere slits. He turned from Lincoln to Highton. "Tell me, Mr. Highton: when you sketched the scene in the consulting-room, how did you know that the red diary was lying in the middle of the blotting-pad? It wasn't there when your mother went to see him, and it was when she returned, and yet you never entered the room after your professional visit! You murdered your father!"

"Why, damn you!"

Highton launched himself forward at Lincoln, still occupying the doorway. A vicious uppercut sent the young clerk tumbling across the hall. Then Highton turned and slammed the door, and the key turned in the lock.

"The window!" yelled Knollis. He reached for the catch and pressed it back. Then Ellis's huge hand went down his collar and pulled him back as the sash fell like a guillotine blade.

"He cut the sash-cords."

"And the telephone wires," grunted Knollis. "Give me a leg up!"

Ellis grabbed him bodily and lifted him towards the open window. Knollis dropped to the path and sprinted towards the front gate in pursuit of Highton. The driver of the police car was lying sprawled across the gateway, and the car, driven by Highton, was drawing away from the kerb.

Knollis ran across the street to the kiosk, pressed the emergency button, and shouted *"Police!"* Thirty seconds later he was hurrying back to the house. The rest of them were already on the pavement, Mrs. Burke tending the driver's eye, hidden as it was behind a mess of blood.

"He was expecting the turn-up this afternoon then!" growled Manson. "Telephone wires cut, windows tampered with, key on the outside of the door, and a 'plane ordered! What a man!"

"He can't get away!" snorted Knollis. "How's Lincoln?"

He came limping up the path to the street. "Hit me clean on the point of the jaw, and I caught my knee on the bottom stair as I fell. If I get hold of him I'll make him look like a jar of mince-meat."

Joan Challoner put an arm round him. "Come back to the house and let me bathe it. You can't do anything!"

"Can't I?" shouted Lincoln. "I'm going with the Inspector. Can I, sir?"

"You can," said Knollis with a grim smile. "I don't expect to get him without a fight, and you may get your chance. Here are the cars!"

Two cars came speeding down the street, and skidded to a halt. Manson and Ellis hurried into the rear one, and Knollis pushed Lincoln into his own before clambering after him.

"Swinnerton Airfield—and if this thing can fly, then make it!"

"Yes, sir!" said the driver. "I'll take the short cuts!"

Knollis had nearly bitten through his lower lip when the airfield came in sight, and by that time a low-wing monoplane was circling the field. He scrambled out at the control tower.

"Didn't you get a message to stop him?" he bawled at the Traffic Manager.

"Your people told us to hold or delay a fellow called Highton. The bloke who's just taken off is called Hodson—a Sturton Lacey lawyer."

"Got red hair?"

"That's him, Inspector!"

"That aircraft got radio?"

"No R/T in it. It's going to Croydon, and he'll change kites there."

"Why's he circling the field?" demanded Knollis.

"Orbiting the field to gain height and check his compass. One orbit and he'll set course for London."

"Any way of getting him down?"

"Well, ye-es, but I mean—!"

"I want your passenger for murder."

"Golly! Right!"

The man ran back into the building. He returned with a Very pistol, into which he rammed a squat cartridge. He ran twenty yards or so from the control tower and fired the cartridge into the air at an angle of forty-five degrees. A long trail of white smoke headed by a red glow sailed up into the air, then five red stars broke from it and came gracefully to earth. The Traffic Manager repeated the performance, and the aircraft rocked as the pilot waggled the main-planes to signal that he understood.

"That's done it," called the man as he returned to Knollis's side. "He'll come in over our heads and land at the opposite side of the field, then taxi round the perimeter to the park at the other side of the control."

"The pilot might," Knollis said dryly. "My man may have different ideas. Get in: we'd better get round the other side."

"Now what's gone wrong?"

Knollis looked up. The aircraft was acting crazily, bucking and tossing and swinging from side to side.

"That's my man trying to persuade your pilot to keep going the way he should go. I don't think he's armed. . . ."

"He's jumping, Inspector!"

A dark figure detached itself from the aircraft and began to fall to earth. Seconds passed, and the white canopy of the parachute opened.

"He'll drift away from us, Inspector."

"Into the car!"

The two cars, followed by the airfield ambulance, sped round the perimeter until they reached the boundary of the field.

"Now what?" demanded Knollis.

"Walk it, I guess! What the devil is he trying to do? The wind's capsized his 'chute! Look! The shroud lines are wrapping round him. He'll drop like a stone!"

One and all, they scrambled over the low fence and began to run across the open field in the direction of a small copse towards which Highton was falling. He came hurtling down like a stone. As he plunged into the copse the twisted canopy of the parachute caught on a high branch. There came a scream from Highton, a strangled cry, and a horrible crack.

Knollis stumbled over the rough ground and through the dead winter undergrowth until he came to a breath-less halt beneath a tall birch. Among the bleak silvery branches hung Highton, the shroud lines twisted round his neck, his head at a curious angle, his whole body twitching and swaying in the icy wind.

Ellis was the first to reach Knollis's side. He stared up through the branches, and shuddered.

"I'm sorry in a way," said Knollis. "He was the only real individual in the bunch. He taught me a valuable lesson, too; that the eyes of a fool are in the ends of the earth—but what a pity he didn't take his own advice!" Manson panted towards them. "Lincoln won't come any closer. Says he can't bear bodies. Say, Knollis, why did he do it?"

"Vengeance, Manson. I don't think he contemplated murder until he discovered that Challoner was going to marry Madeleine Burke. Mother and son were very much alike. She waited years to get her wrong righted legally, and he took the law into his own hands. Yes, they'd a lot in common. Even their handwriting was almost identical. Oh well, that's another case cleared up!"

"Tell me, Knollis," said Manson. "I know you were a wee bit late in pinning him, but what made you suspicious of him at the outset."

"His eyes," said Knollis with a secret smile.

"They were brown," said Manson.

"And his hair was red. There may be such a person, but I've yet to meet a man with red hair and brown eyes. I knew he couldn't change the colour of his eyes, so wondered why he'd dyed his hair."

"Quite a point!" said Manson. He looked up into the leafless branches. "Got a long drop, didn't he? Wonder it didn't pull his head off!"

"It wouldn't have mattered," shrugged Knollis. "He'd already lost it. He must have known it was the end, aircraft or no aircraft, from the moment when he socked Lincoln and made his break for freedom."

"It was perhaps the best way," said Manson, still staring up into the tree.

"It was the only way, and inevitable," said Knollis. He shook his head sadly. "You can't play tricks with life and death and expect 'em to fit in with your own plans."

"They always get the last laugh, eh?"

"That's it," said Knollis. "The last laugh."

THE END